WENDY PERCIVAL's intere
the time honoured 'box of c
became the inspiration beh'
novels and novellas.

Wendy shares the intriguing, so.ۦ
in her own family history on her blog anu ..
articles published in *Shropshire Family History Society*'s quaۦۦ
journal and in *Family Tree* magazine.

She lives in South West England, in a thatched cottage
beside a thirteenth-century church, with her husband and
their particularly talkative cat.

The Esme Quentin Mysteries

Blood-Tied
The Indelible Stain
The Malice of Angels
The Fear of Ravens

Novellas

Death of a Cuckoo
Legacy of Guilt
*(*An Esme Quentin prequel – FREE to subscribers*)*

Blood-Tied

THE FIRST ESME QUENTIN MYSTERY

WENDY
PERCIVAL

OLD KEY PRESS

First published in 2008 by Robert Hale Ltd
Second edition (revised) published in 2013
by SilverWood Books

This edition published in 2021 by Old Key Press
Old Key Press
Worlington
Devon
EX17 4TT

ISBN 978-1-8380860-2-2

British Library Cataloguing in Publication Data A CIP catalogue record for this
book is available from the British Library

Acknowledgements

My thanks to my readers Emily Percival, Diane Owen and Caren Denton for their time and positive feedback, to Margaret James for her sound advice, and to friends and family for their continuous encouragement. Also thanks to Heather Chaddock, Andy Barrett and Andy Szczelkun for allowing me to pick their brains on various technical matters.

Finally, special thanks and love go to my husband Brian, for his constant and enthusiastic support which has made the writing of this novel so enjoyable

Prologue

As soon as the lie left her lips she realised her mistake. She stood behind the armchair avoiding his eyes, her trembling fingers gripping the upholstery and praying that now he would leave. She felt weary suddenly. She groped her way round the chair and painfully lowered herself into it.

He hadn't moved from the window and she risked a glance in his direction. He was leaning back against the window sill, his hands in his trouser pockets. What was he thinking? Would he leave her alone now? His face gave nothing away.

'Was that all you wanted?' she asked, clasping her hands in her lap. 'I'm very tired...'

'I'm glad you recognised the injustice,' he interrupted. 'You understand that, don't you?' He turned to stare at her and she winced under his close scrutiny.

'Of course.' She pulled her eyes from his gaze and looked towards the oxygen cylinder on its trolley in the corner of the room. She must stay calm, yet already she could feel the constriction in her chest. Perhaps now that he had got the reassurance he was seeking he would leave her in peace.

She felt him move and she turned her head. He stepped towards her and crouched down, his knees almost touching hers. She recoiled into her seat.

He smiled but his eyes remained cold and empty. 'It was wrong what he did. It should never have been yours and soon it will be mine. By rights.'

Her breathing was becoming laboured now. With his face so close to hers she could almost imagine that he was pressing against her, his weight pushing down on her lungs. She pulled her head away, arching her neck, trying to take control.

7

'My air...' she gasped, gesturing frantically towards the cylinder in the corner.

He stood up and turned to where she was pointing, but made no indication that he understood her meaning.

She groped for the arm of the chair and pushed herself to a standing position, pausing to catch her ever-diminishing breath.

She stumbled past him but he moved ahead of her. He reached the oxygen cylinder and pulled it away from the corner of the room. She halted, panting, and steadied herself against the back of the sofa.

'Mask...' she wheezed. She reached out towards the contraption. The pain in her chest was intensifying. Time was running out.

And then she saw his face and she knew what he intended.

His black eyes were no longer empty. Malevolence filled them. In spite of everything she'd learned about him, she had underestimated his capacity to hate. Instead of buying herself time, her little indiscretion had merely goaded him into revealing the extent of his vindictiveness.

She watched helplessly as he wheeled the oxygen container away from her and out into the hallway. He turned back and stood on the threshold, observing her. She stared back, struggling for breath, her vision blurring as she weakened, knowing she didn't have the strength to take a step forward, let alone get past him.

He began slowly shaking his head. 'I'm so sorry,' he said.

She could barely hear his words against the rasping sound in her ears as she fought to stay conscious. 'But it's not as though you've years ahead of you. You said it yourself; it's only a matter of time. Why wait? Do it now.' He folded his arms. 'Then everything will be resolved. Everything will...come to an end.'

He laughed out loud at his own witticism.

The sound of his vile laughter was her last memory. The groping for air became too much for her frail breathless body and she slid on to the floor, her damaged lungs expelling the last gasps of life.

1

It began with a telephone call. Not late at night or in the small hours of the morning, which might have served as a harbinger of bad news, but early in the evening. Yet something unnerved Esme Quentin the moment the telephone rang. Perhaps it was a sixth sense which forewarned her, developed over years of being on her guard. Certainly nothing which had gone before, no event that she could recall or snippet of information she could bring to mind had hinted at what she was about to hear and prepared her for what was to follow afterwards. For Esme it was the first step on what would prove to be a strange and bewildering journey.

When the call came Esme was kneeling in the large inglenook fireplace in her cottage, trying to relight the wood-burning stove which she had mistakenly allowed to go out, so engrossed had she been in her current research project. Local Ordnance Survey maps were strewn across the floor and reference books lay open on every available surface in the room. She was plotting the route of the long since defunct Shropton Canal, recording snippets of historical information to put into her report, in accordance with her client's brief.

April had started a cold and wet month and she was glad of the comforting warmth of the woodstove in her living room where she worked. It was only when the chill of the room penetrated her absorbed state that she realised the fire had died.

If it had been later she might have opted to go to bed and tackle the job the next morning but the fascination of her task, and the early hour of the evening prompted her attempt to reignite the embers.

The shrill pitch of the telephone startled her. She frowned and wiped her charcoal-blackened fingers on her jeans. For a moment she didn't move, just stared towards the instrument, gripped by a sense of dread. Then a compelling urgency took over. She scrambled to her feet and stumbled across the room to answer it.

'Esme Quentin. Hello?'

The distress of her niece, Gemma, at the other end of the line was evident.

'I'm at Shropton hospital,' she said, in a shaking voice.

At first Esme didn't understand. Gemma was a theatre nurse, so it was perfectly usual for her to be at Shropton hospital, but as Esme opened her mouth to frame a question Gemma's next words explained everything and sent a stab of horror through Esme's body.

'It's Mum,' Gemma continued, emotion threatening to overpower her. 'She's been beaten up. Badly. You better come.

They don't know if she'll survive.

*

The hush in the intensive care unit was broken only by the relentless rhythm of beeps and clicks from the monitoring machines. Esme stared with dismay at her elder sister's bloodied and swollen face through the tangle of tubes snaking into her nose and mouth. Who had done this? Who had inflicted such injuries to leave her so damaged?

Esme's fingers were instinctively drawn to the disfigurement on her own face and a memory of another time and another place filtered into her consciousness. She thrust it from her mind. Thoughts of such times were inappropriate here. It was Elizabeth she had to concentrate on now.

It wasn't surprising that, amidst the paraphernalia of medical technology, Elizabeth appeared much older than her five years' seniority over Esme, more like sixty than fifty. In addition, the extent of her injuries emphasised a vulnerability that Esme had never before attributed to her.

Esme lowered herself on to a chair. She stared at the pristine white sheets and became aware of the grubbiness of her appearance. Her jeans were streaked with black smudges from kneeling in the fireplace and her unruly hair had escaped its fastening and was sticking out in all directions. She smoothed the loose strands back off her face, tucking them into the clip on the top of her head, and noticed that her fingers smelt of wood smoke. She shuffled uncomfortably on her chair and slid her hands under her thighs. She'd always been the scruffy one in the family. In comparison with Elizabeth, that was. Even with half her face shattered, Elizabeth managed to retain a certain calm elegance.

Esme sighed. This wasn't real. Somehow she had been transported into a false world, where everything was wrong, unnatural, bizarre. She struggled to find the right word but nothing adequately described it.

There was movement from the other side of the bed. Esme looked across at Gemma. She was rocking slightly in her seat.

Even though hospitals were familiar territory to Gemma she looked as bewildered as Esme, as though she didn't recognise where she was.

Gemma looked up. Her thick chestnut hair hung heavily around her face, making her round hazel eyes seem even larger than usual.

'You OK?' said Esme. Her voice sounded disproportionately loud in the hushed tension of the room.

Gemma smiled weakly and nodded.

There was a sound behind them. Esme looked round and saw a nurse in the doorway.

'That's Helen,' said Gemma getting up. 'She might have something to tell us.' She went out into the corridor. Esme followed.

Helen was a hospital colleague of Gemma's. Esme vaguely remembered meeting her once before.

'This must be one hell of a shock, Gem. I'm so sorry.' Helen glanced at Esme, concern showing in her eyes from behind wide-rimmed glasses.

'She's going to be all right, isn't she?' Gemma's voice had an edge of despair.

Helen looked uneasy. 'You know what it's like with head injuries, Gem. Too early to say. The first few hours are the most critical.'

'When will she come round?' asked Esme.

Helen shook her head. 'I'm afraid we don't know that either. I'm sorry I can't be more helpful.'

'They didn't say what exactly happened,' continued Gemma. 'Why was she brought here?'

Helen glanced down at her watch. 'The police should be here soon. They'll fill you in. Apparently she was found in the park.'

'What park?'

'Here, in town.'

'What was she doing there?'

'I don't really know any more. Like I say...' She looked over Gemma's shoulder. 'Ah, looks like the police are here. You can ask them.' She approached two men coming out of the lift and spoke to them.

Esme saw Gemma shudder. 'I could never understand it before, when relatives said they hated hospitals,' Gemma whispered. 'Now I know.'

Esme went over and put an arm round her shoulders.

'You've never been on the other side of the fence before.'

'Why have I never noticed the cold, unsympathetic sense of the place? I've walked these corridors hundreds of times, yet now they seem unfamiliar, even threatening.' She looked blank. 'I don't understand any of this.'

Helen came back up the corridor, the police following behind.

'They'd like a quick word,' said Helen, as she passed. 'I've told them you've only just arrived. They said it won't take long.'

She went back to her duties.

12

Esme turned towards the two policemen. The younger man was skinny with cropped blond hair and bright blue eyes. The older one was shorter and stockier. His grey hair was pushed back off his face but his long fringe had slipped down and partly obscured his left eye.

'Detective Inspector Barry and this is Detective Sergeant Morris,' said the older man. Both men held out their police identity. Esme glanced at both in turn. She was aware of their brief scrutiny of the scar on her face but neither gaze lingered.

'I'm Mrs Holland's sister, Esme Quentin, and this is her daughter.'

'I'm sorry to impose on you at a time like this,' said the older man, 'but if you could answer a couple of questions —'

'What happened to my mother?' said Gemma, her eyes darting from one to the other.

'We're treating it as a mugging, at present,' said the inspector, 'as there was no sign of her handbag. She did carry one, I assume?'

Gemma nodded.

'One of the park staff found her,' said the sergeant. 'There must have been a struggle, which would explain her injuries.'

The inspector addressed Gemma. 'Was your mother meeting someone, do you know, Miss Holland?'

Gemma frowned. 'I've no idea.'

'Does she have business associates in town, friends, relatives whom she may have been visiting?'

Esme answered. 'We're Elizabeth's only relatives, Inspector, and neither of us was expecting a visit from her, were we, Gemma?'

Gemma shook her head. 'I didn't think she ever came to Shropton otherwise. She lives forty miles away. I suppose she might have friends here, but I don't know of any.' She began to move away. 'Look, I'd really like to go and sit with my mother, now.'

'Couldn't you talk to Gemma later, Inspector?' said Esme. 'I can probably answer your questions.'

The inspector hesitated briefly. 'Yes, all right.' He nodded. The wayward flap of hair slipped further down across his eye. He flicked it off his face. Esme wondered why he didn't simply get it cut short. Surely it must irritate him.

Gemma peeled away, back to Elizabeth.

'So,' continued the inspector, 'if you could establish whether she was meeting anyone?'

Esme stared blankly at the inspector. 'I suppose there may be something written on her calendar at home,' she said, trying to concentrate. 'She doesn't normally use a diary. Is it important?'

The sergeant spoke. 'Possibly. A witness saw your sister having a heated argument with a man in the park.'

Esme's mouth fell open. 'Elizabeth?' Esme shook her head. 'I can't believe that. Your witness must be mistaken.'

'Your sister may have made a note of his name,' continued the inspector. 'We need to eliminate him from our inquiries.'

Esme was still trying to take in what they were saying.

'You think Elizabeth was meeting this man?' She immediately felt foolish. Why shouldn't Elizabeth meet a man? She was an attractive woman. Just because Elizabeth had seemed content to remain a widow since the death of Gemma's father didn't mean that her social life excluded men. Yet it seemed inconceivable to her that Elizabeth would arrange to meet an unknown man in a park. But then why assume he was unknown? Perhaps there were things in Elizabeth's life about which she chose not to tell her sister.

Esme shook her head, her thoughts spinning. She felt suddenly exhausted. The last ounce of energy drained from her and she felt her shoulders sag. 'I'm afraid I haven't quite got used to this whole thing yet. It's such a shock.'

'We quite understand,' said the inspector.

Esme suspected that it was a line he must use frequently, though she had no reason to believe he wasn't genuine.

'If you could just check that date, Mrs Quentin,' said the inspector. 'Anything you find out, perhaps you'd pass on to my sergeant.' They turned to go. 'Oh, I nearly forgot.' He slipped his hand into his jacket pocket. 'This was found on the path next to your sister. Is it hers?' He held out a locket.

Esme gathered her bewildered thoughts and concentrated on the necklace. She swallowed. 'Yes, that's Elizabeth's. It was our grandmother's.'

The inspector dropped it into Esme's palm. 'The chain is broken. I expect it snapped in the struggle.'

The policemen expressed their hopes for Elizabeth's imminent recovery and left.

Esme opened her hand and examined the locket. She fingered the small dent on one side where Elizabeth had accidentally trodden on it, years ago. It held miniature pictures of their maternal grandparents and had been left to Elizabeth as the elder grandchild. Instinctively Esme snapped the catch and opened it.

What she saw compounded the whole evening's catalogue of confusion and turmoil. The photographs inside were of two people whom she had never seen before.

2

Elizabeth's condition stabilised overnight and Helen sent them home to get some rest. There were no obvious signs of Elizabeth regaining consciousness but at least, Esme reassured herself, she was off the critical list. That was an important step.

Esme told Gemma of her conversation with the police and the need to establish whether Elizabeth had arranged to meet someone in the park. She hadn't, though, mentioned the argument, only that the police had spoken of a witness. Esme was herself struggling with the idea of Elizabeth being involved in a violent dispute and felt that at this stage it was premature to involve Gemma. She didn't need further complications. If Elizabeth regained consciousness in the next few hours, it might all be explained away soon enough.

Although they hadn't implied it, Esme wondered whether the police secretly suspected Elizabeth of being involved in something underhand. Wasn't that customary? If you spent your working life dealing with criminals did you eventually come to assume that everyone had something to hide? It must be an occupational hazard, surely? With both her and Gemma admitting to the police that they had no idea why Elizabeth had been in the park, and a witness's report of an argument, it was inevitable that suspicions would be aroused. After all, she had questions of her own. Not least, whose pictures were in the locket.

She had handed the necklace to Gemma afterwards wondering whether, like Esme, she would open it and find the same enigma inside, but Gemma nodded her thanks and slipped it into her pocket without giving it a second glance. Esme hadn't felt able to say anything further. Her head was still in turmoil.

If it hadn't been for the distinctive damage which identified it as Elizabeth's she would have convinced herself that it belonged to someone else.

Esme offered to go alone to Elizabeth's house but Gemma seemed keen to accompany her. Perhaps Gemma felt the visit would offer some comfort, being in touch with familiar possessions which she associated with Elizabeth. Or maybe she simply felt it gave her something constructive to do. They set out together, Esme envisaging that the trip would involve no more than a quick scan of the calendar, the picking up of the post and that they would be back at Elizabeth's bedside by late afternoon.

It took an hour to drive to Elizabeth's house. The windscreen wipers droned rhythmically most of the way, but there was a break in the weather as they arrived and a patch of blue appeared between the intimidating clouds. They'd said little on the journey apart from discussing Elizabeth's continuing unconsciousness. The medics were at pains to stress that there were no definitive answers as to how long her recovery would take. Patience, along with hope, was what was needed.

Esme revisited her thoughts on having an early explanation of everything from Elizabeth. Keeping Gemma in the dark about the argument in the park might not be an option she could stick with. Perhaps the opportunity to tell her would present itself shortly.

Esme tried to assess the facts rationally. It seemed possible that the argument was merely the figment of someone's vivid imagination. Elizabeth could simply have been reprimanding someone for dropping litter. That was more Elizabeth's style.

The witness could have misinterpreted what she saw and embellished it. That seemed a reasonable assumption.

But that didn't explain the locket.

As they pulled into the drive of Elizabeth's house and got out of the car Elizabeth's friend and neighbour, Brenda, called to them, waving from her doorstep. She had obviously seen their arrival from the kitchen sink because she was peeling off a pair of pink rubber gloves as she tottered across her driveway to speak to them over the hedge.

'Gemma, dear, we were so shocked to hear about your mum,' said Brenda, shaking her head, her grey, permed hair remaining rigid despite the breeze. Gemma updated her on Elizabeth's condition.

'We've come to sort out a few things,' she explained. 'Deal with Mum's post and stuff.'

'Of course,' said Brenda, nodding gravely. 'But I ought to tell you about the man who called round a few days ago.'

'What man?' said Esme, abruptly.

'Tony saw him while he was in the garden.' Brenda eagerly turned her attention to Esme as Gemma appeared uninterested.

'He was at the front door and Tony called across to him, you know, could he help, sort of thing?'

'So what happened?' Esme threw a glance at Gemma, wondering why she was being so offhand.

'Well, it was a bit odd, really,' continued Brenda, getting into her stride. ' 'Cause, like an idiot – he cursed himself afterwards – Tony said, "were you looking for Mrs Holland?" and the man immediately jumped on it, as if he hadn't known it before. You know what I mean, he said, "ah yes, that's it, Mrs Holland".

Well, of course Tony then felt really stupid. I mean he could have been anyone. Casing the place, sort of thing. I feel a right fool, he said to me. Tony that is, not the man. He left then. Wouldn't give his name. Said he'd come another time.'

Esme frowned. 'When was this?'

Brenda shook her head. 'That's just what I was saying this morning to Tony. I really can't remember which day it was. We were trying to think.'

'So before Elizabeth's...' Esme found it difficult to know what word to use. Attack? Mugging? Accident? 'Before what happened to Elizabeth?' she said, at last.

'Oh yes, before then, definitely.'

Esme immediately thought of the argument. Was there a connection?

'Oh don't worry, Brenda,' Gemma said, dismissively. 'It's probably nothing.'

But then Gemma knew nothing about that information.

Esme realised that she must tell Gemma about the quarrel as soon as she got the chance.

'I'm really sorry, dear,' Brenda was saying. 'We do come over of an evening and draw the curtains, put lights on and that, so it looks like there's someone in, you know.'

Gemma thanked her and Brenda went back indoors.

'What do you make of that?' asked Esme, as soon as Brenda was out of earshot.

'Tony's over-active imagination,' said Gemma decisively. 'He reads too many crime novels. He'd see a conspiracy in the milk delivery.'

'Except there was one thing the police said,' began Esme.

'Yes, I know, that she was meeting someone,' snapped Gemma. 'Isn't that what we're here for?'

Esme looked at Gemma's dark expression. 'You sound as though you don't approve?'

'I don't.'

'But it might help catch them.'

'I don't see how poking about in my Mum's house is going to catch a mugger in a town forty miles away.' She turned towards the car. 'You go ahead. I'll be there in a sec.'

Esme watched her walk away. With Gemma so prickly, perhaps now wasn't the time to mention the argument, but how would she take seriously what Brenda had told them if she remained in ignorance? Esme turned and went over to the house.

She unlocked the front door and picked up the post from the mat. She stepped inside and stood for a moment in the hall.

Elizabeth's house was a large Victorian semi-detached property, brick built with a steep roof. Brenda and Tony's was the mirror image. Esme had never liked the high ceilings but Elizabeth had told her it gave the property elegance. There was never a snug feeling in the house, as far as Esme was concerned. It was too reserved, with too much space for cosiness. Esme preferred the full, almost cluttered, feel of her low-beamed cottage, with packed bookshelves and the eclectic mix of well-worn furniture. Elizabeth's tastes were unfussy and functional, and in Esme's eyes, clinical. Elizabeth would argue they had style.

Gemma joined her, a bottle of milk in her hand. She held it up. 'Cup of tea?'

'Good thinking.' Esme smiled. Gemma seemed to have got over whatever irritation she'd expressed a moment ago, at least for now, though Esme guessed that mentioning the confrontation might provoke its return. But Esme felt they shouldn't dismiss this latest information out of hand and Gemma could only appreciate its significance if she knew the full facts.

She trailed Gemma into the kitchen. 'Joking apart, you don't think Tony's mysterious caller might be connected?'

Gemma huffed, as if to consider another unknown curiosity was the last thing she wanted right now. Esme hesitated. If they did discover that Elizabeth had been meeting someone it would create an opening to mention the episode with the unknown man. She decided to defer the matter for the moment.

Gemma slammed down the teapot on the worktop with such a thump that the lid clattered and threatened to jump off.

'You look tired,' said Esme with concern. 'Did you sleep at all?'

Gemma sighed. 'Fits and starts.' She placed her hands flat down on the counter, on either side of the teapot, and leaned towards Esme. 'Is this weird for you, too? Doesn't it seem odd to you to be standing here, making tea in Mum's house, the two of us, without her being here?' Her forehead was furrowed, her mouth turned down at the corners.

'Of course it does,' said Esme. 'It's bound to. The whole thing does. It will work itself out.'

'You sound like me in my nursing role, talking to distressed relatives.'

'Then take some of your own advice.' Esme turned away.

'Come on. Get on with that tea, then let's see if we can solve the mystery of who your mother was meeting...'

'If anyone.'

'If anyone,' echoed Esme. She scanned the kitchen. 'Let's start with the obvious.' She walked over to the notice board on the wall and inspected it. A business card for a window cleaner, a shopping list pad with a single word 'matches' written on the top sheet and a flyer for a forthcoming event at the local library.

They were all neatly and geometrically arranged next to the calendar. Esme took the calendar off its hook. She stared at it for a second and then flicked back through the pages.

Gemma came and looked over her shoulder. 'What is it? Have you found a name?'

'Nothing so specific, only the initials, W.H.' Esme prodded a finger on the page. 'But on the very day.' She turned back to the previous month. 'And there, and again there.' She looked up at Gemma. 'So who's W.H.?'

'Address book.' Gemma hurried into the living room. The telephone was on a small table by an armchair. Elizabeth's address book was neatly stored in a small shelf underneath.

Gemma pulled it out and began scanning through the entries.

'I'll finish making the tea,' said Esme, turning back to the kitchen. She flipped the switch to re-boil the kettle.

While it did its magic she speculated about the initials. So, who was W.H.? Friend? Lover? Why only put their initials?

Surely you'd write the person's first name? Was this the person she was quarrelling with? On the other hand it could be an aide-mémoir of some sort. But for what?

The kettle boiled and she warmed the pot, swilling the hot water around and tipping it down the sink. Water the Hostas, Hyacinths, Heathers? She dropped the teabag into the pot and poured on the water, racking her brain to think what other things came to mind. Women's...something? Something Holiday?

She sighed. It was pointless to try and guess what it might be. They needed more to go on. She picked up a tray from behind the bread bin and put the teapot down on it. Two mugs followed into which she slopped some milk and then she took the tray into the living room. The room was spotless and smelt of gardenias or something equally cloying.

Esme looked around for somewhere to put the tray. Unlike in her own home, there were plenty of empty surfaces. There were no discarded newspapers and magazines on table tops, piles of reference books with markers sticking out of them or half-read paperbacks face down on the arms of the sofa. She walked over to the middle of the room and placed the tray on the vacant coffee table.

Gemma sat in the armchair, her nose buried in Elizabeth's address book.

'Any luck?' asked Esme.

'Nothing under W or H, or anywhere else that I can see.'

Esme nodded towards the bureau. 'There might be a clue in there somewhere.'

Gemma made to get up. 'Hang on,' said Esme. 'Let's have a think while we have our tea.'

'What sort of a think? We haven't learned anything yet.'

'That's what I mean. We don't even know if W.H. is a person. It might be a reminder to do something.' Esme stirred the pot. 'You know, like –'

'William Hill!' interrupted Gemma. 'She was going to place a bet.'

They both laughed out loud at the absurdity of the image of Elizabeth walking into a betting-shop. The emotional strain they had both been feeling for the past few days dissipated in a burst of uncontrollable giggling.

It was Gemma who recovered first. She rubbed her hand across her face and sighed. 'You don't realise how much our faces must have been in a constant frown for the past few days.

These muscles had almost forgotten how to work. Should we be laughing at a time like this?'

'Don't knock it. It's good therapy.' There was a few moments of silence while they both reflected on Esme's comment.

Gemma took a deep breath. 'So, where were we?'

Esme considered. 'W.H. is on the calendar regularly and she's not been attacked before, so perhaps that means that W.H. is completely irrelevant.'

'Or if she does have a friend with the initials W.H. he or she isn't usually aggressive.'

Esme gave Gemma a wry grin. 'Thank you, Gemma, for that pearl of wisdom.' She gave the teapot a last stir and replaced the lid. 'If W.H. is a friend she was meeting we still need to find out who it was though.'

'Do we?'

Esme gave Gemma a wary glance. She poured the tea and passed Gemma a mug. When Gemma made no further comment Esme continued: 'Telling the police that W.H was written on the calendar won't be any use to them unless we do find out, will it?' She reasoned.

'No,' said Gemma with emphasis. Esme looked at her. Now what?

Suddenly Gemma slammed down her mug on the tray and stood up. The hot tea splashed over the rim and Esme instinctively recoiled.

'This is stupid. We should be sitting with Mum, not poking around in her house. How's this going to solve anything?'

'Because we don't know what she was doing in Shropton,' said Esme gently. 'Because if she was meeting someone, he or she might have seen something.'

'So why haven't they come forward?' Gemma folded her arms defiantly.

'Maybe they don't know it's happened.'

'So what use will they be?'

'Because the more witnesses there are who were around at the time the more chance there is of identifying the culprit.'

'We know the culprit. The police have a witness, you said. They'll have a description. They just need to find him. And we need to stop faffing about here.' She wandered over to the window and stared out on to the front garden.

Esme sipped her tea. Gemma had always had a temper. As a child, and particularly when she was a teenager, Gemma had often been inclined to fly off the handle. But Esme hadn't witnessed such an outburst in recent years. It was an indication of the strain Gemma was under.

Esme finished drinking and put the mug back on the tray.

'OK, out with it. What's bugging you?'

Gemma spun round. 'I don't like this.'

'I don't like it any more than you,' agreed Esme, 'but if we can help the police find out –'

'That's just the point. Why do they need to know about Mum's private life? She hasn't done anything wrong. She's the victim, not the criminal.'

True as that was, it made no difference. Esme was well aware of that. Victim or not, the very crime itself brought unwanted attention into the lives of those involved. But Esme didn't want to get into a row about side issues. And although she sympathised with Gemma's need to protect her mother, she had her own curiosity to satisfy. Why had Elizabeth been in the park at that time? Why hadn't she said she was in the area, as she usually did? And who were the people in the locket? The questions tormented her like grit in a shoe.

*

The old lady was aware that she was being discussed. She watched out of the corner of her eye from her armchair in the residents' lounge until the two staff members glanced her way. She turned her head with deliberate intent and gave them a withering stare. It had the desired effect. They looked uncomfortable and departed. She sighed. She knew they meant well and that they were worried about her but she disliked the loss of privacy and independence since she had moved here. There had been no alternative and she knew it, but she resented the tendency to patronise, to equate frail body with frail mind and to believe that all the elderly residents were of the same character and had the same requirements.

She chastised herself. She was being unfair. They weren't really like that. She couldn't have tolerated it if they were. But now and again a situation would occur which would irritate her to the bone and this was one.

The man's visit had alarmed her but by the time she had collected herself and put the façade in place it had been too late. Abigail had already noticed her distress. Of course she had immediately asked if everything was all right. At least she hadn't gone gossiping behind her back. But despite protestations to the contrary, Abigail wasn't convinced and now she was passing on her worries to others. The old lady knew she would be under scrutiny for a while now. She must try to behave normally.

She sighed. What could she do about it, anyway? And there might be nothing to worry about. She could be over reacting. But the past seemed to have an uncanny way of catching up with her when she least expected it. It had happened before.

Perhaps it was time to talk to Elizabeth. Yes, that was it.

Elizabeth's clear-headed, no nonsense approach was what was needed. Of course it would mean she would have to tell her everything. Could she do that? What would Elizabeth say?

Would she be horrified? She shuddered slightly. She might have to take that risk, if she wanted Elizabeth's help.

Stop it, she told herself. It may never happen. Don't need to cross that bridge yet. But perhaps the time had come to tell Elizabeth anyway. Perhaps it would be good for her soul to share it, after all these years. But she knew she was being dishonest with herself. She knew perfectly well that she would only tell if it became unavoidable, because the idea of confessing disturbed her to her very core.

*

Esme suggested they commit an hour to a search of Elizabeth's bureau and if nothing came to light in that time, they would conclude that there was nothing to find. Gemma had readily agreed, having already made it clear that she didn't expect to find anything.

'At least we can tell the police we looked,' added Esme, which had earned a withering look from Gemma.

Gemma chose to start on the top drawer and took it over to the dining table. Esme dragged a chair up to the bureau and sat herself down. The divisions were all neatly organised. The first appeared to be letters from friends. No W. H., though. The next held letters needing to be answered. Bills filled the next, headed notepaper the next one and unused envelopes on the far right.

Under the pigeonholes the drawer was full of pens, pencils and highlighters. There was nothing out of the ordinary. What did she expect to find? Confession to a crime? Love letters?

Gemma's voice made her jump. 'Esme, what do you make of this? It doesn't make sense.'

Esme went over to the table and sat down next to Gemma.

Adjusting her reading glasses she peered down at what Gemma was studying.

'It's a birth certificate, isn't it?' said Gemma. 'I thought it was you who'd done all the family history stuff. Whose is it?'

Esme frowned. 'It's not one I recognise. Rosie, girl, no father's name, mother's name Daisy Roberts.' She peered at the document. 'Can't quite make out the address, can you?' She sat back and took off her glasses. 'Roberts.' She shook her head.

'Haven't come across that name before and I've done both

sides of the family. Where did you find it?'

'It was in an envelope. Nothing written on it. I almost didn't look inside. Who could it be?'

Esme put her glasses back on and returned her attention to the piece of paper. Suddenly something caught her eye and she felt her stomach lurch. She stared, trying to deny what the document was telling her. Her face grew hot and she felt her heart thudding inside her ribcage. Surely it wasn't what she thought?

'What's the matter? What have you seen?' Gemma looked down at the certificate, her eyes rapidly scanning it. 'Tell me. What should I be seeing?'

There was no way Esme could prevent Gemma from seeing what she herself had just noticed. Sooner or later she'd study it and come to the same conclusion.

Esme laid a finger on the section where the date of the birth was recorded. She hadn't immediately noticed it, being drawn instead to the name.

Gemma read it out loud. 'Twenty-eighth of March 1956.' She looked at Esme. 'That's Mum's birthday.' Her brow puckered.

'I don't get it. Who does this belong to?'

Esme hesitated. She wasn't jumping to conclusions was she? What else could it be? And if Gemma had any idea what Esme was talking about she wouldn't be looking as confused as she was. So she hadn't known either.

Esme looked around. 'Where's the envelope this came out of?'

'Esme, for goodness sake! Tell me. Whose birth certificate is this?' Gemma thrust the document at Esme.

Esme didn't answer. She snatched up the discarded brown envelope and pulled out a second piece of paper. She scanned it and then slumped against the back of the chair. The image of the two people in Elizabeth's locket flashed into her mind. It had to be.

Gemma was staring at her. 'What have you found?' she said, her voice barely above a whisper.

Esme looked up and held out the document in her hand. 'It's an adoption certificate. Your mum was born Rosie Roberts. She was adopted before I was born and renamed Elizabeth.'

The implications of what she'd just said hit her like a door being slammed in her face. Elizabeth wasn't her real sister.

3

From Esme's favourite spot on The Long Mynd in the Shropshire hills, it was often possible to see several counties. But today the weather was hazy, which aptly reflected her state of mind. She stood, hands deep in the pockets of her duffel coat, and stared out across the expanse of the undulating landscape around her.

When she had read Elizabeth's birth certificate she had felt suddenly stupid. She had started dabbling in her family history when she first moved back to Shropshire. Her friend Lucy suggested it as a way of rekindling Esme's talent for investigation which she had rejected following the untimely death of her husband Tim, an investigative journalist. Pursuing it again had proved cathartic. Slowly and tentatively she re-engaged with the world of research. At least, on her own terms.

How cruelly ironic that, while researching her genealogy, she had been completely unaware of the details of her immediate family. It made a mockery of being able to trace your ancestors back to the seventeenth century, when you were ignorant of the fact that your own sister wasn't part of your bloodline. But then who, when starting out, began by checking the legitimacy of their own siblings? Not unless they had cause to suspect something, which she never had. Should she have? The feeling of foolishness had slowly over the past few hours given way to a sense of betrayal. Why had she never been told?

Gemma's first reaction had been one of disbelief until Esme explained about the photographs in the locket. Perhaps she herself had looked inside and been similarly puzzled because she fell silent. When Esme asked the question most pressing in her mind: why neither of them knew of Elizabeth's adoption, Gemma had shrugged and said something about Elizabeth having her reasons. But despite her apparent casual manner she looked to Esme like a person in shock.

After they had returned from Elizabeth's, Esme had felt a compelling urge to visit her parents' grave. In the last couple of hours of daylight she drove out to the village where they had lived. She stood by their headstone in the diminishing light, and the chill of an easterly wind, desperate for some sense of understanding as to why they had kept Elizabeth's past a secret from her. The questions whipped around in her head, mimicking the wind in her hair. Were they protecting Elizabeth?

Had Elizabeth always known or had she found out later?

There was no way of establishing that until Elizabeth woke up and answered the question. The date of the certificate copy was 1977, the year after the act was passed allowing adopted children the right to see their original birth certificate, and so learn the names of their parents. Elizabeth would have been twenty-one.

Was she told then because she had reached a significant age? Or had she grown up with the knowledge that she was adopted and had taken the first opportunity to take up her right to know the details as soon as the act became law?

A couple of hikers came into view. Esme nodded 'Good morning' to them as they passed by. She had hoped that the walk would help her to put the situation into perspective but she had to admit that her usual source of solace wasn't giving any comfort. She decided to retrace her steps and return home.

As she walked she thought back to her childhood. Had anything ever been said, or any event happened which indicated the true relationship? Nothing came to mind. Unless the difference between the two of them was a clue. Elizabeth had always been such an exacting child, whereas Esme was happy-go-lucky in her approach to life. Elizabeth was very particular and everything had to be just so. She hated being called anything but Elizabeth, never Liz, or worse, Lizzie.

Esme used to tease her by calling her 'Lizzie Dripping', from a children's television programme of the time. Elizabeth loathed it. She tried to get her own back by calling Esme by her full name, 'Esmerelda', but Esme would remark that it sounded like a princess's name. She smiled at the memory.

Was there something in Elizabeth's development which was influenced by her knowledge that she had been adopted?

Was her need for everything to be ordered and precise part of her security? Esme tried to understand her parents' role. These days it was assumed that adopting parents were honest with their children about their parentage, but Elizabeth would have been adopted in the 1950s. Attitudes were different then. Esme guessed they had kept it from Elizabeth because if she had been told then surely they would have had to tell Esme. But Elizabeth had known since 1977 at least, in order for her to obtain a copy of her birth certificate. Why hadn't she told Esme? Because she was at university and away from the family home? Was that it? Surely not a good enough excuse. But after that, Esme had hardly been home, working away in London with Tim on the Mail and then going abroad. And later, when Esme was dealing with the trauma of Tim's death and her own disfigurement, Elizabeth might easily conclude that it was not the time to make such a confession to her younger sister.

But Esme was determined not to give Elizabeth an excuse.

She should have told her, whatever the circumstances. Nothing so important should be allowed to stay secret. What had she thought Esme would say? Had she feared rejection?

By the time Esme had stomped her way back to her car she knew what she wanted to do. She fumbled in her pocket for her keys and slid the key into the lock. She had, after all, gained some clarity as a result of her visit. She knew that she would not be able to sit back and wait until Elizabeth was able to explain everything. She wanted to find out the truth for herself.

She stopped abruptly, a particular question reverberating in her head – the attack, the argument in the park, the suspicious visitor at the house. Were these connected to Elizabeth's hidden past? And if so, what exactly had Elizabeth got to hide?

4

Gemma was at Elizabeth's bedside when Esme arrived at the hospital later. Esme stood at the bottom of the bed and studied Elizabeth's face. Were the bruises fading yet? Were there signs that she was coming round? The machines clicked and hummed but Elizabeth lay still, the only movement the barely perceptible rise and fall of her breathing.

Gemma stirred and stretched her arms above her head. She stood up. 'I could do with a cup of coffee.'

'Shall we go to the canteen?' suggested Esme. She draped her coat over the chair that Gemma had vacated. 'I'll sit with her for a while afterwards, if you like. You have a break.'

They took the lift to the basement canteen and seated themselves at a table in the corner.

'How are you?' asked Esme. 'Are you getting enough sleep?'

Gemma shrugged. 'So-so. Helen's on nights at the moment so she kicks me out when she comes on duty and sends me home to bed.'

'What about food? Are you eating?'

Gemma gave a wry grin. 'What's this? Aunty Esme fussing?'

'Your mum wouldn't thank me for allowing you to wither away while she's in the land of the sleeping beauties, now would she?'

'No, perhaps not. But I'm perfectly capable of looking after myself, you know.'

Esme felt the comment was an unnecessary rebuff but perhaps she was being oversensitive, especially under the circumstances. If Gemma didn't see that their relationship had changed, why should Esme? She pushed the thought away.

'There's nothing wrong with being pampered once in a while. Why not come round for something to eat later?'

Gemma wrapped her hands round her coffee mug. 'It's tempting,' she admitted. 'I'm going over to Mum's to pick up her post again tonight. Shall I drop in afterwards?'

'You do that.'

They sipped their drinks in silence.

Esme was aware that someone was walking towards their table. She glanced up and recognised one of the policemen they'd seen on that first day.

She spoke to him as he approached. 'DS Morris, isn't it?'

He grinned. 'That's right. Sorry to spring upon you, ladies, but the nurse upstairs said you were here.' He gestured to a spare seat. 'May I?'

Esme nodded. The sergeant pulled out the chair and sat down. He delved into his pocket and brought out a picture of a man's face. He laid it on the table and slid it across to them.

'Our witness came up with this likeness.'

'Esme said you had a witness.' Gemma drew the paper towards her. 'So this is Mum's attacker?'

'We don't know that,' cautioned the sergeant. 'The witness only saw the argument.'

'What argument?' Gemma looked up at the sergeant and followed his gaze as he glanced across to Esme. 'Do you know something I don't?' she said.

Esme cleared her throat. 'The inspector mentioned an argument that first day. I forgot to tell you.'

'How could you forget something like that?' said Gemma accusingly.

'I was rather preoccupied with how your mum was,' Esme said in her defence. She cursed herself for not dealing with it before. She hoped Gemma wouldn't say any more on the subject in front of the sergeant. The police didn't need to conclude they were dealing with a dysfunctional family or they might start looking into Elizabeth's background. Gemma wouldn't like that.

'Anyway,' interrupted Sergeant Morris, much to Esme's relief.

'If we could just get back to this suspect.' He tapped his finger on the paper. 'Do you know this person, by any chance?'

They leant over and studied the picture on the table. The man was probably about thirty, gaunt face, with wispy collar-length hair.

Gemma shook her head. 'No idea.'

Esme continued to stare at the picture. 'He doesn't ring any bells with me. And they were definitely arguing?'

'The witness was some distance away so she didn't hear what was said, just that it was clear they were quarrelling. She said it looked pretty heated, as we mentioned to Mrs Quentin.'

Gemma threw a sharp look at Esme, but took out her antagonism on the sergeant. She shoved the picture back across the table.

'This is ridiculous. The woman probably went home, watched her favourite soap and a game show before she realised the significance of the man she'd seen. By the time she'd reported him to the police any number of faces could have cluttered up her memory banks. If you match his face to the cast list of Emmerdale, you'll find he's one of the actors.'

The sergeant gave a sardonic smile, but made no comment.

Instead he changed direction. 'Does either of you know the name Leonard Nicholson?'

They both shook their heads. 'Who's he?' asked Esme.

'Someone we'd like to talk to.'

'What's the connection?'

'We don't know there is one. One of my colleagues said he thought there was a likeness but...' he shrugged his shoulders.

'I don't think so, myself. Not his territory.'

'As in the place, or mugging?'

'Both. So did you find anything on the calendar?'

Esme opened her mouth to answer but Gemma cut her off.

'No. Completely blank.'

The sergeant stood up. 'Ah well. If you do come up with

anything, you know where we are. I'll leave you in peace.'

He nodded to them and left.

When he'd gone Esme looked hard at Gemma. 'Why didn't you mention about the W.H. on the calendar?'

'What's the use? We don't know what it means, why should they? More to the point, why didn't you tell me about the argument?' She sounded as though she was trying to control her temper.

Esme cradled her mug. 'Sorry about that. To be honest, at the time I took what they said with a pinch of salt.'

'Why?'

'A bit like you with the photofit, or whatever they call them. Someone's over active imagination.'

Gemma sighed but said nothing.

'So what do you make of it?' prompted Esme.

Gemma shrugged. 'I don't know what to think.'

'Or want to?'

Gemma looked up with narrowed eyes. 'What's that supposed to mean?'

Esme tried to make her voice sound casual. She didn't want her question to sound like an accusation. She simply wanted an honest answer. 'Don't you want to find out what's going on?'

'There's nothing "going on", as you put it.' Gemma's tone was indignant. 'Poor Mum was at the wrong place at the wrong time and some junky got lucky.'

'But aren't you interested in why she was there at all? You've got to admit it's odd, even if we both think the argument idea is unlikely. And now with finding out what we did...'

Gemma stood up and pushed back her chair, the legs scraping noisily on the tiles, drowning out the end of Esme's sentence. 'I'm more interested in Mum getting better,' Gemma said haughtily. 'As you should be.'

And she turned and marched away.

*

Chopping onions allowed Esme's emotional tears to mingle with the onion induced ones and relieve some of her inner turmoil.

Already emotionally confused by the revelation of Elizabeth's secret, there was now Gemma's state of denial to deal with and her determination to remain as blinkered as possible. How was that going to square with Esme's own decision to delve more deeply?

She sighed, sensing there were turbulent times ahead. She might be prepared for them but she didn't expect to relish them.

It was a relief to let the tears run down her face and not feel the need to curb them.

She had no idea whether Gemma would turn up. By the time she had followed her back to the ward after their exchange in the canteen, Gemma had already left. The only clue Esme had that she wasn't completely excommunicated was that Gemma had left a message with the duty nurse to say she'd gone to Elizabeth's house. Esme took that to mean their arrangement still stood.

The doorknocker sounded. She wiped her face with the back of her wrists and went to answer the door.

'Onions,' she said to Gemma's alarmed face. She stepped back to allow Gemma in.

Gemma took off her coat and dropped it over the arm of the sofa. 'Brenda's going to send on the post,' she said. 'Saves me going over.'

'That makes sense. Come on through.' Esme headed for the kitchen, relieved to see that Gemma had decided that their earlier disagreement was a thing of the past. Unless this was her way of avoiding the difficult issues, by pretending they hadn't happened. Time would tell.

Esme grabbed a couple of wineglasses and a bottle of Merlot from the dresser.

'Fancy a glass?'

'Yes please.' Gemma plonked herself down at the kitchen table and dropped the heap of envelopes next to her. Esme handed her a glass of wine.

'Cheers. Here's to Mum's recovery,' toasted Gemma.

'Ditto to that.' Esme sipped her wine and then turned back to the onions. 'I usually chop these things outside, but it's a bit wet for that.'

Gemma glanced out of the window. It had been a day of heavy showers and another was rattling against the window panel of the stable door.

'Outside?'

'Yes. You don't suffer the effects.'

'I suppose not. I've never thought about it. You're a mine of information, Esme, d'you know that?'

Esme gave a weak smile and slid the onions into the pan. They hissed as they hit the hot oil. Whatever mine of information she usually enjoyed seemed to have deserted her for the moment. If there was a mine analogy, it was that she was fumbling around in a dark place like a nineteenth-century collier with only a single candle to light the way.

Esme added the remaining ingredients, turned down the heat and left the pan to simmer. She turned to Gemma who was idly sifting through the post she had collected from Elizabeth's house. Esme picked up her wine and went to join her at the table.

She took a sip and studied Gemma over the top of her glass. She had stopped flicking through the pile and was frowning at one letter.

'What have you got?' asked Esme.

'I don't know. It's the way this is addressed.'

'How d'you mean?'

'Well, you know what a stickler Mum is for convention and her obsession with being Mrs P Holland? I could never see what the problem was.'

'It probably goes back to when we were kids. With both our

names beginning with "E" if a letter was addressed Miss E Meredith, we didn't know if it was for me or her. We'd squabble until your gran intervened.' Esme laughed. 'We'd stand there holding our breath while she opened the letter to establish whose it was. We had to ask people to address letters by our full name so there was no confusion. Your mum preferred the formality of Miss E Meredith so she made a right fuss about it.

She complained that Gran should have thought about it when she chose our names.'

Gemma shook her head. 'She's never told me that, even though I used to ask her why it mattered so much.'

There was a moment's pause while Esme guessed they were both reflecting on the things that Elizabeth never told people.

'So what's odd about this letter, then?'

'It's addressed to her full name. No "Mrs".'

Esme shrugged. 'The writer obviously didn't know her like you and I do.'

'But if she only ever gives her name in the way she prefers, why would it be altered?'

Esme was encouraged that Gemma was raising the question.

Was this an indication that she might change her mind about learning more about Elizabeth's attack?

'What about official forms?' said Esme. 'You have to give your full name then.'

Gemma scoffed. 'You haven't heard Mum on the phone, giving them an earful because they haven't addressed her correctly.'

'Why are we having this discussion?' said Esme, sitting back in her chair. She put her glass on the table and fiddled with the stem. 'Why don't you open it and find out who the culprit is?'

'Open it?' Gemma looked aghast.

'Well, wasn't that the idea of going over there and collecting the post?'

'Only the bills, the things that needed sorting out. The gas, electricity, that sort of thing. Not private correspondence.'

'How do you know it's not a bill?'

Gemma looked at it. 'Because it doesn't look like one.'

'But even if it's not a bill, you can't ignore private correspondence. I'm sure the person writing would want to know what's happened so you'll need to open it to contact them.'

Gemma continued to stare at it but said nothing.

'If you don't open it I will,' challenged Esme. She felt in a strange mood, somewhere between irritation and recklessness.

Her feelings over the past couple of days had ranged from loss to hurt to confusion. And back again. In some ways Elizabeth had become a complete stranger. Who was this woman who had called herself Esme's sister but who wasn't? Perhaps opening her mail would help answer the mound of questions Esme was building. If so, she wasn't going to turn the opportunity down.

The two women stared at the envelope, the ticking of the kitchen clock the dominant sound in the room coupled with the gentle almost undetectable bubbling of the Bolognese sauce in the background.

At last Esme couldn't stand the suspense.

'Give it here, for goodness sake,' she said, reaching over and taking it out of Gemma's hand. She dropped it on the table while she hunted around for her reading glasses. Gemma seemed to be in a daze. If she objected to Esme's intentions she didn't try to stop her. So there was a modicum of curiosity in there, after all.

Esme turned the letter over and looked at it, front and back.

The envelope was slim, white and businesslike with an address window. The postmark was local. Sadly, since the Royal Mail had dispensed with franking marks carrying the identity of individual posting locations, all local mail was now stamped Shropton, so there was no way of telling whether it had been sent from town or country.

'For God's sake, get on with it, if you're going to.'

Esme looked up at Gemma's outburst and saw her gulp a

mouthful of wine. Esme slipped her finger under the corner of the envelope flap and ripped it open. She took out the single sheet of paper and read it.

'Dear Elizabeth,' it began. The letter went on to thank her for her help at a recent fund raising event and was signed by someone who called herself the secretary of the Friends Association.

'So who's it from?' asked Gemma, interrupting Esme's reading.

Esme took off her reading glasses and looked at Gemma.

She realised she was shaking slightly. 'I think we've found out what W.H. stands for,' she said handing the letter to Gemma.

'It's from a residential home called Wisteria House.'

'A residential home?' Gemma took the letter as if it held a contagious disease.

'But there's something more. Towards the end. About who your mother was visiting.'

She watched as Gemma frantically scanned the letter, her eyes halting at the relevant line.

Gemma looked up. 'Roberts, you mean? She visits a Mrs Roberts.'

'Exactly,' said Esme. 'That's the name on the birth certificate. My guess is she's in regular contact with her birth family.'

5

Esme applied certain conditions to her work as a researcher.

She wouldn't touch any job unless its roots were fixed firmly in the past. Finding out about people already dead and what had gone before was by far a safer option than investigating current issues. It was far too easy in the contemporary world to stumble into dangerous territory. She'd seen the catastrophic results of that mistake and wanted no part of it.

One current project was the history of the Shropton Canal.

Although there were contemporary aspects to the brief, it fitted her criterion of being associated with the safe, distant past of the Industrial Revolution of the eighteenth century.

She was already familiar with a rough history of British canal construction, having spent many childhood weekends walking the towpaths with her father, who had his own fascination with the subject. But she had known little of the Shropton Canal, which was of interest to her client.

Esme studied her notes, wondering how much information he required. She preferred it if clients explained their reasons for needing the information as it helped her compile a more relevant report, but he had not been forthcoming on that particular question. She scanned through the summary of what she had put together. The canal had been built in the middle of 'canal mania' when wonder of the new transport system was at its height, and was officially opened in 1797. By 1846 the arrival of the railways had begun its negative effect on the whole canal system. Shropton Canal was eventually left to deteriorate along with many smaller canals in the network. Her client was particularly keen to know about the enthusiasts' society, which had been formed in recent years with the idea of restoring the canal. With the increasing popularity of canal-boat holidays, these societies were becoming more common. She discovered that The Shropton Canal Trust had recently won funds to conduct a feasibility study to determine the cost of carrying out a restoration project. There was every possibility that the old canal might flow once more.

Esme took off her glasses and rubbed her eyes. She had been working since early morning and her brain was feeling distinctly addled. She decided to shelve the arduous task of documenting the current route of the canal, where it was still identifiable, opting instead to take advantage of the break between showers to benefit from some fresh air in the garden.

She was on her knees weeding at the front of the cottage when Gemma arrived unannounced. Esme sat back on her heels, hand fork in mid-air, alarmed by Gemma's early departure from the hospital, and fearing the worst. Had the hospital tried to telephone but she'd not heard it ring? She froze, tableau-like, on her kneeling mat, staring towards her niece, bracing herself for bad news.

'Don't panic,' said Gemma, as she climbed out of the car. 'Change of plan, that's all.'

Esme realised she had been holding her breath. She exhaled and got to her feet.

'For a moment I thought...' She shook her head. 'Never mind.' She dropped the fork on to the grass and peeled off her gardening gloves. 'So what's happened?'

Gemma held aloft a small black leather bag, swinging it as if enticing Esme to snatch it from her. 'Mum's handbag.'

'Where did they find it?' Esme gestured for them to go inside and Gemma followed Esme through the side gate to the back yard and into the kitchen.

'Someone had handed it in.' She shrugged. 'For some reason they've only just made the connection that it might be Mum's.

Something about the person going on holiday and not realising the bag's significance. Anyway, here it is.'

Esme ran the hot water tap and swilled her hands. 'So was

anything missing?'

'That's why I'm not at the hospital. I had to go and see if I could identify whether anything had been taken. Bit pointless. How am I supposed to know what Mum was carrying round in her bag?'

Esme agreed. She'd hardly remember what was in her own bag, let alone someone else's.

'I said to the sergeant,' continued Gemma, '"Would you know what was in your mother's handbag?" He admitted it would be a long shot.'

'But what about her purse, cards and so on?'

'Oh that's all there. Cash, credit cards, keys, the lot.'

'So not a mugging then?' Esme wasn't sure whether that was good or bad.

'They still say they're keeping an open mind, but the sergeant said they have to consider whether she could have slipped and fallen.'

Esme was aghast. 'Surely if she fell she wouldn't have been so badly injured?'

'Or that it was an accident. Someone running from the park could have dashed past her and knocked her over and she hit her head on the edge of the step. Apparently there was a report of someone seen running away but then there was a load of kids leaving around the same time so they can't be sure if it was significant.'

Esme frowned. 'So which is it? Attack or accident?'

Gemma leant her elbow on the kitchen worktop. 'With her handbag turning up intact, they think robbery unlikely.'

'And the row?'

'They didn't mention it. If the police do think it was an accident and nothing was taken...' Gemma sighed. 'That's it then, isn't it?'

'But what about the person she was arguing with?'

Gemma stood up straight. 'No idea. Like you said right at the beginning, he probably dropped a fag-end and Mum told him off.' She turned away and wandered into the living room.

Esme dried her hands and followed Gemma into the other room. Gemma was sitting on the sofa rummaging around in the bag.

'There was one odd thing I did find, though,' said Gemma as Esme walked in. 'A set of keys I didn't recognise. I didn't tell the police, though. No need to get complicated. They might start off on some wild-goose chase again, imagining all sorts of things. In any case, I don't know whether they're meant to be there, do I?' She held them out on her hand for Esme to see.

'They're obviously not for her house,' she added, 'because she's got a latch. They're the old fashioned sort.'

'Mortice,' said Esme. 'Like here.'

'But they're not yours?'

'No.' Esme shook her head. 'Wrong pattern. I think she's got a spare set somewhere for emergencies, but I doubt she'd carry it around with her.'

Gemma dropped the keys back in the bag. 'Oh well, no doubt all will become clear. Maybe she was looking after someone's place while they're on holiday. Perhaps they're something to do with that residential home she was visiting.'

Esme was surprised that Gemma had brought up the subject of Wisteria House. She hoped it was a good omen. She perched on the arm of the sofa and took advantage of the timely opportunity. 'I wanted to talk to you about that.' Gemma looked up but gave nothing away in her expression. 'I've arranged to go and visit Mrs Roberts.'

Immediately Gemma's eyes flared. 'You can't.'

'Of course I can. Mrs Roberts will be wondering why your Mum hasn't been.'

'That's not why you're going. You just want to dig the dirt.' Gemma dumped the handbag on the floor with obvious irritation and folded her arms.

Esme hadn't expected her plan to be greeted with enthusiasm but she was taken aback by Gemma's hostility. 'Don't be so melodramatic, Gemma. I wouldn't be telling the truth if I said I wasn't curious, but digging the dirt's a bit below the belt.'

'Mum will tell you about it when she's well enough.'

Esme knew she couldn't possibly wait that long. How could she explain her feelings to Gemma? She didn't seem to have the same yearning to find out as Esme did. She swallowed and tried to keep calm. 'I'm sorry you feel like that, but I can't wait until then.'

'Or won't.'

Esme stood up and wandered over to the desk. Tim looked out at her from his photograph. Get to it, Ferret, he seemed to say. That's what he used to call her. He told her she was the best researcher he'd ever known. Esme smiled at the memory, then experienced a moment of disquiet on the consequences of her relentless digging. She pushed the thought away. Now it was she who was being melodramatic. This wasn't the same thing at all.

'It makes no difference either way,' she said as calmly as she could.

But Gemma wasn't calm. 'You're prying. Poking your nose into something that doesn't concern you.'

'Doesn't concern me?' Esme spun round. There was going to be no meeting of minds on this issue. She tried to appeal to Gemma's sense of justice. 'But she's never told me the truth.'

'She's never told me either,' protested Gemma.

'But she's still your mother.'

Gemma looked away. They sat in silence for a moment while Esme allowed the implications of what she'd said to sink in.

'I just don't see why you won't wait for Mum to tell you,' grumbled Gemma.

'You know what the doctors say. That could be weeks away.' Or months, or years. Or never. But Esme left those words unsaid. Gemma knew what she was saying, surely. She was a nurse. She should have no misconceptions about Elizabeth's prognosis.' Esme looked pointedly at her niece. 'I can't wait around wondering, Gemma. Not if I can find out. Can't you see that? I'm hoping Mrs Roberts can fill in some of the gaps.' Gemma stared at the floor, saying nothing. 'Aren't you a little curious yourself?' suggested Esme.

'If Mum wanted to tell me, she would have. It's like spying to go behind her back.'

'It's not. It's different. This is a crisis we've been thrown into. If you want to survive a crisis you sometimes have to go down routes you wouldn't normally take.'

Gemma got up and walked over to the window. She stood with her back to Esme.

'What if her past is linked to her attack?' said Esme. 'Don't you think it might help to find out something?'

'It won't,' said Gemma bluntly. 'You're just trying to justify your actions. Anyway, I just told you, the police think it might have been an accident, so there is no mystery.'

Esme realised there was no way she was going to convince Gemma. She didn't want to be convinced. She'd already made up her mind. It was a defence mechanism against the uncertainty she feared would compound her present insecurities. Esme sympathised but that was Gemma's way of dealing with it.

Confronting it was Esme's.

Esme turned back to her cluttered desk and absent mindedly began to arrange things in neat piles. 'I'm going tomorrow afternoon, about three, after I've been to see your mum.'

'Why should I care when you're going?'

'In case you change your mind. If Mrs Roberts is who we think she is, then she's your grandmother.' Esme looked round.

'Wouldn't you like to meet her?'

Gemma swung round and snatched up her coat from the back of the sofa. She stood in front of Esme, her chin up, her expression defiant. 'I already know my grandmother. She died

47

when I was fourteen.' And she swept out of the room. Moments later Esme heard her car drive away down the lane.

Esme looked across the room and noticed that Gemma had left Elizabeth's reclaimed handbag behind. She picked it up and opened it. She took out the unfamiliar keys from inside and held them in her hand. Did these also have a part to play in unravelling the mystery of Elizabeth's past? Perhaps tomorrow she would find out.

6

Wisteria House was an elegant building in the centre of the sleepy village of Bromfield. Esme guessed it had once been the rectory. No doubt it had become too large and too expensive to run as accommodation for the clergy these days. The current vicar's residence was a badly weathered boxlike house next door, suggesting that the plot had once been part of the rectory garden. The old Georgian-style house possessed an air of authority which the new rectory would never achieve. Its solid stone walls had tall windows with low sills which looked out benignly across the land it surveyed.

The risk of destroying the beauty and integrity of such a structure on its conversion into a home for the elderly must have been high, but the architect had managed to retain the dignity of the house's origins, despite the numerous regulations and requirements there would be for such an establishment. The original style of multi-paned sliding sash windows had been retained and not substituted with plastic alternatives, which Esme always felt made a property appear as though its eyes had been poked out.

The house was approached along a short drive opening out into a wide gravelled area in front of the building. Esme parked her Peugeot next to a large Volvo estate. She manoeuvred herself out of her car and adjusted her skirt. She had deliberated for hours about what to wear, cursing herself for being so sensitive on the subject. It was ridiculous, like attending a first job interview. Was she seeking approval from Elizabeth's family, wishing to emulate the smart and sophisticated dress of Elizabeth? She hadn't had to deal with such a question since they were teenagers, vying with an older sister who seemed to have complete confidence in her appearance. Had that been part of Elizabeth's armoury, a form of power dressing to hide the underlying uncertainties? Or was the question irrelevant because at that time Elizabeth hadn't known about her true identity? Esme dismissed her ponderings with impatience and tried to choose her dress according to the criteria she would use when meeting a new client.

In the event she settled for a mid-calf-length bright-green skirt, a plain cream sweater and a scarf, emerald and turquoise, with tiny green beads stitched in wavy rows which Gemma had bought her for Christmas. Esme decided that the outfit had the right balance of smart, which she didn't do very well, and casual, which was more in keeping with her usual style.

She had taken trouble, too, over her make-up. She had been taught the effective techniques to soften the appearance of the ugly scar on her cheek but she had neither the patience nor the inclination to become a daily slave to the procedure. There were occasions, however, when she made use of the know-how and she had judged this to be one of them. While not concealing the disfigurement completely, it went a considerable way to lessening the shock to those she was to meet for the first time.

She had become accustomed over the years to the different responses people gave. They ranged from embarrassment to audacity. She had learnt that a confident smile took the edge off people's discomfort, though it had been a long time before she felt able to react in such a way. To those who were bold enough to ask the inevitable question, 'an accident' usually sufficed and by the time the questioner had absorbed the information he or she had invariably accepted that Esme had no intention of elaborating, as by then she would have steered conversation elsewhere. None of these strategies had come quickly or easily but over time they had been achievable. Only those closest to her were aware of the truth and the effort it had afforded to her to come this far.

Taking a deep breath Esme crunched across the gravel and

walked through the orangery which served as the entrance.

She turned the handle of the partly glazed door at the end and stepped into a long hallway. There was a door to her left, through which she could hear the sounds of clattering crockery. Unusual to have the kitchen at the front of the house. A compromise to a successful conversion, or designed purposely so that staff could assess the comings and goings in and out of the home?

As she paused on the threshold, the kitchen door opened and a slim middle-aged woman with short hair, wearing a white uniform emerged. She smiled on seeing Esme.

'Can I help you?'

'I've arranged to visit Mrs Roberts. I spoke to Mrs Rowcliffe on the telephone.'

The woman nodded and stepped across the hall. She tapped on a door to Esme's right, opened it and put her head inside.

'Christine, someone to see Mrs Roberts.'

'Thanks, Marion,' said a disembodied voice. 'Do send her in.'

Marion stood back and gestured for Esme to enter the room. A striking woman, tall and very erect, walked towards Esme and held out her hand.

'How do you do? Christine Rowcliffe, matron.'

Esme shook her hand and introduced herself. The matron indicated a chair in front of the large wooden desk which dominated the room, and retreated around the other side. She sat down opposite Esme and smiled.

'Matron's a bit of a dated title these days, I know, but my residents seem to like it.' Her curly dark brown hair bounced on her head as she nodded.

'It's becoming more fashionable again, I think,' said Esme.

'Quite.' Mrs Rowcliffe rested her elbows on the desk and wove her fingers together. 'And you are Mrs Holland's sister? How is she?' She leaned over and looked at Esme intently, which at first Esme found disconcerting.

'Still unconscious at the moment, I'm afraid. We just have to wait and hope for the best.' Her head had been spinning that morning as the consultant had been explaining the various tests and procedures they would be carrying out over the next few days to assess Elizabeth's development and prognosis.

Christine Rowcliffe shook her head slowly. 'We are all most concerned for her. She has been such a support since Mrs Roberts's loss.'

'Her loss?' Esme wondered if Mrs Rowcliffe was party to the relationship between her sister and Mrs Roberts but concluded that if Elizabeth couldn't tell her own family it would hardly be the subject of casual comment. Perhaps Elizabeth had allowed Mrs Rowcliffe to assume she was a family friend.

'Yes. And of course she's been such a help in clearing Mrs Roberts's cottage and sorting out everything. Packing it up for the sale. Not an enviable job at the best of times.'

'No,' agreed Esme. It was strange to be talking to someone about a part of Elizabeth's life about which Esme knew nothing.

But unless she was prepared to explain the circumstances she had to maintain the pretence that she was aware that Elizabeth was a regular visitor.

'We are extremely grateful for what she's done,' the matron was saying, 'and it's so good of you to come and see Mrs Roberts.' She smiled broadly at Esme.

'I thought I'd call in and explain what happened,' said Esme, wincing as she recalled Gemma's cutting comments about digging the dirt. Esme was determined not to feel guilty that she had come. Surely under the circumstances it was reasonable to be curious? And as she had said to Gemma, her visit might throw some light on what had happened to Elizabeth.

'She was most concerned to hear of Mrs Holland's accident. She'll be interested to hear the latest news, I'm sure.' She stood up. 'Shall I take you to her?' She inclined her head to one side, her hair bobbing over too.

Esme rose from her chair. 'Thank you. She knows I'm coming?'

The matron strode over to the door and opened it with a flourish. 'Of course. This isn't a boarding school, Mrs Quentin, where the staff vet what's acceptable for the inmates.'

'No, of course. I wasn't implying –'

'Oh there I go again,' said Mrs Rowcliffe, tipping her head back to give a whoop of a laugh. She began to walk down the hall way, bidding Esme accompany her. 'Don't mind me. Bit of a hobby-horse of mine, I'm afraid. You'd be surprised by how many people think so. If one finds that physically one is too worn out to look after oneself, it's bad enough that one has to live dependent on others. Here at Wisteria House we take pride in our philosophy, to remember that however dependent in body, our residents are independent of mind.' She halted at an open door. 'Here we are. I'll introduce you.'

The matron led Esme into a stylish and spacious sitting room with a soft-green carpet. Across the other side of the room long drapes hung at tall windows, tied back with wide sashes. The matron marched across the room and approached an elderly lady sitting in a chair facing the garden.

'Mrs Quentin's here to see you, Mrs Roberts.' She turned to Esme. 'I'll leave you to become acquainted and go and organise some tea.' She strode off.

Esme smiled. 'Hello, Mrs Roberts. I'm Elizabeth's sister, Esme.'

Mrs Roberts was a slight woman with bright blue eyes, neatly dressed in a wide-pleated navy chequered skirt and a pale yellow twin-set, a string of small dark-blue beads around her neck. Her hair was almost white, pulled off her face and tucked into a French pleat at the back of her head.

The old lady took Esme's hand in wide flat fingers and shook it firmly. Her hands were surprisingly large, disproportionately so, considering her build. Could this be Elizabeth's mother?

Esme found herself looking for a likeness, a clue that confirmed her assumptions but saw nothing. She wasn't even sure she was one of the images in Elizabeth's locket. She felt disappointed.

The old lady smiled. 'Pleased to meet you, dear.' She indicated a chair opposite and Esme sat down.

'Mrs Rowcliffe explained why Elizabeth hadn't been to see you as usual, I understand,' said Esme.

The old lady's smile faded into the folds in her long face.

'An accident she said.' She laid her hands in the lap of her skirt. 'I'm afraid she's still unconscious. But we're hopeful she'll come round soon.'

'Dear, dear.' Mrs Roberts shook her head slowly.

Esme hesitated. Now she was here, she was uncertain how much to tell the old lady. Should she explain about the suspicions behind the incident? It might be better that she and the matron continued to believe it was an accident, not an attack. But that would negate one of her reasons for being here, to find out if there was a connection.

Esme looked round at the sound of rattling crockery. A young woman was carrying a tray across the room towards them. She placed it on a small occasional table and then carried both over to the two women. Mrs Roberts gave a friendly smile to the girl.

'Thank you, Abigail, dear. Most kind.' The girl returned the smile and retreated.

Mrs Roberts looked sharply at Esme. 'How's Gemma taken it?' she asked.

Esme was taken aback by the question. Although Gemma might have decided that she was unwilling to acknowledge Mrs Roberts, there was no reason why Mrs Roberts wouldn't know about Elizabeth's family. Before Esme had collected her thoughts to answer the question, Mrs Roberts confounded her with another.

'Elizabeth never told you about us, did she?'

Esme looked into the old lady's bright eyes. 'No,' she admitted eventually. There was nothing else to say. And it was a relief that she didn't have to continue the charade.

'She was going to tell you soon, I think.' Mrs Roberts, lifted the lid of the teapot and peered in. 'It was on her mind.'

The old lady's casual manner implied that the matter was of little importance and for a brief moment Esme felt irked by the misapprehension. But then she realised that Mrs Roberts might not be fully conversant with all the facts. While she may have been aware that Esme and Gemma didn't know that Elizabeth had got in touch with her birth family, she might not realise that they were ignorant of the adoption itself.

'You haven't asked how we found out,' Esme said.

'But you did, and now you're here.'

Esme was puzzled. Wasn't she curious? She watched as Mrs Roberts focused on stirring the pot, her mind drifting back to the dilemma of whether or not to mention that they'd first thought that Elizabeth had been attacked. Or should she say nothing, now that the police weren't treating it as such? She sighed inwardly. This was ridiculous. She was going round in circles.

She wondered suddenly what Mrs Roberts's reaction would be if she told her.

'It may not have been an accident,' said Esme, more abruptly than she had intended.

Mrs Roberts looked up from the pot and stared at Esme, the spoon in her hand hovering in midair, as if confused by the sudden change in direction.

'What, dear?'

Esme swallowed. 'When Elizabeth was first found, the police thought she'd been attacked.'

The spoon clattered on to the tray and Mrs Roberts's hand went to her throat. She grasped her beads and looked straight at Esme. Esme could see the panic in her eyes.

'To be fair, they're not sure,' she continued hastily, alarmed at the old lady's reaction. 'The police thought at first that she'd been mugged because her handbag wasn't with her. Since then it's been found and nothing was taken, so it could have been an accident, someone running past and knocking into her.'

Mrs Roberts's expression remained disconcerting.

Esme immediately felt guilty. 'I'm sorry. I shouldn't have said anything. I know what a shock it was to us.'

The old lady began to shuffle the crockery on the tea tray, evidently trying to compose herself. Her hands were shaking and the porcelain clinked as she placed cups in their saucers.

'No, no. Of course you should have told me.' She tried to smile.

'As you say, it is a shock.'

'Well, you don't expect these things to happen, do you?'

'No, you don't.'

Mrs Roberts fell silent. She abandoned the organisation of the tea tray and slumped back into her chair.

'Shall I pour?' suggested Esme.

Mrs Roberts nodded. Esme dribbled some milk into the cups and picked up the teapot. She poured out the strong brew and with her thoughts on the remedy for shock, lifted the sugar bowl with one hand and gestured with the spoon.

Mrs Roberts gave a brief nod. Esme spooned in the sugar and stirred.

'Do the police know who did it?' asked Mrs Roberts, sitting forward again.

Esme couldn't decide whether it was an odd question to ask so directly about the perpetrator or whether she was simply looking for anomalies which didn't exist. 'They have one of those photo-fit pictures of someone Elizabeth was apparently having an argument with earlier on.'

'Argument? What about?'

'They didn't hear what was said.' Esme watched the old lady carefully as she passed the teacup. 'Of course it might not be important. Elizabeth often plays the keeper of the castle. She likes people to take responsibility. Gemma and I thought she might have taken a litter lout to task.'

Mrs Roberts took the cup. It rattled noisily in the saucer.

'Are you all right, Mrs Roberts?' asked Esme. 'I know it's not a very comforting subject but you seem...disturbed.'

'I'm quite well, dear, thank you. As you say, not a nice subject.' She placed the saucer on her lap and brought the cup to her lips with great care, sipping the sugary tea silently.

'The police wondered whether she was meeting someone.'

Mrs Roberts made no comment. 'I don't suppose you would have any idea who that might be?'

The old lady looked at Esme with astonishment. 'Why should I know that?' Her tone was defensive.

'I wondered if she'd mentioned it, that's all. It was the last day she came here.'

'She never said she was meeting anyone.' Mrs Roberts returned the cup and saucer noisily on the tray, her hands still shaking.

Esme finished her tea and returned her owned cup and saucer.

'As you may imagine,' she began. 'It has been a double shock with Elizabeth's accident and then finding out about her...coming here. With Elizabeth unable to talk to us, I'd love to understand. Know a bit about you.'

The old lady looked down at her hands in her lap. 'It really ought to be Elizabeth who tells you.'

'But we have no idea when that will be.' Esme sensed the first stir of frustration. She couldn't leave without learning something more. 'Surely you can explain something without feeling it was betraying confidences? You did say she was planning to speak to us. After all, the truth's out now, isn't it? The main secret, so to speak.'

Did a shadow pass across the old lady's eyes then?

Mrs Roberts shook her head. 'It's too complicated.' She put her hand across her eyes.

'What's complicated?'

'If only it wasn't now.'

'What do you mean: now? Do you mean because of

Elizabeth's attack?' At the word 'attack' she incurred a sharp glance from the old lady.

'It's best I say no more.' Mrs Roberts put her hands on the arms of the chair and pushed herself into a standing position. Esme got to her feet and moved the tray and table. She came around to the side and put her arm under the old lady's elbow.

'I don't understand,' said Esme. She lowered her voice. The conversation seemed to have taken on an air of conspiracy.

'Why can't you talk to me?' Esme gave a short gasp and looked wide-eyed at the old lady. 'You know something, don't you? You know something about Elizabeth's attack?'

Mrs Roberts's reply was terse. 'Of course I don't.' She reached for her stick by the side of the chair and pulled her arm, none too gently, out of Esme's grasp. Esme stood back. She cursed herself. She shouldn't have pressed the old lady. Instead of learning more she had panicked her into erecting a barrier between them.

'I'm sorry. I didn't mean to offend you.'

Mrs Roberts turned towards Esme and leant closer. Esme braced herself for a brusque censure but it never came. The old lady grabbed Esme's arm and spoke in an exaggerated whisper.

'Please,' she pleaded. 'All I can say is, it can't be now. I can't say anything now.'

'But it might help. Find Elizabeth's attacker I mean...' whispered Esme, even though she knew she had nothing to suggest that was anywhere close to the truth. 'Surely...'

The old lady shook her head firmly. 'Leave it.' She gripped Esme's arm. Her face was pale with anxiety. Esme could see fear in her eyes.

'Please,' Mrs Roberts begged. 'Best not get involved.'

7

Esme was unloading the car outside her cottage, foolishly trying to carry books, food and research files in one trip. She had one eye on the rapidly approaching weather and did not relish being caught in another tumultuous shower as she went back and forth to the car.

A black Audi glided past her in the lane as she manoeuvred herself around the bonnet. She glanced to see who it was but couldn't make out anyone through the heavily tinted windows. It was probably the new people who were doing up the farmhouse at the end of the lane. Village gossip was they were spending money like water. Esme hoped the uncharitable assessment meant that they were investing sufficient funds to do a decent job. The old house was in need of both TLC and an aesthetic eye to ensure that what was done wasn't to its detriment.

The telephone started ringing as Esme bundled her way through the door. In her effort to get to the telephone before answer-phone cut in, she lost the battle to balance her load and the pile cascaded from her arms and crashed on to the floor. She swore and snatched the receiver off its cradle.

'Hello?'

'Mrs Quentin?'

Esme recognised the voice but couldn't place it. 'Yes. This is Esme Quentin.' Someone from the hospital, perhaps? She felt her insides tighten as she anticipated the reason for the call.

'It's Christine Rowcliffe, Mrs Quentin, Wisteria House.'

Esme relaxed and sat herself down on the arm of the sofa. They exchanged pleasantries.

'We're in a bit of bother here and I'm hoping you can help us out.'

'Oh? Well, if I can...' She remembered that the letter to Elizabeth had mentioned fund-raising. Was Mrs Rowcliffe enlisting volunteers? Fêtes and coffee mornings were not her forte.

'I've just been on the phone to Mrs Roberts's solicitor, Mr Evans. You remember your sister had been clearing the cottage where Mrs Roberts lived?'

'Yes, so I understand.'

'Mr Evans telephoned to see how things were progressing, having not heard from Mrs Holland recently. Obviously he was unaware of the latest turn of events, which of course I was able to explain to him.'

'Oh, I assumed Elizabeth had finished everything.'

'Not completely as far as I know. The thing is,' Mrs Rowcliffe continued, 'we are unable to take matters into our own hands at the moment, not least because we are short-staffed. But there's a more pressing complication. Mrs Roberts is adamant that she does not hold a key to the cottage.' Esme felt a surge of adrenaline shoot through her system as she thought of the keys at the bottom of Elizabeth's retrieved handbag. Ironic that it was Gemma who had suggested there was a link with Wisteria House.

'I'm sure she had her own set,' the matron was saying, 'but Mrs Roberts says not. I think she may have mislaid them and is too embarrassed to say. But it means that I have no way of getting into the cottage to appraise things. Obviously Mrs Holland would have had a key. I don't suppose you know where it is, do you?'

'As it happens I do,' said Esme, walking over to the desk where Elizabeth's bag was sitting. 'Is there something I could do to help? Do you want me to call in to the cottage and report back?' She slipped her hand inside the bag and pulled out the keys, clasping them in the palm of her hand. 'If there are still things left to do, I could carry on where Elizabeth left off, if you like.'

'Really?' said Mrs Rowcliffe. The matron sounded greatly relieved. 'We are so pushed at the moment. I can't deny it would be an enormous help.'

'You're sure Mrs Roberts won't mind?' added Esme, suddenly. For a moment she imagined the matron consulting Mrs Roberts and receiving a definite 'no', given the old lady's reticence at their meeting, but Mrs Rowcliffe didn't flinch.

'No, of course not. She understands these things need to be sorted out. I'll let her know you've offered your help. I'm sure she'll be relieved to have the clearance of the cottage completed.'

Esme wasn't entirely convinced but accepted Mrs Rowcliffe's reassurance. She wouldn't like going against the old lady's wishes, despite the compelling idea of visiting the cottage of Elizabeth's family. Perhaps it was where Elizabeth had been born.

Esme reached over to grab pen and paper. 'Where is the cottage? I'd better take down the details.'

Mrs Rowcliffe gave her the address and directions. 'This is so good of you. I can't thank you enough.'

'It's no problem, really.'

'Do you want to report directly to Mrs Roberts's solicitor?'

'I can do if you like.' Esme took his details, too.

'Well, I'll leave it with you, then,' said the matron, preparing to end the conversation.

'Just one more thing,' said Esme, as a thought flashed into her head. Stupidly, it was the most obvious piece of information she'd failed to establish on her visit. 'Is Mrs Roberts's first name Daisy?'

'No, dear. It's Polly. Polly Roberts.' Esme felt strangely deflated. So this old lady wasn't Elizabeth's mother after all. She ought to have known it wouldn't be that simple.

'You're thinking of her daughter,' said Mrs Rowcliffe.

'Her daughter?'

'Yes. You remember I mentioned her when we met. She was called Daisy. She died recently, rather unexpectedly.'

Esme recalled the matron's words about Mrs Robert's loss.

So that was who she'd been talking about. Elizabeth's mother was not Mrs Roberts but the old lady's daughter.

As Esme replaced the receiver she felt a pang of empathy with Elizabeth. Not to meet your real mother until you were an adult and then to lose her a short time later was very hard.

And because she had been unable to tell her family, she couldn't engage their support when her mother had died.

Esme began to wonder what other trials Elizabeth had endured in her need to keep her secret from them all. Perhaps she shouldn't judge her so harshly, after all.

8

The only part of 'Keeper's Cottage' which Esme could see as she approached was its gable end. Both front and back gardens were flanked by tall hedges running parallel to the road.

Esme slowed the car looking for somewhere to park. There was no drive or obvious place to pull in beside it. She decided she approved. There was something appealing about walking up to the cottage unannounced by the revving of a car engine.

She found a lay-by further down the lane, at the entrance to a wood.

She got out of the car and wandered over to the gate. A public footpath sign pointed into the trees. She leant on the gate and gazed into the shadows. The path looked well-used.

The cottage's namesake, the gamekeeper, would have patrolled in here, protecting the estate's wildlife and game birds from poachers. She thought of the poor souls who had been transported to the colonies in the late eighteenth century for catching a rabbit to feed their hungry families. She wondered if these woods had seen such events, whether the landowner had been a benevolent soul or a strict upholder of the law of the land. She turned away and took the path to the cottage.

A privet hedge screened the cottage from the road. Esme stood at the picket gate and contemplated the front elevation.

It was the child's quintessential image of a house. Brick-built, it had a door in the middle, a window either side, and two above.

Esme pushed open the gate and walked up the path.

The front door was wide but squat. Anyone nearing six foot would have to bend their head to walk under the lintel. Esme put the key in the lock and rotated it. It made a satisfying click.

She turned the handle, pushed open the door and stepped inside.

Standing in the hall, the front door ajar, she silently absorbed the scene. Through the open door to the sitting room she could see cardboard boxes of various sizes on the floor and on tables.

She closed the front door behind her and shivered involuntarily. Strange to come into someone's house and pack away a lifetime into cardboard boxes. Until recently Esme's life had been nomadic; short term lets and changing locations. She hadn't accrued many personal belongings. But years living in the same house would surely result in a plethora of possessions.

How to choose what to keep and what to dispense with?

She stepped through the doorway into the sitting room. The room was a pleasant mix of furniture pieces, an old squashy sofa with a loose chintz cover, an armchair in a plain bottle-green and a wooden railed high-backed chair piled with cushions.

The rest consisted of a side table and two small stools, a large wooden trunk in the window and a round 'what-not' in the corner, green baize on each shelf. A few books and ornaments still adorned the shelves on either side of the fireplace.

She asked herself if she should feel guilty at being there.

Gemma would think she should. Esme had tried to tell her about her visit to Polly Roberts, but Gemma was still occupying the moral high ground, waiting for Elizabeth's explanation and pretending she didn't want to know. She was scathing about Esme's observations of Mrs Roberts's apparent anxiety.

Gemma cited privacy and the respect of confidences, implying Esme's disregard for such matters. She poured scorn on Esme's suspicions, accusing Esme of exaggerating in an attempt to justify her actions.

'You're being neurotic,' Gemma scoffed. 'Get a grip, Esme. You're letting past experiences distort your sense of reality.'

Esme had been shocked by the attack. Perhaps she did look at the world differently since Tim had been killed but that was because it had taught her not to take things at face value. Don't believe everything people tell you. Or did she mean don't believe anything people tell you? She shook herself. Gemma was wrong.

Esme had learned from her bad experiences, not been destroyed by them. How could Gemma be expected to understand that? She was still young with the lessons of life's experiences yet to grasp.

Esme knew Gemma hadn't yet come to terms with what had happened to her mother and what she had since learnt about her. Not that Elizabeth's being adopted troubled her, because, as Esme had already pointed out, it didn't change the fact that Elizabeth was her mother. It was the deception Gemma was struggling with, as was Esme herself.

But Esme had few qualms about prying, as Gemma termed it. She was desperate for some answers and if Elizabeth wasn't able to give them at present, Esme saw no harm in making her own enquiries.

She peered into the boxes on the floor. There was obviously still some work to do in this room; there were still items on the shelves. But she wanted to explore the rest of the cottage first.

There were three rooms downstairs, the sitting room which she had already explored, an empty room to the left and a tiny kitchen to the rear. There was a bathroom extension beyond, obviously installed long ago. The atmosphere was cold and uninviting, and the smell of damp palpable.

Upstairs there were two bedrooms. In the first, the only furniture remaining was a wooden trunk pushed against a wall.

Esme guessed this had been Mrs Roberts's room. There was no evidence of her presence, of course. Her clothes and personal things would have gone with her to the home, but the wallpaper was brighter above the trunk than on the remainder of the wall, indicating that there had once been a different piece of furniture there, a chest of drawers or a dressing-table perhaps, which Mrs Roberts might have taken with her. Christine Rowcliffe had explained that residents were encouraged to bring items of their own furniture where feasible.

The trunk held no secrets, being completely empty, so Esme wandered across the tiny landing into the next bedroom. This room held more furniture. The bed had been stripped. A patchwork eiderdown lay concertina-style across the end of the bed. Esme stroked the fabric squares. She wondered if each piece had a story. She'd once been in a school play called The Patchwork Quilt. She couldn't recall the details, only that every square held something about the past: a piece from a favourite summer skirt, another from child's dress, another square made from a cushion cover, one side faded but the other side serviceable enough for reuse, such as rag rugs. It was more than 'mend and make do'. The homes of the women who made these furnishings had soul. Now society simply swept into a high-street store and chose furniture on a whim, or because of a television advertisement. In times past, wardrobes, trunks, tables and chairs were lovingly cared for and passed down through the generations, like threads which joined their living histories.

Boxes on the bed held folded blankets and sheets. Esme glanced around the room. Objects were piled up on the dressing-table: brushes, gloves, lavender bags and scarves. In the wardrobe there were clothes still hanging, and the drawers of the dressing-table were still full. This room must have been Daisy's, Elizabeth's mother.

Esme decided to begin here and spent the next couple of hours folding, packing, and clearing the wardrobe. As she stood back to congratulate herself on a job well done, she looked up at the deep cornice around the top of the wardrobe.

She ought to check that nothing had been left on top, obscured from view.

She reached up and felt over the cornice, cringing as the sticky texture of dust and cobwebs clung to her fingers. Her fingertip touched something hard. She stretched as far as she could, trying to curl her fingers around the edge of whatever it was and bring it closer, but the object refused to co-operate.

She looked around the room. There was a walking stick propped up in the corner of the room. She picked it up and tried to use it as an extended arm but it was too inflexible. She was concerned that she might knock the object on to the floor. She propped the walking stick against the wardrobe door while she considered her best course of action.

She could reach if she stood on the bed but it was too far away and she couldn't budge it. Iron-framed, probably. She remembered she'd seen an outhouse as she'd arrived. Maybe there was a stepladder. She headed off down the stairs.

Half-way down she stopped. There was someone at the front door. She could see their outline through the glass panel. Whoever it was appeared to be slipping a key into the lock.

Who was this? The house clearance people? No, couldn't be. They didn't have any keys. That was the reason Esme was to drop them off at Mrs Roberts's solicitor once the packing was finished.

The front door slowly opened a few inches. Suddenly there came a loud clatter from upstairs. The sound echoed around the empty house. The walking stick must have slipped from where Esme had propped it up against the wardrobe and hit the wooden floor.

The door was yanked shut and the figure behind the glass disappeared from view. Esme dashed down the rest of the stairs and wrenched open the door. No one in sight. Whoever it was didn't wish to be seen, that was obvious.

She rushed down the path, scanning in every direction.

Nothing. Where the hell had they gone? Behind the cottage?

She ran back up the path and round the side towards the road.

She sprinted up to the opening in the hedge and looked through, glancing up and down the lane. Someone was moving away from her in the distance but it could be someone out for a walk. They weren't in any hurry.

Esme stood for a moment to catch her breath. Who else would have a set of keys? Christine Rowcliffe believed that Mrs Roberts had once had a set but now was claiming she didn't.

Had she mislaid them and wouldn't admit it, as Christine suspected, or had she given them to someone? But who? And surely if she had, she would have said so. Wouldn't she?

Esme retraced her steps, unnerved by the experience.

What should she do? There could be a hundred perfectly good reasons why someone else had a key. Except that at that particular moment she couldn't think of any. And if the reason was genuine, why had the person run away? She thought of Gemma's remarks about Esme seeing mysteries where none existed. She sighed. She hadn't time to contemplate Gemma's blinkered opinions. She had a job to do.

She resumed her search for a stepladder in the outhouse.

There wasn't one but she remembered the small table in the sitting room. She went to fetch it and carried it up to the bedroom.

It wobbled alarmingly but she managed to stabilize it by wedging it against the wardrobe with the box of bedding.

She tentatively climbed on. Even with the extra height she still couldn't see over the cornice but she was able to reach further.

She grabbed hold of the object and stepped down from her perch.

It was a picture frame, thick with dust. She blew across it, making herself sneeze. She used the sleeve of her sweater as a duster. The frame was silver, about the size of a paperback book, and heavy. The glass was cracked across the bottom right-hand corner. Behind it was a black-and-white photograph, an elegant head and shoulders portrait of a young woman in soft focus.

The photographer's name was embossed in the corner.

Who was she? She was very pretty. Beautiful, even. She wore a pearl necklace. Her hair was short and full, cut level with her chin, 1920s style.

Esme turned it over hoping for a date, but there were no clues on the frame itself, or on the front of the photograph. It looked easy enough to open up. Perhaps it was written on the back.

Taking care not to loosen the broken glass, she placed the frame face down on the floor. Esme pushed at the swivel clips around the edge with her thumb. They were rusting and stiff, but she felt them move. Gingerly she removed the back from the frame.

She couldn't see anything written on the reverse of the picture. She teased at a corner of the photograph with her finger.

Then she realised that this was another photo on top of the first.

She slid her finger underneath, lifting them both carefully out of the frame, and turned them over.

The second picture was of a group of people dressed in uniform, standing on the front steps of a large house. She took it over to the window and studied the people in the better light. Judging by the dress and hairstyle she guessed that the photograph had been taken in the 1930s. Had Polly Roberts ever been in service? Was she in the photograph? She must be, otherwise why keep a copy?

Esme squinted again at the picture. There was something written in the corner? The name of the house, perhaps? The writing was faded but she could just make out an 'M' and possibly 'Hall'. Then she noticed a date. 1937. So her estimate was correct. She looked at the house. There was something familiar about the building. She was sure she'd seen it recently.

She turned back to the portrait. Perhaps the woman was Daisy. Esme was intrigued. Why was it on top of the wardrobe?

Had it been discarded because of its broken glass and overlooked when Mrs Roberts moved out? If it was of Daisy, surely Mrs Roberts would have taken it with her and replaced the glass?

And why hide one picture behind another? If it was hidden.

Perhaps the frame was required and someone hadn't bothered to remove the first photograph.

Esme moved away from the window. She could try asking Mrs

Roberts but, considering her current reticent behaviour, Esme couldn't help feeling that she was unlikely to tell her anything. She gathered up the photos, carefully put the frame back together again, and put them in her bag. It was worth a try, anyway.

The more Esme thought about the old lady's behaviour, the more baffling it became. What was it that was too complicated to explain? No matter how she looked at it Esme couldn't see it as anything other than suspicious. Gemma's explanation of it being a simple case of respecting Elizabeth's privacy was perfectly rational. Except that Gemma hadn't seen Mrs Roberts's alarmed reaction when Esme had mentioned the attack and her further distress when Esme had added that Elizabeth had been seen arguing with someone.

Esme was becoming more convinced. The old lady knew something about Elizabeth's attack. Or, if she didn't know about the attack itself, maybe she knew the identity of the attacker?

9

Reports on Elizabeth were encouraging when Esme next went to the hospital. Various tests had been carried out, the results of which, the house doctor said, allowed them a degree of optimism that Elizabeth might make a full recovery. The question they couldn't answer was when. The burden of uncertainty hovered like a black cloud on a dull day.

A morning visit was becoming routine now for Esme. A pattern had been established which meant that Esme rarely saw Gemma, who had developed her own habit of coming up from theatre at the end of her day shift. Esme felt that they should reconcile matters between them, for Elizabeth's sake at least, but she guessed that Gemma would only be receptive to the idea if Esme agreed not to pursue her investigation. And she couldn't agree to that.

Elizabeth had been moved from the intensive care unit to a general ward, though continued to be monitored closely.

That felt like progress of a sort. There was a physiotherapist at Elizabeth's bedside when Esme arrived, working on Elizabeth's limbs. She told Esme that inactivity was the greatest threat to her long-term recovery and keeping her muscles working was crucial.

When the physio left, Esme sat for a while, simply watching Elizabeth. The bruising was less acute, though the change in colour barely improved Elizabeth's appearance. Esme had been assured that the bones were slowly knitting back together.

Leads and tubes remained but the clutter had lessened. The atmosphere seemed calmer, more reflective, as though Elizabeth was taking stock and deciding upon her next move.

Since Esme had learned of Daisy's death she had tried to imagine how Elizabeth had dealt with it. When Esme's mother had died she and Elizabeth had leaned on one another, sharing their memories. That helped deaden the sense of severance from the past. How would Elizabeth have coped with Daisy's death? Their past, however long ago Elizabeth had found her, would have been brief compared with that of a whole childhood. How had that affected her? Esme found that there was more she wanted to ask Elizabeth, that had less to do with her initial hurt at being lied to and more about the emotions of Elizabeth's circumstances. And in a way it had changed the nature of Esme's quest. It was no longer about discovering the truth for its own sake, but in order to understand Elizabeth.

Of course, there was still the issue of the attack and Mrs Roberts's disquiet. Esme intended to deliver the photographs to Mrs Roberts later that morning. Whether there was a chance that the old lady would reveal anything about them was another matter, but Esme wasn't going to give up. Not until she'd found out what was behind the argument in the park, and what Mrs Roberts was hiding.

*

Esme was greeted with the pungent smell of lilies when she arrived at Wisteria House. Christine Rowcliffe was arranging flowers in the reception hall. She glanced up as Esme came through the door.

'Ah, Mrs Quentin,' she said, pausing. 'I'm afraid Mrs Roberts has got a visitor at the moment. I did say that you planned to drop by.'

'Oh, don't worry,' said Esme, turning to go. 'I'll call in later.'

'Er, actually...' Mrs Rowcliffe put down the blooms and came over to Esme. She lowered her voice. 'I don't think she'd mind you interrupting her. Between you, me and the gatepost, I don't think Mrs Roberts was that pleased to see her.'

Esme was immediately intrigued. 'Who is it?' she asked.

'A lady friend. Well, I say friend. She's not a regular visitor, though it's not the first time she's been. But she told me they go back years. Used to work together. But I don't think there's any love lost there.' She shook her head to confirm her assessment.

'Work colleagues, you say?' Esme immediately thought of the photograph of the servants in front of the big house which she was holding, and instinctively glanced down.

'Yes, from donkey's years ago, so she was telling me. Oh, are those photographs?' said the matron. 'I love old photos, don't you?'

'I came across them while I was sorting through things at the cottage. I thought she might have missed them.'

Mrs Rowcliffe smiled. 'Thank you for doing that for us. I did explain to Mrs Roberts that you saved our bacon, with us being so short staffed.'

Esme saw the matron's eyes fixed on the pictures, as if she was eager to look but felt it inappropriate to ask to do so.

Esme put her out of her misery. 'Would you like to see?' She held them out to her. 'Be careful with the one in the frame, the glass needs replacing.'

Mrs Rowcliffe barely glanced at the portrait of the young woman which Esme had replaced on its own in the frame but instantly seized upon on the staff photograph.

'Goodness, do you think this is Mrs Roberts when she first worked in service?'

'So she was in service, then. I wondered if that was the case.'

'Yes, indeed and from what her friend's just told me, they could both be on this photograph.' Mrs Rowcliffe looked up at Esme with a smile. 'Strange that you should come across this now when her old work colleague has turned up.'

'Yes, isn't it?' Esme had the feeling it was one of many oddities. The friend not being welcome, the photograph of her and Mrs Roberts in their service days hidden behind another picture and left out of sight on top of a wardrobe, Mrs Roberts's nervous behaviour. What did they all mean?

'I do believe I've seen this house somewhere recently,' said the matron, frowning. 'Something very similar, anyway.'

'I thought so too,' said Esme. 'Do you know where?'

'Well, I'm just trying to remember. In the local paper, I think. Hasn't some trust or other just taken it on to make a library or something?'

'That may be it. I'll have to ask around.' Esme made a mental note to speak to Lucy. She worked in the county records office. She would know about any local history issue which had been in the press.

'I'd be fascinated to hear all about "life below stairs" from Mrs Roberts,' Mrs Rowcliffe was saying. 'History is so much more interesting from those who lived it, don't you think?'

Esme nodded. 'Have you ever asked her about it?'

'Once or twice, but she was most evasive. And then, of course, there was the journalist.'

'Journalist?'

'Well, that's what I assumed he was. I saw an article in the paper a week or so later about domestic service in one of the National Trust houses nearby so I put two and two together. Of course I may have been mistaken.'

'About what?'

'Whether he was indeed a journalist,' said Mrs Rowcliffe with an open-handed gesture.

'But someone did come. To see Mrs Roberts?'

'Yes, indeed. He wanted to talk to her about when she worked with the family he was researching. I don't remember their name. She worked for them for a very long time, that I do know.' She tapped the picture with her forefinger. 'Probably right from when this was taken. In the 1930s, would you say?'

'1937. You can just make out the date in the corner. So did Mrs Roberts talk to this journalist?' Maybe if she could find out who he was Esme could glean some information from him.

Mrs Rowcliffe shook her head furiously. 'Goodness me, no.

On the contrary. She wouldn't give him the time of day. Sent him off with a flea in his ear.' The matron frowned. 'She seemed most upset by his visit. I can't imagine why she was so uncharitable with him.'

Esme was learning so much and yet only collecting more questions. Why would someone keep a photograph of when they were in service with a family and then be so reluctant to talk about them? Had something traumatic happened during her time there? Was that why a visiting friend from the past was such an unwelcome guest?

Mrs Rowcliffe was studying the staff photograph again.

'So this must be when she was with *the* family,' she said, emphasising 'the' as 'thee'.

'*The* family?'

Mrs Rowcliffe looked up and handed Esme back the pictures.

'Yes, the one I mentioned, where she worked for years. That's how she got her cottage, you know. The family left it to her.'

10

Lucy, reliable as ever, remembered the piece in the paper to which Mrs Rowcliffe had referred and promised to track down a copy. When she phoned back with the details Esme realised at once why the house was familiar. The project was to convert a dilapidated, fire-damaged old building into a new museum and library for a botanical trust, and the reason it had caught her eye was because the architect involved was an old friend of hers, Andy Patterson. She phoned him immediately and he'd suggested she should call in at his office. He might know something about the house's history which would be useful to her. She had taken a copy of the photograph of the house to bring with her. She had felt a certain sense of duplicity in doing so but if she was to make any progress in her quest she needed some leads and this was the only one she had at the moment.

As Esme had feared, Mrs Roberts was unhelpful regarding the photographs. She confirmed that she was in the staff photograph but immediately looked as though she regretted saying anything. She made no comment about it being out of the frame. Esme explained she'd planned to replace the broken glass, and had discovered it when she dismantled the picture.

Mrs Roberts nodded, but showed no further interest.

She'd been dismissive about the name of the house, insisting that it was a long time ago and best not to look back. Neither did she give anything away on the portrait of the young woman, only that it was someone she'd once known. She then announced that the visit from her friend had tired her and she intended to rest in her room. Esme stood and watched her shuffle out of the lounge. She felt frustrated, yet she was not surprised. The old lady had her reasons for keeping such information locked in the past and

Esme's curiosity was not good enough grounds for her to change her mind.

Esme sat in the swivel chair in Andy's office waiting for the architect to emerge. She could hear the sounds of frenetic activity down the corridor. Telephones ringing, photocopiers humming and footsteps up and down the stairs as Andrew's colleagues went to and fro carrying out their business. The hectic pace would suit Andy. He'd always done everything at speed, even at school, where Esme had first met him. Since her return to the area she had bumped into him at the history society she occasionally attended. He had been conducting a seminar on vernacular architecture. It was one of his passions.

Esme glanced at the clock on the wall. Andy was with a client elsewhere in the building but would be free shortly. Esme absent-mindedly picked up a booklet from Andy's desk and began flicking through it, hardly focusing.

Instead she was wondering whether Gemma had moved any closer towards seeing how things were from Esme's point of view. Perhaps she should try to talk to her again. She'd left a couple of messages on Gemma's phone but her niece hadn't as yet chosen to respond. Maybe she was expecting too much, too soon. Once Elizabeth's condition improved, that would be the time to readdress their differences, when they weren't under so much pressure.

The door flew open and Andy characteristically burst into the room, tie flung over his shoulder as if he'd done a hundred metres sprint to get there.

'Esme.' He beamed. 'Great to see you.' He came round the desk and gave her a bear hug.

'You haven't learnt how to slow down yet, then?' said Esme.

Andy grinned. 'Slow down? What's that? Never get anything done.'

'I can believe that. You wouldn't know how to function at a lesser speed.'

Andy sat down on the end of the desk. 'So what can I do for you?' He gestured towards the document in Esme's hand. 'Something about the Local Development Plan?'

'What?' Esme glanced down at what she'd been reading. 'No, I was just browsing. Sorry, I shouldn't be nosing at stuff on your desk.'

'Oh don't worry. That's for public consumption. You can buy your very own copy from the local planning authority. Fascinating bedtime reading about where's favourable for development. I'll get you a copy for Christmas.'

Esme laughed. 'I'll pass, if you don't mind. There's plenty else I should be reading.'

'So, fire away. You said something about a newspaper article.'

'Yes, in the Chronicle a few weeks ago. Isn't it your outfit that's involved in that place which burnt down and is being renovated for some sort of research library? Some botanical trust?'

'Markham House, you mean?'

'Could be. I've got a photo of a house taken in the 1930s and it looks like the same place as in the newspaper, but I want to be sure.' She dipped into her bag and pulled out the copy she'd made. She passed it over to Andy, who examined it with interest.

'It certainly looks familiar. We could do with the other to compare it with.' He picked up the phone. 'There'll be a photo on the file. Hang on, I'll see if someone can dig it out.'

He gave the necessary instructions over the phone and replaced the receiver. 'So how are things with you? Is this one of your research projects?'

'Sort of.' She didn't want to go in to details. She changed the subject. 'So how's business?'

'Oh, you know. Either getting thin and giving us palpitations over staff levels or too much work giving us...'

'Palpitations over staff levels,' laughed Esme. 'It's never nice and steady is it?'

'No it's not. I remind myself that when it's busy, like now, I should be thankful but it's exhausting. Talking of which, Esme, you look a tad done in yourself. You're not working too hard, I trust?'

Esme was surprised at what he could read in her face. She told him briefly about Elizabeth.

He was shocked. 'Poor thing. Hope they get the bastard.'

There was a brief knock on the door and a young woman entered. She acknowledged Esme with a nod. 'Is this the photo you wanted, Andy?' she said, passing him a manila envelope.

He took it and delved inside. 'Is this the one which the press used?'

'Far as I know.'

'Thanks, Jill.' The young woman smiled and left.

They compared the two photographs.

'Well, it certainly looks like the same place,' said Esme.

'What do you know about it?'

'Not a lot. I'm not involved, myself. One of the other guys is working on it. But what I do know is that there were heaps of documents found by the trust who bought the place. Most got passed to the Records Office, so you'll have a field day browsing through it all. Just up your street.'

Esme returned her photograph to her bag. 'I'd better get on to it then, instead of holding you up.' She stood up.

'Did you read the article?'

'Not really. It was the photo I saw. I read the headlines and saw your name. Why d'you ask?'

'The paper tracked down one of the members of staff who used to work there years ago. The gardener, I think. He might be able to give you an angle on the place.'

'Now that really would be useful,' said Esme with undisguised enthusiasm. Another member of staff might be able to throw some light on why Polly Roberts was so reluctant to talk about the old days.

She threw her bag over her shoulder and thanked Andy for his help. She couldn't wait to get started.

*

Gemma walked over to the bed and watched her mother's breathing for a moment or two. Was it less shallow than the last time she was here? The nurse said her fingers had twitched slightly yesterday, but though Gemma focused on them for a while she could discern no sign of movement.

A large vase of flowers on top of the cabinet in the corner of the room caught her eye. It was a beautiful arrangement of narcissi. They were almost white, lemony-sherbet in the centre.

Surely they hadn't been there yesterday or she would have noticed. She wandered over for a closer look.

A card was tucked inside. It read: 'Looking forward to chatting with you again soon.' She turned it over. There was no name. She frowned. Who would send such a gorgeous bouquet of flowers and then not say who it was from? Maybe the flower shop made a mistake and missed off the name. It was an odd message. Surely a friend would make some comment about getting well soon, or some similar sentiment. Chatting?

It suggested gossiping, chitchat, having a natter. Not something Gemma identified with her mother's activities.

A disturbing thought occurred to her. That person she was seen arguing with – was the word 'chatting' a reference to the argument they had been having? She spun round and walked over to the nurses' station. A young fresh-faced nurse was on the telephone. Gemma hadn't seen her before. Perhaps she was agency staff. Gemma paced up and down until she'd finished her call.

'Who brought the flowers?' asked Gemma before the nurse had replaced the receiver.

'No idea. I only came on duty at two. I can ask. Was there no message?'

'Yes, but it's a bit odd, and there was no name.' She held the card out towards the nurse, who took it from her and read it.

'Yes, I see what you mean.' She handed it back to Gemma.

She smiled. 'Maybe it wouldn't need a name if your mum could read it.' Clearly she'd been briefed as to who Gemma was.

'Maybe it was an "in-joke".'

'Why write an in-joke to someone who's still unconscious?'

'True.' The nurse slid off her chair. 'I'll go and see what I can find out and let you know.'

Gemma nodded. 'OK. Thanks.'

She wandered back into her mother's ward and pulled up a chair by the bed. Watching her mother made her think of Esme and this obsession with seeing things where there was none. Trouble was with Esme, if she got her teeth stuck into something, she was terrier-like in her tenacity. She'd always been like that, apparently. Gemma remembered comments her mother had made about it getting her into hot water. At the time she hadn't understood what she'd meant. She'd probably been too young. Now she could see how it could happen.

Gemma shifted in her chair. Had her reaction to the flower message been caused by Esme creating doubts in Gemma's mind?

Her mother was here because of an accident, which had been misconstrued as something more sinister. That was all. Wasn't it? Or was that just wishful thinking, because she couldn't deal with the idea of anything else? She felt a flash of irritation. Esme's assumptions were clouding her own reasoning.

She sighed and glanced at her watch. Only eight o'clock. It felt like the middle of the night. She rubbed her eyes and slid herself down in the chair so she could rest her head on the back.

In a couple of minutes she was feeling drowsy. No problem. She might as well take a nap if her body was telling her to. She let her mind drift.

She had no way of telling how long she had been dozing but it couldn't have been more than a few seconds. She woke with a start, and with the distinct impression that someone was in the room. She sat up, blinking, expecting to see the nurse returning with information.

'Did you establish anything?' said Gemma groggily, but the room was empty. She shifted in her chair and looked towards the door. Had someone just left the room? She forced herself off her chair and staggered to the door. She snatched it open and peered frantically up and down the corridor.

The nurse she had spoken to earlier was walking towards her from further up the ward.

'Did you see anyone, just then?' asked Gemma.

'No, why?'

Gemma looked back down the corridor. The swing doors at the entrance to the ward were twitching slightly. Had someone just gone through them? Gemma dashed down the passageway and burst through the doors. The lift was closing but she was too late to see whether anyone was inside. She banged her hand on the call button, but the lift carried on its journey. The lift next door gave an audible indication that it was on its way.

'That's no bloody use, is it?' she shouted at it. She turned to see the nurse at her shoulder.

'You OK?'

Gemma sighed. 'I think there was someone in Mum's room.'

'Do you want me to call security?'

Gemma shook her head. 'To say what? I was half asleep in the chair. I could be dreaming for all I know. That's why I wanted to see if there was anyone. To see if it was my imagination.' She began to walk back up the ward.

'Sorry. I didn't see anyone.' The nurse fell in step along side her. 'And I'm afraid I drew a blank with the flowers. No one saw them arrive. They were left at the nurses' station while my colleague was called to a patient. He found them when he got back a few moments later.'

'Phantom flower deliverer and now phantom visitor.'

Gemma wrinkled her nose. 'Ah, well, thanks anyway. It's

probably nothing.' She watched as the nurse went back to her duties. Was she making something of nothing? For goodness' sake, she was getting as bad as Esme, seeing mysteries where there was none. She mustn't let it get to her.

She marched into her mother's room and glared at the flowers. Then she hoisted them out of the vase and shoved them, blooms downward, into the dustbin.

11

Lucy found the name of the old gardener who, Andy had mentioned, had been interviewed by the newspaper. He was Albert Jennings and Esme soon located him in the telephone directory. The next stage was less fruitful. She failed to get an answer on three separate occasions during the morning and there was no facility for leaving a message. At the third attempt Esme dropped the receiver back on to its cradle with a sigh of frustration. She decided to visit the records office instead. Andy said that the documents relevant to Markham Hall had been deposited there.

When Esme arrived it was quiet. Lucy had warned her that as the record office had only recently acquired the documents no one had yet begun the onerous task of cataloguing everything.

Consequently there was no way of knowing whether there was anything there relevant to Esme's cause. The one positive note, however, was that there were several estate maps amongst the collection. Esme decided that a study of these would be a good place to start so Lucy promised to have them available for Esme's arrival.

Lucy was on the reception desk when Esme arrived. She was in her early forties but was one of those enigmatic individuals, whose age was difficult to assess, looking anything from twenty-five to fifty. Her straight shoulder-length hair was cut with a fringe and she wore plain, old fashioned clothes. Considering the enthusiasm Lucy showed in her work, Esme thought she ought to be dressed in flamboyant patterned fabrics of bright colours, not the grey functional outfits she invariably wore.

Perhaps it had something to do with being influenced by the sober environment of archive establishments.

Esme signed herself in at the reception desk.

'Not rushed off your feet this morning, then?' she said, indicating the short list of names on the pad.

'Must be the rain,' said Lucy, wrinkling her nose. It had been wet for days now. Esme couldn't remember the last time she'd left the house without a waterproof and an umbrella.

'I've put the maps out,' said Lucy. 'What is it you're looking for exactly?'

'No idea,' said Esme. 'I'm interested in finding out about the family who owned the estate before it was sold to the trust.'

'They were called Monkleigh,' said Lucy. 'Sir Charles Monkleigh would be the one relevant for you, I think. He inherited the estate in 1930.' She slid a thick book across the counter towards Esme. 'I looked him up in an old Who's Who but it doesn't say much.'

Esme opened the book where Lucy had marked it with a slip of paper. She ran her finger down the page until she came to his name. *Monkleigh, Sir Charles Edward Mortimer.* She scanned through the significant items. *Born 3 Sept 1904...married 1937 Rosalind James-Barrington...one daughter.* The remainder of the entry was details of his education and a long list of activities associated with his political life.

'He was a bit of a philanthropist, apparently,' said Lucy. 'Well into his nineties when he died, which wasn't that long ago, actually. He was involved with all sorts of projects right up to the end.' She handed Esme a photograph. 'Here he is at some local fund-raising event in the seventies.'

Esme took it from her. 'Where did you get this?' She looked at the man in the picture, tall and upright in a suit, with a head of thick white hair. He was standing beside a thin woman holding a toddler's hand.

'It was on file in our photograph collection. Taken by the local paper.' She gave Esme a smug smile. 'Our new computer cataloguing system is showing its mettle. I put in his name and, bingo, it referred me to this.'

'That's great,' said Esme. 'What else did it throw up?'

Lucy looked crestfallen. 'Give us a chance, it's an on-going project. Not everything's logged on the system yet.'

Esme looked back at the photograph. 'Is this his wife?' she said pointing to the woman and child. 'The entry said they had a daughter, but this looks like a boy to me.'

'No, that's his sister and her son, apparently.'

Esme put the photograph down on the counter. She scrutinized the old gentleman's face, wondering what he would be able to tell her if he'd been alive. She slid the photograph back towards Lucy. 'That's a great find, Lu. I'd better go and see what else I can learn from the maps.' She turned to go into the search room.

'By the way, I've got the copy of that newspaper article you were after about the botanical trust,' said Lucy, scanning the desk. 'I'll bring it over to you when I put my hands on it.'

Esme raised a hand in thanks and went through the double doors into the main search room. She passed microfiche readers, filing cabinets and shelves of box files. People were engrossed at their screens, scribbling notes or poring over lists.

She continued into the next room. Here there were huge layout tables. In the far corner there was a large, grey, faded roll which stretched the width of the table. She put her notebook and pencil down and unrolled the maps, holding the corners down with weights so she could examine them more easily.

The area covered a huge part of the county. She peeled back the top map to reveal another of a larger scale which showed the heart of the estate. She could identify the main house and other outlines identified as 'dwellings' in several places on the periphery. She studied the map carefully, trying to get her bearings as to where the land extended and to see whether she could identify any places she knew.

Then she saw it. Almost on the boundary, in the far corner of the map. It was clearly identified with its name, Keeper's Cottage. If what Mrs Rowcliffe said was true, that Polly Roberts had worked with the family for many years, this might have been her home for a long time. At the time of the photograph she might have lived in the staff quarters, of course. Perhaps over the years she had moved into the cottage and then on her retirement it had been made over to her. It was a very generous gesture. A secure tenure for life would have been the more usual arrangement. She must have had a significant part to play in the life of the family to warrant such consideration.

Esme glanced up and saw Lucy coming towards her with a newspaper in her hand.

'Here's that article,' said Lucy. 'I've just had a quick sneak look at the heap of stuff. The Monkleighs were obviously considerable landowners in their time.'

'So I see, looking at these maps. What state's the "heap of stuff" in?'

Lucy rolled her eyes to the ceiling. 'The proverbial haystack. It'll be a slow job to go through all that lot. I don't think it had been organised for years, so there's no sense of order, just boxes of papers and books.'

Esme was disappointed. The staff would be hard-pressed to trawl through such a collection of documents quickly, despite the enthusiasm they might feel about the fascination of such a valuable historical source. Their time and expertise were called upon from many quarters and they were always under pressure one way or another. She was tempted to offer her own services but she had to be realistic. Her days were already stretched visiting the hospital and working on her paid research. Her personal investigations would be time-consuming enough without getting sucked into such a project. Besides, if the documents proved irrelevant to her case, she might learn nothing for her efforts.

'I do intend to make a start, though,' said Lucy, with her usual optimism. 'You never know. I might throw up something of note.'

She looked over Esme's shoulder. 'Found anything?'

Esme shrugged. 'Nothing of any great significance. Just confirmed the location of a cottage of someone I know who lived on the estate. Polly Roberts. She worked for the family for years, from around 1937.'

'On the estate?'

'No, she was part of the household staff.'

'Not for long she wasn't.'

'How do you mean?' Esme took off her reading glasses.

'Markham Hall burnt down, you know.'

'Yes, I know. But wasn't that recently?'

Lucy shook her head and held up the paper. 'It's all in this article. There wouldn't have been household staff after the fire, because the house was never rebuilt.'

Esme sensed she was about to learn that her information didn't add up.

'So when was the fire?' she asked.

Lucy handed her the newspaper. '1942.'

12

Esme cursed the lack of clarity of the microfiche she was studying, not to mention its small print. Even with the magnification of the reading machine as high as it would go, it was still difficult to decipher and extremely tiring to look at. She sat back in her chair and rubbed her sore eyes. Her shoulders were beginning to ache too, from crouching over the machine for so long. And she hadn't even learnt anything to compensate for her discomfort.

What Lucy had told Esme of the fire at Markham Hall completely undermined Mrs Rowcliffe's theory that Polly's cottage had been left to her for 'long and loyal service'. If the house where Polly was working had burned down in 1942, she would only have been employed there for a few years. Had the matron been misinformed or had she simply jumped to a false conclusion?

Lucy proffered a suggestion that some staff might have moved down to the south east after the fire, to the other family home. It was possible. But would they have needed the extra staff? Or perhaps Polly had found different work on the estate and remained. But if the family had moved permanently down south, in what way would she have managed to establish such a close relationship, resulting in her being left an estate cottage?

There was something here that wasn't quite right.

It was then that Esme had thought of Daisy. Esme hoped that if she could find the record of Daisy's birth and send for her birth certificate, it would show where her parents were living at the time and thus establish whether Polly had moved down to Brighton as additional staff or whether Daisy was born on the estate in Shropshire. That was the theory, but it was not proving an easy task.

The filming of thousands of records on to neat postcard- sized pieces of celluloid was a brilliant device, saving time- consuming journeys to see the original documents which were held all over the country. But the quality of the film varied considerably. There was nothing to better scanning through the originals, large journals in the Family Record Centre in London which listed all births, marriages and deaths across the country since 1837. Esme's favourite volumes were the earlier issues when entries were written in beautiful copperplate handwriting. Later on the records were typewritten and for entries of recent events access was via a computer screen.

But despite her checks and rechecks she could find no record of a Daisy Roberts being born in the time period that would fit the facts as she knew them.

She did the calculations again in her head to check that she hadn't got the time wrong. If Daisy was, say, twenty years old when she had Elizabeth, who was born in 1956, that would mean that Daisy was born around 1936. Adjust the date to take account of the fact that she could have been younger or older and the dates would be somewhere from 1925 to 1940.

Esme had searched the four quarterly records of births in each of those years. Twice. And come up with nothing. Nothing that fitted, anyway. There were several Daisy Roberts listed but they were born in Yorkshire, or Cornwall or Suffolk. It wasn't impossible that Daisy had been born in one of these counties but there needed to be something else in Esme's information armoury to link them before she could order a copy of the birth certificate with any hope that it was the Daisy she was looking for.

After rechecking the last few fiches once more, in case her concentration had lapsed, she switched off the microfiche reader, returned the fiche to its envelope and took it back to the filing cabinet.

Esme replaced the packet, slid the drawer shut and rested her elbows on the top of the cabinet. If Daisy's birth wasn't in the index there could be a number of reasons. Perhaps it was never registered. By law, births had to be registered within a period of forty-two days. If too much time had passed and the parents were concerned about the fine they would incur, they might have decided not to bother with the formalities at all. Or it could be that she was registered in some name other than Daisy. Esme made a mental note to look Daisy up in her name dictionary and see if it was short for something.

Alternatively, it could be an administrative error. There was ample opportunity for human error when the indexes were compiled. Maybe it was a simple matter of someone having missed her off the list.

Something caught Esme's eye and she realised Lucy was waving at her from the main desk. She stood up and walked over. Lucy's face was beaming and she was clutching a brown leather-bound book to her chest.

'You look pleased with yourself,' said Esme, glancing at the book. 'What's all the excitement?'

'You'll love this,' said Lucy. She was almost hopping about, much to Esme's amusement. 'I've been trawling through the Monkleigh documents.'

Esme felt that surge of expectancy she always got when she knew she was on the brink of discovering something new after a long and unproductive search. 'What? What have you got?'

Lucy held out the book. 'It's some sort of household record from 1937. Isn't that the date you mentioned? I don't know if there's more but this is the only one I've come across so far.'

Esme took it from her. 'Look towards the back pages. There's a list of the wages paid out and the names of some of the staff.'

Esme laid the book open on the desk and began slowly turning the pages, guided by Lucy's instructions.

'A bit further on. There!' She pointed to a name on the list. 'Look. That's the name you said, isn't it?'

Esme adjusted her reading glasses and focused on the line

Lucy was indicating. In neat, careful handwriting was written: *Wages 10s paid to Miss Polly Roberts.*

She read it again. There was no question. Polly Roberts was unmarried.

*

'Lunch is on its way,' said Esme, edging around the café table. She slid into the chair opposite Lucy and set down two glasses of white wine.

'Thanks, Esme.' Lucy raised her glass. 'Here's to mystery and intrigue.'

'You're incorrigible.' Esme grinned. 'Don't they warn you as part of your training not to get emotionally involved with your clients?'

'Most definitely not. That's the whole point of the job, delving into the past and getting worked up about the people you find out about. So what have we got? What's the significance of Polly Roberts?'

Esme hesitated. A stab of loyalty to Gemma? More likely her own protection mechanism. She still felt predominantly foolish about her ignorance of Elizabeth's adoption. But Lucy was a good friend and a discreet one, too. If there was anyone she should be able to confide in, it ought to be Lucy. She knew Esme better than anyone.

'It's rather difficult,' began Esme, fiddling with the stem of her glass.

'Oh, I see. Don't worry if it's confidential.' Lucy smiled but didn't fail to look disappointed.

'No, you don't understand. I didn't mean that.'

Lucy smiled. 'Don't look so distraught, Esme. I just thought this was some more of your family history you were looking into.'

Esme felt uncomfortable. 'Well, it is in a way, but not as I might have imagined.'

Understandably Lucy looked puzzled. Esme gave a half-laugh.

'I'm sorry, this is sounding quite ridiculous and I'm not making any sense.'

The waitress arrived at the table with their meals. By the time they had organised their food Lucy had either forgotten Esme's confusing remarks or had chosen to disregard them. The perfect opening for Esme to explain the situation had evaporated.

Esme concentrated on her salad, asking herself whether she should simply spill out everything. But if that was her intention her brain and mouth didn't seem to want to co-operate with one another. She kept eating.

'So do I get to know who Polly Roberts is?' asked Lucy casually.

Esme told herself to come right out with it and say, she's Elizabeth's grandmother, but the words stuck in her throat. If she said that much, she would have to explain everything and she didn't feel she could cope with Lucy's reaction, right now.

She lost the second opportunity.

'Elizabeth knows her. She lives in a residential home not far from here.' Esme tried to lighten the cool atmosphere which she sensed was gathering between them. 'They know her there as Mrs Roberts,' she added with a wink.

Lucy smiled and seemed to relax. 'Ah, now I see why her name was significant. Roberts was her maiden name and so it looks like she never married. So her daughter was illegitimate.'

Esme tried to ignore the fact that it was Elizabeth's mother they were talking about. She carried on as if she were discussing someone else's life history.

'Which could explain why I couldn't find her birth in the indexes. Maybe it was never registered, under the circumstances.'

Lucy shrugged. 'So what else? There must be something. Babies born out of wedlock are not exactly a new phenomenon.'

'I'm not really sure, but Mrs Roberts is fretting about something and she's not letting on what. Of course, she doesn't know me very well, so she's hardly going to pour her heart out so...'

'So you thought you'd do a bit of digging.'

Esme flashed Lucy a look. She recalled Gemma's comment about digging the dirt. 'You make it sound unethical.'

Lucy laughed and shook her head. 'No, not at all. I know you. You hate not knowing things. That's why you're good at what you do.' She paused with her fork in midair and looked hard at Esme. 'But I get the impression there is something more to this.'

Esme put down her knife and fork and stared at her plate. Go on, she told herself. Just tell her. 'It's about Eizabeth...'

'Yes?'

Esme paused, not knowing how to proceed. She picked up a roll and tore off a piece. 'You remember they thought Elizabeth had been attacked?'

Lucy looked concerned. 'But they think it was an accident now, don't they?'

'Apparently the doctor said she could have got her injuries in a fall, if someone had pushed past and knocked her over.' She shrugged. 'So it could have been accidental.'

Lucy frowned. 'Could have, but they can't be absolutely sure. Is that what you're saying?'

Esme nodded. 'And of course there's still the matter of the argument with someone.'

'Have the police said any more on that?'

Esme slumped back in her chair. 'Apparently not. As Gemma said, if everything's pointing to it's being an accident, why look for a crime that doesn't exist? I'm sure they've plenty else to do.'

Lucy took a mouthful of food and chewed it. Esme could feel Lucy's eyes on her.

'Go on then,' said Lucy, when Esme didn't say anything. 'I'm guessing you were about to tell me why you think there's a connection with Elizabeth's attack and this old lady?'

'It was when I went to visit her,' Esme explained, recalling Gemma's reaction to the proposed visit. 'I thought I ought to go as she'd wonder why Elizabeth hadn't been to see her.'

'And?'

Esme picked up her wineglass and took a sip, debating how best to convey her concerns. 'It was her reaction when I told her the police had thought it was an attack rather than an accident.' She shrugged. 'Maybe I should have dismissed it as over-imagination but she seemed genuinely alarmed.'

'Well, hearing that someone you know has been attacked is going to be alarming, isn't it?'

Esme shook her head. 'It was more than that. Elizabeth had visited her that day, you see, and I got the idea that Mrs Roberts knew something about it.'

Lucy's eyes widened. 'Are you sure? Have you told the police?'

Esme sighed. 'What could I say? It's a feeling, that's all.'

'So you thought if you could get some background on this lady, you might find something you could use to persuade the police to take your concerns seriously?'

'Something like that.' Esme didn't like to think what Gemma's reaction would be. Would she welcome the fact that the perpetrator of the crime might be caught, or would she be angry that her mother's life was being intruded upon all over again?

'So what have you got so far?' said Lucy, clearly warming to the task. Esme relaxed a little. For Lucy this was just another intriguing research project. She wasn't going to bother about the whys and the wherefores of Esme's interest. She didn't need to get caught up in the anxiety and emotion. Lucy would only worry about Esme's sensitivities if she knew the full story. Better that she enjoy the detective work for its own sake. Esme could tell her everything another time.

Esme rested her elbows on the table and counted off the items she had accumulated to date. 'An unmarried mother, a child whose birth appears to be unregistered and a link with a family whom the mother used to work for. The link being the cottage which she now owns but which once belonged to the estate where she worked.'

'Sounds like a good story. What's next?'

'But hang on. There's more.'

Lucy leant closer, conspiratorially. 'I'm all ears.'

'The matron where Polly Roberts lives says that the cottage was left to her by the family, but she told me that Polly worked for them for years and years.'

'That's why you were thrown by finding that Markham Hall burned down in 1942? Because you assumed she still worked at the house and she couldn't have?'

'Exactly.' Esme picked up her glass and drained her wine.

'Of course, there were several farms on the estate which would have been unaffected by the fire. Maybe she married a farm worker and lived on one of them.'

'Except it looks like she didn't marry, and had Daisy as an unmarried mum.' Lucy wrinkled her nose. 'Not an enviable situation to be in, in those days.'

'So the obvious next question is, though I don't know whether I'm likely to find the answer very easily...'

'I know what you're going to say,' said Lucy, pushing her plate to the side and wiping her fingers on her napkin. 'Who was Daisy's father?'

13

Esme eventually managed to get in touch with the gardener, Albert Jennings, through his wife Ada. She arranged to visit him, Albert being apparently unwilling to leave his cherished greenhouse to come to the phone. Ada explained that the greenhouse was where Albert was usually to be found, save for meals and the hours he was asleep in bed, and so it was when Esme arrived.

The Jennings home was a narrow Victorian terrace house on a busy road on the edge of town. Ada answered the door and showed Esme through the house and out into the garden.

The greenhouse, which almost enveloped the entire back yard, had been a present on his retirement, Ada told Esme proudly.

Albert had his plants and his very own greenhouse for the first time in his life and was content. Esme wondered whether his retirement had coincided with Sir Charles's death or whether he had left before then, but decided it wasn't relevant to the reason she was here. Her enquiries were about the distant past, not the recent.

She and Lucy had speculated as to whether Daisy was the result of the amorous attentions of Polly's employer, Sir Charles Monkleigh, and whether he had left Polly the cottage for her to live there and bring up Daisy. But they dismissed the idea as doubtful. Wouldn't he more likely have whisked Polly away to some remote location to have the baby in secret? Keeping her in a cottage on the estate for all to see would have only added to the scandal. Perhaps Daisy's father was someone else in Sir Charles's employ and Sir Charles had felt obliged in some way to intervene?

However intriguing it was to hypothesize, they decided to keep an open mind, for the time being. That Polly Roberts had, in some form or other, worked for the family and had been rewarded would remain their main theory, unless Albert Jennings revealed something to enlighten their speculation. Esme was optimistic.

Ada ushered Esme in through the open greenhouse door and coughed loudly to attract Albert's attention. Albert looked up, his fingers blackened by the potting compost.

'Close the door, woman, for goodness sake. My angels will take chill.'

Ada hastily shepherded Esme further inside and followed, pulling the door to behind her.

'Angels?' mouthed Esme to Ada.

'Angel pelargoniums, dear,' Ada said under her breath, indicating the beautiful array of small-leaved plants on the right-hand shelf. Esme detected the distinctive scent of the foliage and was reminded of her grandfather.

'Mrs Quentin's here, Albert,' said Ada. 'You remember. It's about the family.' She smiled up at Esme and with a clever manoeuvre reversed her round, dumpy shape out of the door rapidly and closed it again.

'Good afternoon, Mr Jennings,' said Esme. She was about to extend her hand but then she noticed the state of the gardener's own hands and dropped her arm to her side instead. 'I telephoned yesterday. I'm researching some family history and it seems to link in with the family you used to work for. I read about you in the local paper, in the article about the house.'

'Oh ay,' said Albert. 'You said as much to Ada on the telephone.'

Esme couldn't decide whether he was flattered to be in demand or irritated by another intrusion, mainly because he was studying her face with a frown. Occasionally people expressed concern about her scarred skin. Some even suggested remedies or treatments. Being approached in this way was something she had yet to come to terms with.

Esme cleared her throat and hurried on in case Albert was

prompted to say something on the matter. 'Would you mind if I ask you a few questions?'

'Ask away,' replied Albert, his face relaxing into a gentle smile. 'Don't mind if I carry on, do you?' he added, turning back to his task of stuffing compost into clay pots and setting them in a neat row on the slatted bench in front of him.

'I'm interested to find out a little more about the family,' Esme began. 'Sir Charles was married with a daughter, I believe?'

'That's right. I never knew her, though, if that's what you've come about.'

'Who's that? The wife or the daughter?'

'Neither, as it happens. Of course there was all the gossip and that when I first started, but it all happened before my time.'

'Gossip?'

Albert completed the line of pots on the bench in front of him and started a new one on the shelf above. 'I don't remember much. I was only a young lad, you see. It had just happened when I went there.'

He seemed to assume she already knew much more than she actually did.

'You'll have to fill me in a bit, Mr Jennings, I'm afraid. I'm not quite —'

'Albert.'

'Albert,' she repeated. 'You said it had just happened when you went there. What was it that had just happened? Where?'

'At the Brighton house. I was there with old Fred on some errand or other from up here. Only for a few days, like. I hadn't long started, see. And the missis had been at Brighton since I'd been started. So, like I said, I never knew her.'

Esme tried to grasp what he was saying but it didn't make sense. She decided to start at the beginning.

'What year did you start working for the family?'

'1939.'

Before the fire, then. 'And something happened soon after,

while you were in Brighton?'

'The women was on about it for weeks, but it didn't mean much to me, not never seeing her. She was the little 'un wasn't she? Catherine.'

'The daughter, you mean? Her name was Catherine?' Esme fished out a notebook from her bag and noted the name.

'That's right.' Albert turned towards her. He leant against the bench and folded his arms across his chest, expertly avoiding resting his soiled hands on his shirt. He chuckled.

'I do remember there being a bit of a kerfuffle. It must have been the day after, I'm pretty sure. Yes, that's right.' He wagged a grubby finger in the air. 'A young girl got the sack. I dunno what for, but I'm sure it was something to do with her ladyship and the little 'un going off.' He smiled to himself at the memory. 'She was pretty sore about it, I can tell you. I was rather glad she was going, I remember thinking at the time: wouldn't want to get in to her bad books, I thought. She'd already walloped me one for leaving a muddy footprint on 'er clean floor.'

'What did you mean about her ladyship and the little one going off? They left?'

'Buggered off the day before, apparently. Went abroad, so they say. Her ladyship had family somewhere foreign. India, I reckon it was. Left a note for his lordship, like, and was never heard of again.'

'Never?'

Albert shrugged. 'Not as I know, anyhow.'

'How old was Catherine when this happened?'

He scratched his head. Getting compost in his hair clearly didn't incur the same wrath as on his shirt. 'Ooh, now you're asking. Couldn't a been more than a few month old, from what they all said.'

Esme had a sudden thought. Was Polly the member of staff who had been sacked? Was that why she was trying so desperately to avoid talking about the past? Maybe she had been ignominiously sent away without references. It wouldn't support the theory of a legacy for long service, but they already had their doubts on that one.

'The girl who was sacked,' she said, 'was she called Polly Roberts?'

Albert shook his head.

'But you do remember Polly Roberts?'

Another shake. Esme frowned. So much for Albert throwing light on Polly's background. Had her journey been a waste of time?

She tried another direction. 'Do you remember the name of the girl who was sacked?'

Albert laughed. 'Are you joking? It was over fifty years ago!'

Esme smiled. 'Sorry, that was asking a bit much.'

'Hang on a minute, though. Now you come to say...' He began tapping his forehead with a grubby finger. Suddenly he pointed at her. 'Griffin. That's it.' He seemed quite excited.

'Mary, I think. That's right. Mary Griffin.'

Esme was sceptical. 'Are you sure? As you said, it was a long time ago.'

'She had the same name as my cousins. I remember having the horrible thought that she was a relative or something, though I'd never seen her before.'

'I don't suppose you know what happened to her?'

He shrugged. 'No idea. Went back to where she came from, I s'pose. Probably back up here. There's lots that went down there as 'ad worked up here, you know, over time.'

Esme noted the name Mary Griffin in her book and dropped it back in her bag. Wasn't that so-called friend who'd recently visited Mrs Roberts called Mary? She'd have to check. It might just be a coincidence. Mary wasn't an unusual name. 'Well, thank you, Albert. You've been very helpful.'

Albert acknowledged her gratitude with a nod and turned his attention back to his plants. 'You with the other bloke?' he asked nonchalantly, facing away from Esme now.

'Do you mean the journalist who did the piece in the paper?' Esme asked to his back.

'Nah, not him. He only wanted to know what the old place was like before it burned down. No, him as was trying to find the little 'un.'

Esme frowned. 'You mean Catherine? When was this?'

Albert stood up and stared out into the garden. 'Now let me see. Got to be a fair few months back now.' He shook his head.

'Can't remember now. Never mind.' He went back to the bench and began scooping compost into the next pot. 'Well, now, if you don't mind, I'd better be getting on.'

'Yes, of course,' said Esme, her thoughts galloping. She turned to go, then paused. 'This person? Did he say who he was?'

'Some sort of investigator. Private. Like on the tele.'

'And he was definitely trying to find the daughter, Catherine?'

'That's what he said.'

For some reason the idea that someone else was asking questions made Esme nervous. Should she read anything into it? Did it have any bearing on Polly's anxious state of mind? And who was it who was looking? And why?

Esme decided she needed to find out more about Catherine Monkleigh.

Albert cleared his throat and Esme realised where she was.

'Sorry, Albert. I was thinking through what you said. I'll leave you in peace.'

'You'll make sure you close the door when you go, won't you?' he called after her.

14

Esme found Catherine M. Monkleigh's birth listed in the first quarter of the year 1939. That would mean her birth was registered between January and March of that year, which matched Albert's assumption that she was only a few months old when she left. She noted the reference so that she could make the necessary arrangements to receive a copy of her birth certificate by post. The certificate itself would give her the exact birth date, where Catherine was born and her parents' details.

Whether that would give her another lead, though, remained to be seen. She lived in hope.

The records office was humming this morning. If the rain had kept them away last time it was having the opposite effect today. There was a musty scent of damp clothes in the reception area as people arrived and shook themselves to dispel the rain from their coats.

Esme went to find Lucy at the desk. She was giving a brief explanation of the layout of the office to a middle-aged woman with a fraught expression, clutching a notebook and copy of *Practical Family History*. She declared her bewilderment as to where to start. Esme sympathised. There had seemed to be so much to grasp when she set out on her own family history trail. The terminology was like a foreign language and it had taken her some while to wrap her head round everything, before feeling able to make the first step. It was a slow, if enthralling, learning curve and what you did learn was invariably dependent on which direction your research took you. If you discovered that your great-great-grandfather was convicted for assault, then you became an expert in scouring sources on criminality and the justice system. If one of your ancestors left a will, probate records became familiar territory. And the more you grasped, the more you realised how much more there was to learn. No wonder that for some it became a lifetime's work.

Lucy directed the newcomer to her colleague across the room and the woman set off with a look of excited anticipation.

'Did you find it?' asked Lucy, seeing Esme waiting.

'Yes.' She tapped her notebook. 'I've got all the details. I'll order it priority service so I should get it the day after tomorrow. I didn't find a record of her death, so with luck she's still with us.'

'I've got the maps out again for you,' said Lucy. 'What do you have in mind?'

Esme shrugged. 'I don't know till I see it. I hope looking a second time will stir something which I can't quite grasp at the moment.'

'I tracked down a copy of the sales particulars as well, from when the botanical trust bought the estate. I thought you might like a look.'

Esme went through to the search room. There was something about this cottage which she'd missed, though she couldn't think what. After all, it was a cottage on the estate of an employer, which had been bequeathed to an employee.

There was nothing inherently wrong in that. Unusual maybe, but dubious?

The date when it had been legally removed from the estate might give a clue as to why Polly had been left the cottage. If it happened around the time that Daisy was born it might indicate a link with Sir Charles but as she didn't yet have a specific date for Daisy's birth, she couldn't yet confirm that as a possibility.

Lucy appeared with the maps and the other documents and laid them down on the table.

'Good luck,' she said with a wink. 'Let me know how you get on.'

Esme stared at the yellowing map roll and wondered whether any other properties had been sold off in the past. Or perhaps Keeper's Cottage hadn't been left to Polly at all? Maybe that was only rumour and speculation. Maybe Polly had simply bought the cottage at some point. She picked up the sales particulars.

Perhaps they would clarify matters.

She sat down on a nearby chair and read them through, glancing now and again at the estate map in front of her. As far as she could make out with a quick calculation of the number of properties across the immediate area surrounding the house site, the estate was sold intact, apart from that one item, Keeper's Cottage.

She checked the date on the sales document advertising the auction. It was more than a year since the sale and the estate had been sold off after Sir Charles's death. Had anyone wondered about the estate being complete except for one cottage? Probably not. It had been broken up into several lots, though the Trust had eventually bought all of them.

She wondered how long the estate had been in the family, and whether there was anyone left who had cared that it had been sold off. If the main house hadn't been occupied since 1942 when it burnt down, maybe there was no emotional link with it any more. Esme thought of Albert who had been at Markham Hall at the start of his career and moved down south later. He implied that many staff members came from what he might have termed 'the old place'. Many might have returned to Shropshire on retirement, just as he had. Strong emotional ties with the house and estate might have continued for various reasons, such as the same family being on the staff for several generations.

Esme's mind drifted on to Catherine and the fact that someone was looking for her. Was that because she was a beneficiary to Sir Charles's estate and was being sought by his solicitor? It was a bit late in the day, though. Unless they had been looking all this time since his death and so far had drawn a blank.

Esme considered. Was there someone who would have been directly affected by the reappearance of Catherine, after a considerable period of time? Someone who hadn't even been aware of her existence? A new wife, perhaps? Esme discounted that. Surely Albert would have mentioned it if Sir Charles had remarried. But then again, why should he? Esme had been intrigued by the story of his absconding wife and daughter.

She hadn't asked about Sir Charles and what happened to him after his wife and daughter had left. If there was a divorce, or Catherine's mother had died, he would have been free to marry.

Perhaps the new lady of the house was unaware that he'd had a daughter, though that seemed unlikely. There it was in Who's Who for one thing, so it would be public knowledge.

Though it might be that she had been aware of Catherine's existence but then was suddenly confronted with her in the flesh.

Or perhaps Sir Charles was. His long-lost daughter arrives home but he decides to keep it from his new wife. Albert had said that to his knowledge Catherine had never again made contact with the family but that may not have been the case. The fact that Albert didn't know didn't mean it hadn't happened.

Esme sighed. This wasn't getting her anywhere because she as yet had no facts to back anything up. She stood up and went over to the desk. Lucy's colleague said she was busy elsewhere sorting through documents. Esme hoped they were of the Monkleigh estate. She needed something else to go on in order to make progress.

She left a note for Lucy asking if she knew when exactly Sir Charles had died and whether there had been an obituary in the local press. Something there might give them a lead. She left it at the desk and went to her locker to find her coat.

She'd already spent far too much time in the records office that morning and she had other pressing obligations to attend to, though one less than she might have had. The Shropton Canal client had dispensed with her services when she was only half-way through the brief. He hadn't given any reason.

As she dragged her bag out of the locker she heard the jangle of the keys to Keeper's Cottage. She'd promised to drop them off

at Polly's solicitors now that she'd completed the packing.
She'd been walking round with them for days. She'd better
hand them in before they came chasing her.

She pulled up her hood and hurried out of the building and up
the street, aware that something was brewing in her head about
Catherine and whether or not she'd ever re-established contact
with her father before he died. It would come to her eventually.
She just needed to give it the time.

*

Esme hurried along the street debating whether to brave the
queue in the post office first or call at the solicitor's to drop off
the keys. The rain hadn't eased and the pavements were doubly
hazardous as people struggled along with reduced vision from
hoods and umbrellas.

At one point Esme thought she spied Gemma through the
window of Waterstones but when she pushed open the door she
realised it wasn't Gemma after all. She was disappointed not to
have the opportunity to sort things out between them. Gemma
had left a message on Esme's answering machine to ask whether
Esme had sent some flowers to Elizabeth. The question seemed
contrived and Esme wondered whether it was Gemma's attempt
to make amends between them. But when Esme returned the call
Gemma had not been at home and Esme could only leave her
own message, confirming that she hadn't sent flowers. Why would
she, when Elizabeth wasn't in a state to appreciate them? She
asked Gemma to ring again sometime soon.

A quick glance at the snake of people in the post office
indicated a long wait, so Esme headed for Smith, Evans & Dart,
Solicitors, instead.

There was a young mother with two noisy children in
reception. The mother was trying to conduct a conversation with
the receptionist above the din of the older child, a boy of about
three, entertaining his younger sister by pretending to be a

particularly loud vehicle driving round and round her pushchair. She was giggling with uncontained delight. The receptionist was battling away bravely with the conversation, throwing the occasional agitated glance in the direction of the children. At least they weren't whingeing, thought Esme, even if it wasn't the right place and time for such a boisterous game. The mother was evidently oblivious to the noise, having perfected the ability to blot it out. By the time the exchange was complete the receptionist looked exhausted.

The party left and calm descended. Esme approached the desk and held out the keys, explaining what they were.

'Ah, yes. It's Mrs Quentin, isn't it?' Esme confirmed that it was and moved to leave.

'Could you hang on one moment? I'll just let Mr Evans know.' The receptionist picked up the telephone.

Esme turned and gazed out into the street. The rain was coming down more heavily, now. People on the pavement were moving more quickly, flashing past the glazed door, heads down, shoulders hunched.

The receptionist coughed and Esme turned back to her.

'Mr Evans would like a quick word, if you have a moment?' she said, smiling.

'Yes, I suppose so.' Esme couldn't imagine why he would want to see her but she was happy to keep out of the wet for a while longer.

The receptionist gestured over to a waiting area to her left.

'If you'd like to take a seat.'

Esme sat down and appraised the décor. The room was long and narrow with the receptionist's desk tucked into one corner, immediately opposite the entrance. The seating area for waiting clients ran along one wall, facing away from the entrance. It felt like a railway station platform which had been recently carpeted, and the track filled in. Esme imagined the 10.54 to Crewe bursting through the wall, sweeping away everything in its path.

After a few minutes a young woman in a smart black suit emerged from a door at the end of the room and led Esme out of the reception area, through a side door and up a staircase to the first floor. She showed her into a large room with a huge bay window looking on to the street below.

A tall, grey-haired man behind a large desk stood up and held out his hand.

'Mrs Quentin, thank you for waiting. My name is Evans.'

'Hello, pleased to meet you.' She shook his hand and returned his smile.

He indicated a chair and they both sat down. He was an elderly man, clearly near retirement age, if he hadn't already passed it. But he seemed bright and cheerful and evidently not one to lay down his pen just because the calendar signified a particular birth-date.

'I am greatly indebted to you for acting in place of your sister while she's in hospital.'

Esme shook her head. 'Not at all. Elizabeth had all but finished, so there wasn't much left to do.'

He leant his elbows on the desk and brought his fingertips together. He looked at Esme over the top of them. 'I was very perturbed to hear about your sister's unfortunate predicament.'

'Thank you. Hopefully things will improve soon.'

He nodded slowly. 'Indeed. Indeed.'

He seemed to be mulling something over in his mind.

'I've left the keys with your receptionist,' said Esme, hoping it would prompt him to explain his wishing to see her.

'Ah, yes. I was going to ask you about that.' He sat back in his chair.

Esme was puzzled. 'I understood you needed them to arrange for the house clearance.'

'Yes, you are quite right. That was the original plan.'

'Has something changed?'

'I'm in a difficult position here, Mrs Quentin, and as you are Mrs Roberts's representative, so to speak, I feel I ought to ask

109

your advice.'

Esme was taken aback. Wasn't it usually the other way around?

'Of course, if I can –'

'I really don't know what to make of it,' began Mr Evans, palms pressed together as if in prayer. For a moment he looked almost distressed.

He searched through a pile of papers on his desk. 'A letter arrived this morning from Mrs Roberts. Ah, here it is.' He studied it carefully and then looked at Esme over the top of his glasses. 'She wishes to dispense with my services, she says.' He laid down the letter and sat back in his chair. 'Well, of course she has that right. I was engaged by her daughter. She may wish to make her own arrangements.'

Esme struggled to grasp the implications of what he was saying. 'Yes, I suppose...'

Mr Evans laid his hands on the desk. 'Perhaps I should explain. Miss Roberts was most concerned that the necessary procedures were in place to ensure that Mrs Roberts was adequately provided for after Miss Roberts's death. The cottage would be sold and the proceeds secured to ensure her long-term care. I was led to understand that all this had been agreed between them. Your sister certainly never gave me the impression that Mrs Roberts would have any reason to dispute the arrangements.'

'And the letter clearly suggests otherwise.'

'And it's the nature of her request which troubles me,' continued Mr Evans. 'Ordinarily I would have expected to pass over the deeds of the cottage to the buyer's solicitor after the sale, or if a mortgage is involved to the relevant building society or bank, but Mrs Roberts is quite adamant that, not only has she no need of legal representation, but I am to forward the deeds directly to her as she has secured a buyer and will conduct the transaction herself.'

'Herself?' Esme was alarmed. Immediately she thought of the old lady's anxious behaviour. The two things must be linked. It was too much of a coincidence. The need to uncover exactly what was causing Mrs Roberts's anxiety was becoming ever more pressing.

Mr Evans laid one hand over the other across the letter on his desk. 'I am most concerned, Mrs Quentin. Her daughter was most insistent that Mrs Roberts's affairs should be dealt with as a matter of urgency following her death. I did my best to adhere to her request, so far as the procedure allows, you understand. Perhaps Mrs Roberts felt I hadn't moved hastily enough.'

Esme inclined her head. 'Did Miss Roberts say why there was such a need for urgency?'

'Not directly. People these days always want everything done yesterday, as is the way of the world, but Miss Roberts didn't strike me as that type of person.'

'You said, she didn't say directly,' noted Esme. 'Did she imply something, though?'

'It was a feeling I had. There was a nervousness about her manner which was quite disconcerting. I put it down to her illness at first. She explained that, of course. I could fully understand things needed to be put in place urgently because she had little time left, but as to afterwards it made no sense.'

'Would you like me to speak to Mrs Roberts?' Esme wondered whether she should involve Christine Rowcliffe but decided against it. If Mr Evans had felt that course of action to be appropriate he would have already followed it himself.

'I will write, of course,' Mr Evans was saying. 'But if you could impress upon her that there is no reason why I can't do the conveyance for the cottage in respect of the buyer she says she has. Of course the current buyers will be disappointed, but contracts hadn't been exchanged so...'

'You already have a buyer?'

'Yes, indeed. Miss Roberts had been in negotiation with the History & Heritage Association. The cottage is quite a gem, I believe. From a historical perspective, I mean. The trust saves and

111

renovates old properties of interest, apparently, and rents them out to raise money for their work.'

'Yes, so I understand,' murmured Esme. Why was Mrs Roberts so determined to sell to someone else when a buyer was all lined up? Mr Evans had been led to believe that everything had been agreed between them. So why question it now? What had changed?

'I assume she also intends to sell the other land to this buyer,' added Mr Evans.

'Other land?'

'The wood. The Woodland Trust was to take that on.'

Mr Evans gave a casual shrug of the shoulders. 'Perhaps Mrs Roberts and her daughter hadn't seen eye to eye on the potential purchasers. Maybe it's as simple as that.'

Esme assured Mr Evans that she would see what she could do to clarify Mrs Roberts's motives. By the time she left his office her head was reeling. Why reject buyers who must, by now, be close to the point when a sale could go through? Why start again? And who was this other buyer?

As she stepped into the street her earlier thoughts came to mind, about whether the cottage no longer being owned by Sir Charles had come as a surprise to his beneficiary, whoever he was, or she, or even they.

What if he, she or they had believed the cottage to be still part of the estate? Or had reason to believe that it should still be?

Had Daisy had doubts as to the legitimacy of Polly's ownership?

If Sir Charles was Daisy's father and he'd passed the cottage on to Polly without going through the proper channels, would that explain Daisy's instructions to Mr Evans to hurry the legalities along? Mr Evans's words had been, It made no sense. But it made perfect sense if Daisy was afraid someone else had a claim on the cottage.

Esme shook her head. This was completely beside the point. The estate had already been sold. Surely it was too late for any such challenge? And anyway, if there had been any legal anomalies Mr Evans would have uncovered them by now.

She stopped suddenly in mid-step, causing a man in a suit and in a hurry to crash into her. They both uttered flustered apologies, Esme smothering a grimace at the injury she'd sustained in her leg from the corner of his briefcase. But she assured him she was fine and he sped off, presumably late for a meeting, looking distinctly wet without the benefit of a raincoat. Esme made for the park-and-ride bus-stop opposite and slumped against the semi-bench on one side of the Perspex wall.

It wouldn't be in Mr Evans's remit to query the ownership of the cottage, it would be that of any potential purchaser's legal representative. Had Polly been forced to switch buyers because questions might arise about the legal anomalies that Daisy had feared? And what sort of buyer would be undeterred by such inconsistencies?

She let out a long sigh. Hadn't she already worked that out?

The one person who believed herself to be the rightful owner of the cottage in the first place? Someone who had come back into the family fold after many years, to claim her inheritance. That someone had to be Catherine Monkleigh.

15

'That female blackbird is spending so much energy seeing off the other birds,' commented Polly as Esme arrived at her bench in the garden at Wisteria House, 'she'll need twice as much food as she would if she just let them be and got on with it.'

Polly was wrapped up against the damp spring air watching the bird feeders across the other side of the lawn.

'I didn't realise they were so territorial,' said Esme quietly, so as not to disturb the birds. Not that they seemed bothered by her arrival. They were obviously quite tame and used to human activity nearby.

'Robins are usually the worst, but this blackbird has really got a bee in her bonnet.' Polly looked up at Esme. 'Have you found something else we overlooked in the cottage? Is that why you're here again?'

Esme shook her head. 'No, it isn't that. I called in on Mr Evans yesterday.'

'Who, dear?' Polly's eyes followed the sparrows flitting from the bushes to the bird table and back.

'Of Smith, Evans and Dart,' said Esme. 'Your solicitors. I went to drop off the keys of the cottage.' Was she being deliberately evasive?

Polly continued to study the birds.

'Mr Evans was rather distressed,' continued Esme. No response. 'He told me you'd written to him.' The old lady still didn't say anything. Esme walked in front of Polly and bent down so their faces were level. 'Is everything all right? Mr Evans was most concerned that your daughter's instructions weren't being carried out as she'd asked.'

Polly flashed a look at Esme. 'Daisy would quite understand,' she said pursing her lips.

'But to sell a house without legal representation...'

Polly smoothed the blanket across her knee. 'Nonsense. It's all taken care of.'

'But why change things?'

'I don't see as it's any of your business,' said Polly. 'I think I'll go back inside now.' She started to remove the blanket. Esme took it from her and helped her up from the bench. She picked up the old lady's walking stick and handed it to her.

'Had you talked to Elizabeth about it?' continued Esme as they began their slow journey down the path.

Polly halted. 'Elizabeth will be pleased that there isn't anything more to worry about,' she said decisively.

Esme didn't doubt that but she suspected that Polly was being obtuse and deliberately missing the point. She sighed.

Polly wasn't going to reveal anything. Her body language told Esme that the matter had been concluded and that was the end of it. Esme couldn't see what else she could do. It was exactly as she had said to Lucy. All she had were suspicions.

'Reassure me on one thing, at least,' urged Esme. 'Have you had it valued properly? You aren't underselling it are you? You're not being...swindled.' It was the only word which came to mind. It sounded silly.

Polly patted her arm. Perhaps she sensed that Esme was about to accept the situation and relaxed. 'There's enough for me to see out my days here. That's all I need.'

As they made their way back to the house, Esme desperately tried to think of something she could say to overcome the old lady's stubbornness. She asked herself whether she should she put her concerns to Mrs Rowcliffe? But then if her policy was that the residents were not children and were, unless medically diagnosed otherwise, capable of making their own decisions, she would be dismissive. The situation was exactly the same as involving the police. What evidence did she have that there was anything illegal going on? If Polly was insistent that everything was above board, perhaps there was nothing to worry about.

Esme thought of Gemma's comment. Maybe it was Esme's naturally suspicious tendencies. Perhaps Gemma had a point.

But Esme didn't believe it. There were too many unanswered questions. Why had Polly seemed so anxious? Why was she so reticent about her past? Esme was still convinced that Polly knew something about Elizabeth's accident. If only she would tell her what she knew, it might lead them to the possible attacker.

Esme felt a surge of desperation. It was like being in a bad dream when you couldn't run fast enough to get away from the danger. She felt something was slipping away from her but she had no idea what it was. She only sensed that it was vitally important.

They reached the side entrance and Esme held the open door for Polly and assisted her into the corridor.

'Ah, there you are, Mrs Roberts.' Abigail was walking towards them. 'There's someone to see you.'

'Who?' Polly asked, halting abruptly. Her tone was suspicious.

'Mrs Watts.' Polly's grip tightened on Esme's arm. 'I've shown her into the lounge, OK?' The girl turned and headed back down the corridor.

Esme closed the outside door and looked at the old lady's face. It was drained of colour.

'What does she want?' Polly muttered under her breath.

'What is it?' whispered Esme. 'Do you want me to send her away? I can say you aren't feeling well.'

Polly shook her head. 'I can't. I'll have to see her. She wouldn't believe you anyway. She's got a nasty suspicious mind, has Mary.'

So Esme had remembered correctly, the name was Mary.

'Is this the lady you used to work with?'

Polly gave a hollow laugh. 'Lady? She's no lady.'

'Is she Mary Griffin, that was?'

Polly flashed an alarmed look at Esme, but didn't answer.

She didn't need to. Her reaction confirmed it. It said, how did you know?

'Why has she suddenly decided to visit you?' continued Esme. 'If she upsets you so much –'

'She won't be coming for much longer. I told you. Soon it will be all sorted out.' She made a move towards the door.

Esme took a step alongside her. 'Do you want me to stay for a while? Let me take your coat, at least. Shall I go and organise some tea?'

Polly leant on her stick and looked Esme in the eye. 'I know you mean well, Esme. But I don't have any choice. I have to do this my way. Please leave now.' She reached out and touched Esme's arm. 'Don't worry, it's nearly over.' Esme watched as Polly walked carefully down the passageway and turned into the lounge.

Well, you could take a horse to water and all that, but if someone wouldn't co-operate what could you do? Sighing, Esme buttoned her coat and walked towards the way out. As she passed the entrance to the lounge she slowed her pace. No one was about. She hovered at the partly open doorway. She could hear voices coming from inside the room. She heard Polly complaining about the intrusion.

'Now don't be like that,' a whining voice answered, which she assumed to be that of Mary Watts. 'I just wanted to check that you weren't thinking of pulling out of our little arrangement.'

'Why should I?' she heard Polly say.

'A little bird tells me that someone has been poking their nose...'

At that moment Esme looked up to see Mrs Rowcliffe coming round the corner and she was obliged to move away from the door or be caught eavesdropping. She acknowledged the matron and hurriedly made her way through the front door and on to the drive.

She stopped and took a few deep breaths to ease her exasperation with Polly's reticence. She couldn't take at face value what Polly said, that everything would be sorted out in due course. It couldn't be that simple. There was still so much to understand.

But it was important that she moved fast. Everything had to be linked to this unorthodox sale of Keeper's Cottage. It was vital that she unearthed something before the sale went through or it would be too late. But where to go from here? It was so frustrating.

Esme delved into her bag for her mobile phone and turned it on. Perhaps Lucy had come up with something. She scrolled to the records office number and made the connection. While she waited to be put through to Lucy she wandered over to her Peugeot. The morning's early rain had left a clean fresh smell in the air and she ran her forefinger through the beads of water on the bonnet as she went through everything.

Why was the cottage such an issue? She'd asked herself the same question over and over. If the estate hadn't already been sold on it might have been of concern to someone. Either because they disliked the idea of the original estate being broken up or were excessively greedy and wanted their full pound of flesh. But the estate had already been sold to the botanical trust and their project concerned only the ruin of the hall. They might have plans to sell the remainder of the estate to help fund the project but she couldn't see how that would affect anything.

The phone crackled and Lucy came on the line.

'Where've you been?' she complained. 'I've been leaving messages all morning.'

'I've had the phone switched off. Why? What've you got?'

'I found out when Sir Charles died and rooted out the obituary in the local rag.'

'Thanks, Lu. That's great. I'll call in and read it.'

'I've already read it and there's something you should know.'

'What did it say?'

'The usual stuff, of course, but I found out something else. You remember the photo I got from the local rag?'

'Of the charity event? Yes, what about it?'

'His sister and nephew were in the picture, remember? Apparently his sister died later that year and because the lad's father was dead, Sir Charles brought him up as his own.'

So it wasn't a wife who had her nose put out of joint by the return of Catherine. It was a nephew.

'Strange that the gardener didn't mention him,' said Esme. 'I might go and have another word. This is beginning to get interesting. I've thought of something else, too, since I saw the solicitor. Where shall we meet? I'll fill you in.'

'Wait a minute. There's more. I also checked back in the probate reports in *The Times*. It reports the values of estates.'

'Yes, I know. I bet it was worth a quite a bit, wasn't it?'

'That's just it. It was hardly worth anything. It must have been mortgaged to kingdom come. Dear old Sir Charles Monkleigh, for all his apparent wealth, was as poor as a church mouse.'

16

Esme pressed 'send' on her computer and e-mailed her final report to the Shropton Canal client, who had abruptly dispensed with her services. It was already written so she might as well pass it on to him. Especially as his cheque had arrived that morning.

It was odd, though, that he had pulled out when she was barely half-way through the job. She shrugged it off. There was always the occasional eccentric client, she'd learnt, in this line of work.

At least he'd paid his dues. Everyone was entitled to change their minds, as long as they paid for what she'd done.

She gathered up her notes from the floor, along with the Ordnance Survey map she'd been studying. Folding the map prompted her to recall the Monkleigh estate plans she'd been examining the day before. There was something definitely bugging her about Polly's cottage, but when she had tried to identify it she had drawn a complete blank. It was frustrating because she knew that time was running out and if she was to discover anything useful it was going to have to be soon or it would be of no value whatsoever.

She was meeting Lucy later to go through everything, sincerely hoping that between them they could unravel something which might establish their next move.

She went over to the window to draw the curtains. Dusk was creeping in and the dull day had resulted in an early darkfall.

She glanced out into the lane. A car was slowly crawling past the cottage. She peered into the gloom. It looked like that black Audi again from the old farmhouse, currently being renovated.

It looked as though the driver hadn't got used to the narrow lanes, yet. Some people found them as intimidating as she found fast multi-lane motorways, particularly if they'd moved from a part of the country where roads had wide carriageways. They braked at every slight curve in the road, even stopping in panic when another road user came the other way. And that was on a two-way road. They probably never ventured down single-track lanes.

As she turned away from the window something clicked. She stopped dead. Of course. Why hadn't she thought of it before?

She cursed herself for being so slow. She glanced at the clock.

It was about to strike five. Just enough time. She grabbed the telephone and dialled, crossing her fingers that the receptionist hadn't gone home early.

*

Andy was in reception when Esme burst through the door. He was alone. The desks were empty, equipment shrouded, and a single desk lamp burning next to him.

Esme gasped to get her breath back. 'Thanks for this. I hope I'm not holding you up. I got here as fast as I could.'

'Not at all. I'm intrigued,' said Andy, coming behind Esme to bolt the front door. 'Come on in, tell me all.'

He gestured for her to sit down in the waiting area. She dropped into a soft sofa by the window.

'That booklet that was in your office. The one I was flicking through when I came before.'

'The Local Development Plan, you mean?'

'Yes that's it. Can I take a look again?'

'Sure.' Andy got up and ferreted around behind the reception desk. 'I thought there was one down here, but I can't see it.

Hang on, I'll nip upstairs and get my copy.' He disappeared around the corner and bounded up the stairs.

Now Esme was convinced that she knew why the cottage was a key. But she still didn't understand why Polly had found herself so vulnerable. It could only be that there was some irregularity with Polly's ownership of the property which put her in a weak position. Why else would someone persuade her to be so secretive about selling it? Why else would she be so willing to indulge whoever it was? The word 'persuade' floated around in her head.

She had previously concluded that the old lady was under some sort of pressure. What if 'persuade' was too weak a word? What if the true situation was blackmail? Was this why she was unable to enlist Esme's help? It couldn't be simply a matter of privacy or she wouldn't have reassured Esme by telling her she knew Esme meant well. The poor old lady was boxed in. Hadn't she said that she had no choice? Blackmail. It made perfect sense.

Esme felt hot and stupid. Why hadn't she realised ages ago?

Polly had assured Esme that all would be sorted satisfactorily because she had been resigned to the fact that selling the cottage would conclude the episode. She had also told Esme that she believed the settlement to be completely fair.

But if Esme was right, what Andy was going to tell her was going to put a completely different slant on things. And it would suggest that however 'fairly' Polly thought she was being treated, the intention of the purchaser couldn't be further from the truth.

Andy reappeared and handed Esme the document. She took it from him and began riffling through the pages.

'You're being very furtive,' he teased. 'Aren't you going to fill me in?'

'There's a map, isn't there?'

'At the back.'

Esme found it and laid it open on her lap. She pored over it for a few silent moments. 'There!' She swivelled the map around and handed it over to him, pointing to a spot on the page. 'Tell me about that bit.'

Andy looked at her, mildly amused, and took the booklet.

He looked at the place she had indicated and flicked back and forth. He set the booklet down on the low table next to Esme and sat down.

'This is Heathley.' He placed his finger on a shaded area. 'I'm assuming this is the bit you're interested in, the village envelope. This is the area in which, in the opinion of the local planners, planning permission would be favourably considered.'

'So if you owned this land, it would be worth a fair bit, would it?'

'If you had a plot big enough to build on, yes. You could apply for planning permission and sell it on at a good price.'

'That's exactly what I thought.' She sat back against the seat and folded her arms. 'I know someone who owns a cottage which used to belong to the estate, years ago.'

'They own land here?' He gestured to the shaded area on the plan.

'Yes. The owner is an old lady who used to work for the family. The cottage is slap bang in the middle.'

Andy pulled the plan closer. 'Whereabouts exactly?'

Esme pointed out where the cottage was situated.

Andy looked at her. 'Are you sure about that?'

'Definitely. I've been there. Why?'

Andy raised his eyebrows. 'We've just got permission for clients for new housing a bit further along.'

Esme studied Andy's face. 'Go on.'

Andy indicated another area of land on the page.

'This area is also ideal for development, on the other side of your cottage.'

Esme looked carefully, trying to match the plan with what she could remember of the area surrounding the cottage.

'But at the moment,' continued Andy, 'there is no access to the site except through there.' He tapped his finger on the map.

Esme stared down at where he was pointing. 'That's the land which goes with the cottage,' she explained. 'It's a wood. Well, apart from a patch of rough ground at the end.'

'Without access to the road the land beyond is virtually worthless.'

Esme suddenly realised the implications of what Andy was

saying. 'So whoever owns that piece of scrub holds the key to realising the true value of the land beyond.' Esme thought of Daisy's apparent careful planning to sell to the Woodland Trust. She must have been aware of the risk the wood was under and had done everything she could to protect it.

'Got it in one. These guys have been buying up land for a while, ready for when the market is right to cash in on it. And that piece of land,' he stabbed at the page again, 'is crucial to their plans. It could be worth millions. In these sorts of cases owners can find themselves under enormous pressure to sell, even if they don't want to and have no plans to move.'

Esme sat back in her seat, trying to take everything in.

Although Polly hadn't been put under pressure to move, she was certainly under pressure to sell. To one particular buyer. Esme was convinced now. Blackmail was the only thing which made sense.

'We often come across situations like this one,' said Andy standing up. 'They're referred to as ransom strips.'

Ransom and blackmail, thought Esme. No wonder Polly appeared so vulnerable.

17

Esme sat in her car and digested everything that Andy had told her. She would need to establish whether Polly was aware of the true value of the cottage she was about to sell to her anonymous buyer. If the information Esme had discovered was unknown to Polly, would it change her intentions?

But how could it if Esme was right and Polly was being blackmailed? Whatever Mary was threateningly whispering into Polly's ear, it was having the desired effect. Whatever Esme told Polly wouldn't make any difference, though it might persuade the police to look into the matter. But where did that leave Polly and her hidden secrets? The old lady wouldn't relish having her dirty linen picked over by the police.

She dug her mobile phone out of her bag and made a call to Wisteria House. Mrs Roberts was having tea, she was told, would she like to telephone later? Esme toyed with leaving a message but 'don't sign anything until I've spoken to you', would have sounded mildly ridiculous. Besides she didn't want to create an opportunity for starting any more rumours about Polly's affairs. She knew there was already plenty of speculation about Mary to get tongues wagging. She owed Polly some discretion. She said she'd phone again in the morning. Esme reassured herself with the thought that Polly was unlikely to have a further visit from Mary this evening, and mulling over the situation with Lucy might help Esme decide her best plan of action.

Esme was seeing Lucy after work in one of Esme's favourite pubs, The Loggerheads. It had secret little nooks and crannies perfect for conducting conversations without being overheard.

Not that the frequenters of The Loggerheads would be that bothered about what two women were gossiping about over half a pint of bitter and a glass of wine. They were there for the beer and possibly the unique historical atmosphere, which was the other reason that the place was a favourite of Esme's. It hadn't changed in decades, it was an escape back in time.

The pub was already busy when they arrived. Esme got in the drinks and they found an empty table in the room at the back.

They drank to success, without being sure what 'success' actually meant in practice. At the moment they were gathering snippets of knowledge but nothing which gave them answers, only prompted more questions.

Lucy sipped her wine. 'I double-checked, by the way. There was no mention of the name of the nephew in the obituary.'

'I'm hoping I might find that out tomorrow. I'm paying Albert Jennings another visit.'

'Couldn't you just telephone him?'

Esme shook her head. 'He won't come to the phone. I made the appointment through his wife. He hardly ever comes out of his greenhouse.'

'Wouldn't his wife know about the nephew?'

Esme considered. 'She might, but I'd prefer to speak face to face. It can reveal things that conversations over the telephone don't.'

'Body language, you mean?'

'Partly that, but something more.' Feel the vibes, Tim had always said. Vibes to a journalist were like a hunch to a detective. So he said. Pity they could be lethal, too.

Esme took a sip of beer and dismissed the direction her thoughts were taking. 'I found out something about the cottage which puts things in to an interesting light.' She related what she had been told by Andy.

Lucy was open mouthed. 'Well, that would explain why someone might be miffed that it wasn't part of the estate.'

'Assuming that they knew about its potential value.'

'Surely they must, if it's the centre of everything, which is what

126

it's looking like.'

'If Sir Charles's estate wasn't worth much, the value of the cottage, whatever it is, wouldn't be sneezed at, even under ordinary circumstances.'

Lucy twiddled with the stem of her glass. 'Yes but the potential value of that strip of land changes everything. It might have tempted someone to raise the stakes.'

Esme felt a pinprick of apprehension. 'You mean, resorting to blackmail and coercion to get it?' She wondered how far they would be prepared to go, and shivered.

'Do you think Mrs Roberts knows what it's worth?'

Esme shrugged. 'I don't know but I doubt it. I tried to get hold of her but she couldn't come to the phone. I'll call her tomorrow. She mustn't go ahead with this sale, without at least knowing the circumstances.' She stared pensively into her beer, mentally reiterating what she'd been thinking earlier, about whether Polly's knowing would change anything. If they were right and Polly was being coerced over something in her past, she wouldn't have any room to manoeuvre, whatever Esme said.

But there was still a chance.

'Are you staying to eat?' asked Lucy, half getting up. 'Or are you off home?'

They decided to indulge and Lucy went to place two orders for fish and chips. Esme listened to the hum of the bar and thought over things in her mind again. Having convinced herself that she now had something more tangible to take to the police, her confidence was ebbing. Surely the problem remained the same? She still had no real evidence that there was anything improper going on, just suspicions. It didn't really amount to anything of any worth. And even if she managed to find a receptive policeman to humour her ideas, Polly would simply dismiss the idea that she was being coerced and that Esme's interference was an infringement of her privacy.

Esme's only hope was to find out what it was that Mary was

using against Polly and persuade Polly to seek help from the police herself. But that would only happen if Polly was prepared to admit that the problem existed in the first place. It was wearisome to keep circling endlessly without making progress. Maybe she should confront Mary. Find out what she had to say for herself. Esme's guess was that although she was the one applying the pressure, she wasn't working alone. Not if this whole business linked in with the past history of the Monkleigh family and its estate. There must be someone else involved.

'So who do you reckon's behind this?' Esme said as Lucy slipped back into her seat.

'You're still thinking it could be Catherine emerging from the woodwork to claim her rightful inheritance?'

'Makes sense to me. Don't you think so?'

'I can see the logic, but we could do with knowing what she's been doing all this time or where she's been, before we malign the poor woman.'

Esme considered. 'Albert said her mother had taken her abroad when they left. There's no knowing when she came back. It could have been last month, or years ago.'

'If it was last month, she'd hardly be on the ball with planning policy, would she?' pointed out Lucy. 'So the likelihood is she's been back for some time. If she is involved.'

'I got the impression from Albert that once they'd left they were as good as dead. Figuratively speaking, I mean. No one ever mentioned them again. Apart from the staff gossip of course, but not talked about officially.'

Lucy rested her chin on her elbow. 'If it was a big family secret maybe the nephew never knew about her. He could have had a bit of a shock at her sudden appearance.'

'You mean he could be involved?'

'It's possible.'

Esme sighed. 'We don't know anything, really. What I can't work out is a theory to explain where Polly Roberts comes in to it. Surely you wouldn't pick on someone just because they happened to own a property you want? Her connection with the family has got to be significant.'

'Well, you do hear about people being offered huge sums of money to move out of their homes,' Lucy pointed out.

'That's what Andy said, but that's my point. Large sums of money. I don't think this is the case here. I'm sure it's Polly's link with the family which is key. And this Mary woman, Mary Griffin that was. How does she fit into the frame? Albert Jennings didn't remember Polly Roberts, and as he started work at the place Mary Griffin was just leaving, having been given the boot. So neither Polly or Mary could have worked there for very long.'

'Long enough to discover they didn't get on. That could be apparent after a couple of weeks, you don't need years.'

'That's true. In a way it's surprising that they even remember one another, never mind Mary looking Polly up and visiting her.' Esme looked at Lucy. 'There's something we're missing about those two. I'm sure of it.'

'They could have bumped into one another years later and developed their differences then.'

Esme picked up her glass. 'I think you might have something there.' What had Polly said? She's got a nasty suspicious mind, has Mary. That sounded more like a comment born of weary experience than teenage distaste. What had she meant by it?

'We've gone off at such a tangent,' mused Esme, thinking out loud. 'I've not even got close to finding out who Elizabeth's father was.'

Esme froze as soon as the words were out of her mouth. In all the ways she had rehearsed telling Lucy about Elizabeth, this hadn't been any one of them. She could feel Lucy's eyes on her.

'Elizabeth's father?' Lucy was saying slowly. 'What do you mean, Elizabeth's father?'

Esme bit her lip and then turned and faced Lucy. Her face felt hot with shame. 'I should have told you, but I felt so stupid.'

Lucy was frowning. 'Stupid? What do you mean? Are you trying to tell me that your mother had an affair...'

Esme shook her head frantically. 'No, nothing like that.' She looked down and stared into her glass. 'It was when we were trying to find out who Elizabeth was meeting when she was attacked. I found all the papers. I didn't know.'

'What papers?'

Esme lined up her glass in the centre of the beer-mat.

'Elizabeth was adopted. I never knew.'

Lucy was silent for a moment, digesting the information, Esme assumed. Esme filled the silence, explaining how they'd discovered the certificates.

'I can't believe you never said anything.' Lucy said quietly.

'The sentence wouldn't form itself.' Esme threw her head back and sighed. 'That sounds pathetic. What I mean is, I couldn't put it into words. It was all a jumble.'

Lucy was gripping the stem of her glass. Her brow knotted tightly as she stared into her wine. 'It's as though you couldn't trust me.' She sounded hurt.

'No, it wasn't like that, really.' Esme swallowed. 'I'm sorry. I wanted to tell you but...' Esme's excuse fizzled out, the knot in her insides tightening. They sat in limbo, neither speaking.

'I knew there was something,' said Lucy after a while, 'but I couldn't put my finger on it.' Esme thought back to the occasion in the café when her answers to Lucy's questions had been deliberately vague and she'd joked about sounding ridiculous.

Lucy exhaled noisily and slumped back against the settle.

'God, you must have been bloody cross with me.'

Esme was aghast. 'You? Why with you?' She sensed a momentary stab of panic. 'You didn't know, did you?'

But Lucy was on a different track, berating herself about something. Esme tried to concentrate on her words. 'You came back here because you needed some security after Tim's death, some stability.' She stabbed at herself in the chest with her forefinger. 'And I was the one who persuaded you that your family could give it to you.' She was sounding increasingly annoyed, now.

Esme put her hand on Lucy's arm. 'Hey, it's me who's been the self-centred individual,' she said, with half a laugh. 'Not you. My family's short comings aren't your fault, you idiot.'

Lucy looked at her with a wan smile. 'No. Perhaps not.'

'There's no "perhaps" about it. You convinced me that roaming around the country in and out of bed-sits and unsuitable jobs was neither going to bring back Tim, or get my life in order.

You can't take the rap for the deceit of my family.' Esme realised she had said the word deceit with noticeable resentment.

'I can understand you being bitter about it,' sympathised Lucy. 'Especially as Elizabeth could have set the record straight, but hadn't done so.'

Esme managed to nod. She daren't trust herself to say anything. There was too much close to the surface for it not to spill out. Lucy would understand that. Esme was grateful that she understood why she'd found it so hard to tell her. But Esme didn't let herself off the hook so easily. For all that she had rebuked her own family for their betrayal, this was a betrayal of her own and Lucy deserved more.

Their food arrived as a welcome diversion. They discussed safe topics over their meal. Lucy's planned holiday in Peru later in the year, the hospital's optimistic assessment to Elizabeth's condition and inevitably the weather, neither of them being able to recall such a wet April as it was proving to be.

'I forgot to tell you,' said Esme, pushing her plate to one side. 'Catherine's birth certificate arrived.'

'Anything interesting?'

'Nothing we didn't already know. Full name Catherine Marguerite Monkleigh. Born 8th February 1939, at Markham Hall.'

'So where now?'

'Albert Jennings. I'm seeing him again tomorrow. Hopefully

he'll have something which will give us another lead. Something about the nephew.' Esme paused. 'I wonder why he didn't mention him when I was there last time?'

'Because you were asking about the past not the present?' suggested Lucy.

They returned their glasses to the bar and left the pub. As they stepped out into the street Esme turned to Lucy.

'Thanks for not giving me my just desserts about blanking you. I guess that's why you're such a good friend.'

Lucy reached out and squeezed Esme's arm. 'I've known you and your protective shield for a long time, remember. I don't take it personally any more.'

Esme smiled. 'Thanks, anyway. I'm lucky to know you.'

Lucy laughed. 'Well, that's pushing it a bit, but I accept the compliment in the manner in which it was meant.' She gave a theatrical bow of her head.

As they said their goodbyes and parted, a sense of unease stirred in Esme. Was it something Lucy had said? She pushed the thought to the back of her mind. She shouldn't feel uneasy, but optimistic. They were on the brink of a breakthrough. She was sure of it.

18

'You know where he'll be, Mrs Quentin,' said Albert's wife gesturing through the kitchen after she showed Esme in. 'Do go through.' She went back to her mixing-bowl on the kitchen table. Esme thanked her and made her way to the greenhouse.

As she'd told Lucy, she could believe that Albert lived, slept and ate in his greenhouse, and a comment from Ada implied that she thought it only a matter of time before he would.

This time his 'angels' were on the high shelves above him. The pots on the bench were full of grey-leaved daisy-like plants.

Esme made sure she made a quick efficient entry into the greenhouse so as not to arouse Albert's displeasure by letting in cold air on his precious horticultural stock.

Albert turned and peered at the incomer over the top of his glasses.

'Ah, Mrs Q,' he said, extending his hand.

'Hello again, Mr Jennings,' said Esme, shaking it. 'I mean, Albert.'

He gave no indication as to whether her second visit in such a short a time was an imposition. He received her well enough.

'I'm a bit cleaner than last time,' he said, indicating the pencil in his hand. 'Writing labels today.'

'I'm sorry to trouble you for a second time.'

Albert flapped his hand, giving the impression that he quite liked being in demand. 'No trouble. Did you forget to ask me something?'

'It's about Sir Charles's nephew.'

The welcoming smile faded and Albert rolled his eyes to the roof. 'Huh. What d'you want to know about him for?'

Esme was immediately curious. 'I take that to mean you didn't think a lot of him.'

Albert wagged his finger. 'Hit the nail on the head, Mrs Q. Nasty piece of work. Made his uncle's life a misery with all his goings on.'

'You never mentioned him last time.'

'You never asked. I thought you were wanting to know about the young 'un.'

'Yes I was, but when I came before I didn't know the nephew existed.'

'Pity he does, ungrateful blighter!' Albert sniffed. He picked up a small piece of rag and began cleaning off some of the grubby labels piled on the bench. 'When his mother died – that was the master's sister – the master brought him up as his own. Caused him nothing but trouble.'

'How old was he?'

'When he took him on, you mean?' Esme nodded. 'Only a nipper. Two or three, I suppose.'

'And this was when?' continued Esme. She needed to confirm that they were talking about the same child who'd been in the press photograph which Lucy had found.

Albert paused and scratched his head. 'The master was getting on a bit even then. His sister was much younger than he was, you see, and she'd had the baby when she was a bit long in the tooth herself. Let me think.'

'Maybe it'd be easier to say how old he is now?' suggested Esme.

'Well, he must be about thirty by now, I suppose, but that's a guess. He's kept his head down these past couple of years after all the palaver. Haven't seen hide nor hair of him for a good long time.'

'All the palaver?'

'Police trouble,' said Albert, pursing his lips. 'All sorts. You name it, he was in to it. Drugs, gambling debts. Worse, some say.' He shook his head. 'The master didn't deserve that, after all he'd done.' He put the labels and cloth down and folded his arms. 'Me and the missis reckoned he was quite tickled to have a son, so to speak. You know having his daughter leave an' all. He spoilt him rotten, see.' He pulled a face. 'Nasty little bugger he was when he was a kid. No nanny'd stay more 'n a few months. And it got no better as he got older, either. Grew up to be a selfish know-all, and that's a fact. Bled the master dry, by all accounts.'

So that fitted with Lucy's information of the impoverished estate and from what Albert had said about him, the nephew sounded like the sort who might be irked that his inheritance was worth a pittance.

Albert turned back to his labelling. 'Can't tell you much more than that though. Haven't set eyes on him for years, like I said.'

'Was there anything in the press about the "palaver"?' asked Esme.

'I know they did all they could to keep it out,' said Albert. 'There was something about the police wanting to question him about something after they'd arrested some of his pals.' He shrugged. 'I think he'd already done a bunk by then.'

'How long ago was this?'

'Like I said, two or three years, I reckon. Time flies don't it?'

'So before Sir Charles died?'

'Oh yes. Before then.' He held out a few of the labels he'd been writing. 'Could you just pop those in the pots behind you?'

'What?' Esme spun round. 'Oh, yes, of course.' She took the labels and glanced down at his spidery writing. She gently slid each label into a corresponding pot on the bench. She really ought to be as organised as this. She was always taking cuttings of plants in her garden, and in friends' gardens but more often than not omitted to label them. Then they'd die down in the winter and she'd never know what they were.

She'd wait for growth to emerge in the spring in the hope that the leaves would give her a clue as to their identity. Rarely did she get it right. Hence her garden was a haphazard collection of misplaced perennials. Sometimes she liked it that way, at other times she wished she could be more orderly.

'Do you have a garden, Mrs Quentin?' asked Albert, as though he had read her thoughts. 'It's a worthy hobby.'

'Yes, I do. It's good therapy when my brain is scrambled. But I'm no good at remembering plant names, apart from daffodils and roses and the ones everybody knows. I tend to think of them as the white ones with the frilly petals, or the orange ones with a yellow blob in the middle. '

Albert chuckled and passed her some more labels. 'Never worry about that, my dear. Enjoying yourself, that's the most important part.'

'I'm sure you're right.' Something was buzzing in her head.

Was there something she wanted to ask? An image of being in the pub came to mind but nothing which clarified her thoughts.

There was one thing she did need to ask, though. 'Sir Charles's nephew, Mr Jennings. What's his name?'

It seemed as though Albert found difficulty allowing himself to speak it. 'Can't think why you want be doing with him,' he muttered.

She gave a little laugh. 'Neither do I, after what you've told me about him, but nevertheless it would be helpful to know.'

He seemed reluctant to say anything at first. Esme wondered if he was going to refuse and tried to think of a specific reason why she needed to know, other than the real one. She could hardly tell him she was concerned that he was part of a blackmail conspiracy, not when it was pure speculation as yet. She started to think who else she could ask. Ada was the obvious alternative.

Suddenly the name seemed to escape unbidden from Albert's lips, as though he had been striving to keep it confined for fear of what would happen should he allow it to burst forth.

Esme's heart gave a sudden lurch. Where had she heard that name before? Then she remembered. It was when the police sergeant came to the hospital to show her and Gemma that artist's impression of the man who'd been seen arguing with Elizabeth. After he'd shown them the photograph he'd asked, do you know the name Leonard Nicholson?

*

Esme knew that she now had something with which she could to go to the police. But first she needed to speak to Polly. Whatever Mary was using against Polly might have to come out in order to find out what happened to Elizabeth. The least she could do was warn Polly what was about to happen. She just hoped that the old lady would understand that there was no other way. Not now. Not after what Esme had learnt from Albert Jennings.

And after all, wasn't Elizabeth her own granddaughter? Surely she also would want to know, if Leonard Nicholson had been her attacker?

She pulled out her mobile and rang Wisteria House. It was no more than ten minutes drive but it was probably better to give some warning of her imminent arrival.

The phone rang for an unusually long time. Esme was beginning to wonder whether there was a fault on the line when at last Mrs Rowcliffe answered.

Esme said who was calling. 'I was about to drop in on Mrs Roberts. It's rather on spec, I thought I'd better let her know. Is that OK?'

Mrs Rowcliffe seemed to hesitate. Esme heard her clear her throat. 'Well, I suppose so. I'm not really sure what to say.'

Esme sensed her anxiety. 'Why? What's the matter?'

'It's all rather alarming,' said the matron distractedly.

Her usual calm authority seemed to have deserted her for the moment. 'The police have just arrived. They were most insistent that they needed to talk to Mrs Roberts. They're with her now.

19

Despite her being so close to Wisteria House, the journey there felt painfully slow. Making it more uncomfortable still was the fact that Esme's brain was churning with questions, seriously reducing her ability to concentrate fully on driving. What did the police want with Mrs Roberts? Did she already know about the 'ransom strip' and the true worth of the land? Maybe Esme had stumbled across a different conspiracy with Polly at the centre. Had Polly been implying that she was under pressure to sell in order to conceal the true circumstances? But then why pretend? She owned the cottage and could openly sell it to whomever she chose. Perhaps she felt badly about the sale, given that Daisy had been so instrumental in lining up potential buyers who would ensure protection from developers.

The traffic lights at the approaching junction turned red two cars ahead of her and she almost slammed into the back of the estate car in front. She told herself to calm down and deal with the matter in hand, to arrive at Wisteria House in one piece. Nevertheless, as she focused on the lights in front and willed them to change, another thought came to mind. What if Mary's blackmail was about something Polly had done in the past? Something illegal? Perhaps the visit by the police was because her past had finally caught up with her. If that was the case, then warning Polly in advance of Esme speaking to the police was irrelevant. By now the story would be out. There would be no further need for Polly to conceal everything from her. She might yet be prepared to reveal to Esme that which she had been reluctant to do before.

Even as she framed these thoughts, Esme felt the whole thing was ridiculous. It couldn't be as simple as that. Did she seriously think Polly Roberts was a fraudulent manipulator? And then the original question returned to her thoughts. Why hadn't Elizabeth ever told Esme about her natural family? What had she got to hide? Was she already aware of what was going on?

The last mile was uneventful and Esme arrived at last at the home. She swept into the drive, spraying gravel in every direction. She didn't stop to lock the car but bounded across the car park and in through the front door like a woman demented.

She stopped to get her breath in the hall. Mrs Rowcliffe was standing at the doorway of her office, no doubt having heard Esme's noisy approach.

'Where is she?' panted Esme.

'Visitors' lounge. But are you sure you should be...'

The matron's voice faded as Esme hurried down the passageway and towards the lounge. Several members of staff were near the door, engaged in a variety of superfluous tasks, straightening curtains or rearranging floral displays, no doubt desperate to hover close to the action in case something interesting happened. They turned towards her as she approached. Ignoring the affronted expressions on their faces, Esme brushed past, pushed open the door and marched unannounced into the lounge.

All eyes in the room turned towards her. It was clear that her arrival had halted the conversation in mid-flow. Esme closed the door behind her.

There were two policemen, one on a footstool and the other perched on the arm of a chair. They were seated opposite Polly who was poised on the edge of the seat of the armchair closest to the fireplace. She had her right hand upon her walking stick, almost as though she had been about to rise, prompted by something that had just been said.

Esme glanced from one policeman to the other. Did they look hostile, as though they were interviewing a suspect? If anything, they looked more concerned than severe. She recognised the one on the stool as Inspector Barry whom she had met at the hospital. He obviously recognised her too, and stood up.

'Mrs Quentin, isn't it?' Esme nodded. He looked at Polly, implying that he expected an explanation. She obliged.

'Mrs Quentin's a friend of mine, as is her sister.'

'Rather a coincidence,' commented the inspector, raising his eyebrows. What did he mean by that?

Esme moved further into the room and looked at the old lady. Her face was white. She turned towards the inspector.

'What's going on?'

'They want...' began Polly but faltered.

Esme took a step closer and laid a hand on Polly's arm. 'Are you all right?' she asked. Polly gave a little nod.

Esme turned and looked enquiringly at the inspector.

'We've had some information concerning a suspect,' he said. 'We need to speak to a particular witness.'

'A witness? Witness to what?' Esme's thoughts were racing.

Did he mean Polly was a witness? She glanced at Polly for some clarification but she appeared lost in her own thoughts.

'Someone came forward having seen our suspect's picture in the local press. She'd recognised him,' continued the inspector.

'She'd thought he was a taxi driver collecting a client from the solicitor's where she works, but later realised that he may have been following their client.'

Esme frowned. 'What has this got to do with Mrs Roberts?'

'The address that the solicitor had for the client in question was care of Miss Daisy Roberts.'

Esme struggled to digest the information and make sense of it. It explained in part why Polly was looking so distraught, having had to tell the policemen that Daisy was dead. She felt a surge of sympathy for the old lady. But who was the client for whom Daisy had been the contact?

'We were hoping that Mrs Roberts might be able to tell us the client's whereabouts,' explained Inspector Barry.

'Obviously Mrs Roberts will have explained that her daughter sadly died a short time ago,' said Esme.

'Yes, and I'm sorry that we may have caused Mrs Roberts some distress. We understand it was her daughter who dealt with the lady's correspondence, so unfortunately she isn't able to help us. Regrettably the receptionist has only recently recalled the incident, which happened some time ago now, back on the first of December last year.'

Something suddenly clicked in Esme's mind. 'When I arrived you mentioned a coincidence, Inspector. This suspect you're talking about? Has he got something to do with my sister's... attack?'

Esme deliberately kept her eyes averted from Polly. Keen though she was to see Polly's reaction to the question, she didn't want to bring the inspector's attention to it.

Inspector Barry looked at her. 'Indeed he has, Mrs Quentin.'

He looked surprised at her deduction. Esme noticed that he didn't challenge her wording, 'attack' rather than 'accident'. So what had happened for them to revert to the original assumption? Had they informed Gemma of this change of direction?

'You had a name for this suspect, didn't you?' said Esme. 'Is he who you thought he was?'

He was looking at her carefully. 'We believe it's likely, given the connection.'

'Connection?' Now she'd lost the thread. 'What connection?'

'With the client we are trying to trace, for whom Miss Roberts acted as contact. She's the suspect's cousin, Catherine Monkleigh.'

141

20

The moment the police left Polly was surrounded by an enthusiastic inrush of concerned staff. Esme could only watch from the sidelines as tea was brought, cushions were plumped up and words of sympathy were offered. Mrs Rowcliffe arrived and Esme decided it was time to withdraw from the bustle of professional tendering. She escaped into the hall and made her way towards the side door and out into the garden.

For the moment there was a lull in the showers, though the darkened sky indicated that the respite was to be short.

She meandered along the wide paths, appraising the borders.

They were well tended and weed-free. She had the urge to rush back home and get out into her own green space which was desperately in need of a complete revamp. Plants had outgrown their allotted spaces and were flattening one another in a sort of horticultural civil war. She also craved the regenerative benefits that gardening would bestow, to counter the feeling of dejection which descended upon her in unguarded moments. But, even if present circumstances allowed her the time, it was unlikely to stop raining long enough for her to get started.

As she wandered the paths she reviewed her theories, which had been thrown in to complete disarray with what she had just learnt from the police. She had been convinced that it was Catherine Monkleigh who was responsible for applying pressure on Polly to part with the cottage. Yet now it appeared that Catherine had been in Daisy's confidence. At least this latest piece of information had confirmed one thing of significance; that there was a loyal, and possibly enduring, connection with the Monkleigh family, as Mrs Rowcliffe had implied. But the reason why Polly was so reluctant to discuss her past association with the family remained stubbornly elusive.

Esme shivered and decided to return indoors. She re-entered the building the way she had come and made her way down the corridor towards the matron's office. She heard a door open behind her and turned to see a member of staff emerge from the lounge. Mrs Rowcliffe followed briskly behind.

'Is everything all right?' asked Esme, turning back towards her.

The matron hesitated. 'Mrs Roberts seems a little distressed,' she said in a low voice. 'We thought it prudent to ask the doctor to call.'

So Esme wasn't going to get her chance to discuss the land values and urge Polly to resist signing any documents. If she was under the doctor, though, at least she wouldn't be seeing visitors so Mary was unlikely to trouble her for a day or two. That gave them some breathing space.

Esme and Mrs Rowcliffe began walking down the corridor towards the matron's office.

'It's understandable she's upset,' said Esme. 'It was really her daughter the police wanted to talk to, about a friend. They obviously weren't aware of the circumstances, so she had to explain.'

The matron shook her head. 'Poor dear. Such a strange few days.' She lowered her voice. 'That awful woman was in again yesterday. The one who used to work with Mrs Roberts.'

Esme frowned. 'Mrs Watts?'

'The same. I do think it most odd that she agrees to her visits, they seem to upset her so. Mind you, she did tell Abigail that Mrs Watts would only be coming once more and then that would be it.'

'Did they have an argument?' asked Esme.

'Not that I'm aware of. I think it's simply that Mrs Roberts has at last seen sense. I can't for the life of me think why she didn't put a stop to her coming before. The woman clearly annoyed her.'

They arrived at the door to Mrs Rowcliffe's office as the front door opened.

'Ah, Dr Parker,' called the matron to a short balding man in a creased suit. 'Good of you to pop round. Such an advantage that you are so close.' Esme wondered whether the doctor shared these sentiments but he seemed convivial enough. Perhaps it boosted his professional ego for the matron to be so dependent on him.

The doctor nodded an acknowledgment to Esme as he passed and Mrs Rowcliffe accompanied him to Mrs Roberts.

Esme hovered in the front entrance uncertain whether to stay or go. She didn't want to leave if there was still a chance that she could speak to Polly, however briefly. She thought again about the issue of blackmail. To what extent had Polly's distress been due to the presence of the police? Had she thought they had come on some other errand, and that Mary had informed on her?

But Esme herself had heard Polly assure Mary that she had no intention of breaking their arrangement, whatever it was. So, if informing on Polly was indeed Mary's threat, why would Mary lose whatever advantage she had by carrying it out prematurely? Esme sighed. If only she knew what this was all about. Having only fragments of information meant she could only speculate. And what good was that proving to be? The most promising conclusion she'd arrived at so far had just been discredited. So much for her investigative skills.

There was a chair outside Mrs Rowcliffe's office. Esme sat down on it, trying to dispel the image forming in her head of waiting to see the headmistress. If Mary Watts had still to visit for a last time it meant that Polly hadn't yet signed the necessary documentation to sell the cottage. She had no doubt that Mary was only the intermediary of whatever deal had been agreed.

Someone else was involved and if it wasn't Catherine, who else did that leave?

Esme rubbed her eyes and ran her fingers through her hair.

But could she persuade Polly not to sign? Only if she learnt what was being used against Polly could she hope to change Polly's mind. But if Esme did learn what it was, what guarantee was there that she could do anything about it? The prognosis looked hopeless.

Abigail came past and offered her a cup of tea which Esme gladly accepted. She was leaning against the doorway of the kitchen chatting to Abigail, a mug of tea in her hand when the matron returned.

'The doctor's given her something to help her sleep,' Mrs Rowcliffe informed Esme when she saw she was still waiting.

'How is she?' asked Esme.

'Dr Parker said she'll be right as rain by the morning,' said the matron. Then something caught her eye and, frowning, she directed her gaze down the hall towards the front door.

Esme turned and looked to see what had caused the matron to harden her expression. A short, round, elderly woman was pushing open the front door. Her hair was covered by a brown headscarf and she clutched a fawn coloured leatherette shopping bag to her as she shuffled into the hall.

The old lady had barely crossed the threshold before Mrs Rowcliffe had swept down the corridor and accosted her.

'I'm afraid Mrs Roberts is indisposed,' she announced, as though addressing a crowd of onlookers.

The woman looked affronted. She stared up at the matron, as though lost for words.

'Eh? What's up with her?' she managed, at last.

'The doctor's been to see her. She's asleep at the moment. I'll tell her you called.'

The woman considered this for a moment. 'You do that,' she said in a manner which implied hidden meaning. Then she turned on the step and walked away.

Esme put down her mug on the kitchen counter and joined the matron, who was standing watching the old lady walk down the drive.

'Who's that?' said Esme. Did she need to ask?

'Mrs Watts,' said the matron through gritted teeth.

'I thought so. Excuse me.' Esme pushed passed Mrs Rowcliffe. 'Tell Mrs Roberts I'll see her tomorrow,' she called over her shoulder.

It took Esme no more than five seconds to catch up with Mary Watts. As Esme came alongside her she received a cold glance from the old woman.

'Mrs Watts?' She wasn't sure what she was going to say but she hoped she would think of something if she could get her talking.

'Who's asking?' The woman showed no inclination to slacken her pace and carried on down the drive towards the road.

'I'm a friend of Mrs Roberts,' said Esme.

'What's that to me?' The old lady kept walking, continuing to look ahead. Esme had to increase her stride to keep up. Either the woman was making a determined effort to get away or she was more nimble than she looked and this was her usual speed.

Whichever it was, she clearly had no desire to make Esme's acquaintance. Did that imply culpability on her part?

'Mrs Roberts seems to be rather troubled about something,' began Esme.

'She's got plenty to be troubled by.'

'Oh?' They had almost reached the end of the drive now. As they approached Esme could see the wing of a black car parked at the roadside. Was it waiting for Mary?

Mary was becoming breathless now as the pace was beginning to tell. She stopped abruptly. Esme halted alongside, turning to look at her, waiting for a response.

'Always gets to us in the end, doesn't it?' said Mary, her breathing laboured.

'What does?'

Mary looked up at Esme, with narrowed eyes. 'A guilty conscience.'

21

Esme had a restless night, full of dreams of old ladies with evil intent, greenhouses and newspaper articles. She put the last of these down to Lucy's telephone call about her success at tracking down reports of Leonard Nicholson's 'pals', as Albert had referred to them, and their criminal activities. The headlines were along the lines of, Rich Kids' Games, and Public schoolboys Rampage. Their idea of fun had been to disguise themselves with balaclavas and then break in to houses of the parents of their peers. Not satisfied with simple theft – none of them was short of money – they then proceeded to terrorise the occupants for several hours until they got bored and left with a bag full of valuable items, presumably in order to lead the police to conclude that the motive was burglary. Their antics backfired when they made the flawed decision of targeting the parents of one of the gang. Unsurprisingly it was their arrogance which was their undoing. The mother of the gang member in question recognised her son's badly disguised voice and, such was her abhorrence of the behaviour, had no qualms about reporting him to the police.

As soon as it was light Esme got out of bed. It was unlikely that she would benefit by fitful dozing, so she got dressed and went down to the kitchen to put the kettle on.

Since speaking to Mary Watts the previous day she had been thinking about the old woman's remark. Was it really a matter of guilt? There were always two sides to a story. Did Mary have an unbiased view of the circumstances? Esme doubted it. She could talk to the police about the implications – the link with Leonard Nicholson and the implied value of Polly's cottage – but she still felt she owed Polly warning of the can of worms she might be opening. And perhaps in a way she also owed Elizabeth. Polly was her grandmother, after all, however bizarre that idea still seemed.

Esme brewed coffee and poured herself a bowl of cereal and a glass of orange juice. Apart from during her student days, breakfast was a meal she rarely missed, not since she realised how weak and unproductive she got in the middle of the morning if she didn't eat anything. She'd almost fainted once.

Everyone wrongly assumed she was pregnant and it took a long time to live it down where she worked at the time. Since then breakfast had become a favourite meal. She was also convinced that it directly stirred her brain cells. And her brain cells were in desperate need of stirring at this moment.

When she'd finished her muesli and toast, she put the crockery in the sink and slipped on her coat. Fresh air was the next necessity. Her head was still muggy and it was too early to make telephone calls. Besides, there was something she needed to get her head round, even though she didn't know what it was.

A good walk was often effective in releasing the subconscious.

She decided on a stroll around the village. It was so beautiful first thing in the morning, quiet and restful with no one around.

She came out of her front door and turned right towards the old priory. The smell in the air was exhilarating. The trees in the lane were sodden with the overnight rain. The evergreen shrubs in the rectory garden were sulking, overwhelmed with the weight of water. The oaks were yet to show their leaves but the branches dripped with moisture as Esme wandered underneath, causing her to pull her coat closer around her neck to avoid the water droplets seeping down her collar.

She spent a few moments looking across at the ruins of the priory and then turned back towards her cottage. She glanced at her watch. The newsagent would be open by now. She'd call in and buy a paper. She took a diversion through the churchyard gate and across the grass to the way out at the bottom of the High Street. The maintenance workers had been at work the previous day with their first cut of the season. Grass cuttings were strewn across the pathway and small heaps of clippings lay in curved channels in corners. They'd missed a few bits, through haste or apathy. Clusters of early daisies were pushing up amongst the new blades of grass on the overlooked edges of the lawn.

Esme stopped abruptly on the path. Daisies. Now she realised what had been nagging her.

She spun round and hurried back to her cottage. She rushed indoors, grabbed the telephone and dialled Lucy's number. She paced up and down while it rang.

After a few moments a croaky voice came on the line.

'Lucy, it's Esme.'

There was a groan. 'God, Esme. It's the middle of the night.'

'I've just worked it out.'

'Worked out what? This better be good. It's my day off.'

'Sorry, but it was seeing the daisies. And then I remembered Albert Jennings's greenhouse. He was writing labels and passing them to me. I should have thought about it before. It all adds up.'

'Esme, what are you talking about?'

'The plants in the greenhouse. They were marguerites. The name of the plants. And they were like little daisies.'

'Esme, I've no idea what...'

'Catherine Monkleigh's middle name was Marguerite,' said Esme with undisguised excitement. 'Daisy and Catherine. They're both the same person.'

22

'I hope that's for me,' said Lucy sniffing, as Esme showed her through to the warm fug of her kitchen, overlaid with the aroma of freshly brewed coffee. 'I need something to drag me into the real world this morning.'

Esme felt a stab of guilt. 'I'm sorry, Lu, but I desperately needed to tell someone. Have I really messed up your day?'

Lucy shook her head. 'You've done me a favour. I've got a good excuse to avoid the usual day-off chores.' She took off her coat and hung it over the back of a chair. She nodded towards the sheets of paper on the table. 'Someone's been busy.'

'I've just assembled everything we've gathered so far, to see if there was anything else which jumped to the fore.'

Lucy sat down and began scanning Esme's notes. 'And did it?'

'Not so far. But everything fits in with Daisy being Catherine – Catherine's correspondence being sent care of Daisy, the fact that I couldn't find a birth for Daisy Roberts.

But the real clue is in the name. Daisy is a diminutive of Margaret, Marguerite being the French version, and it being Catherine's middle name. I should have twigged that ages ago.'

'You didn't know Marguerite was her name until you got the birth certificate,' pointed out Lucy, charitably.

Esme smiled. 'True. It's quite ironic, though. We'd speculated that Daisy's father was Sir Charles and though it's not in the way we thought, we now know that he was.'

'Not necessarily.'

Esme placed a mug of coffee next to Lucy and sat down opposite her. 'How do you mean?'

'Catherine's mother could have been playing away and he wasn't the father.'

'That's possible, I suppose. Would it change anything, though, from a legal perspective? Her birth certificate records Sir Charles as her father, so officially he was.'

Lucy shrugged. 'Only if someone disputes it, I suppose. Bit late for DNA testing, though, I grant you.'

They both sipped their coffees, deep in thought.

'The other day,' said Lucy, 'when you told me about Elizabeth, you never said whether Gemma knew.'

Esme shook her head. 'No, she didn't.'

'Why do you think Elizabeth kept it quiet? Sorry, Esme, I've been thinking about it a lot, that's all. If you'd rather not talk about it...'

'Don't be silly. It's all part of the mystery, isn't it? If I want to work out what's going on I have to deal with it.' She traced the pattern on her mug with her forefinger. 'I don't know why she kept it quiet. I've no idea when she first found out. That in itself might be a clue.'

'She might have only found out recently.'

'No. The copy of the certificate is dated 1977. Only she could have got that, when the law changed. Perhaps she already knew by then. I don't have any idea how long ago she made contact with Daisy, either.'

'And Polly hasn't been exactly forthcoming.'

'When I first went to see her, she implied Elizabeth had been plucking up courage to tell us, but I don't know whether that's true or not. She may have used it as an excuse for keeping me in the dark.'

Esme leant over the table and waved her hand across her page of notes. 'I've always said it's got to be linked with the family and now we have the connection, in the fact that Daisy was really Catherine.' She leant her elbow on the table. 'But how does that vital clue move us on?'

'Well,' said Lucy, considering, 'the first question is when did Catherine become Daisy?'

'When she got pregnant with Elizabeth, I thought.'

'That would make sense.'

Esme continued with her theory. 'And say Polly had been her nurse, or nanny or whatever when Catherine and her mother had left Sir Charles, then it would be quite straightforward for Catherine to pretend to be Polly's daughter and go away somewhere to have the baby, incognito. Elizabeth was born in Cheshire, so well away from the Monkleigh area.'

'But why not go back to the family afterwards?'

'Perhaps it was only when she got pregnant that she came back from abroad and had never re-established a link with the family since they left. Maybe the reunion came later.'

Lucy sipped her coffee. 'And you haven't any idea who Elizabeth's father was?'

'None.'

'What about this nephew?' said Lucy. 'He couldn't be the missing link, could he?'

'Too young. According to the gardener he's only in his thirties, so he wouldn't even have been born then.'

Lucy began drumming her fingers on the table top, absent-mindedly. Esme got up and went and stood by the kitchen door, looking out across the garden. 'Mary Watts, the woman Polly used to work with years ago, told me that Polly had a guilty conscience.'

'About what?'

'She didn't say. Something that happened when they worked together, maybe? Mary was the employee who was sacked just after Catherine and her mother left.'

'What for, do you know?'

'No, but Albert seemed to think it had got something to do with the wife and daughter leaving.'

Lucy put her elbows on the table and rested her chin on her hand. 'So what could it be? She knew something about the imminent departure and didn't tell?'

'I hadn't thought of that but it's hardly a sacking offence. But it can't be a coincidence that Mary was sacked at the same time as Polly left, with the departing Catherine and her mother.'

'Whatever Mary considers Polly is guilty of could still be connected with her sacking.'

'But it's so long ago,' said Esme. 'Surely there's more to it than that?'

Esme came back over to the table. She collected up the used mugs and took them over to the sink. 'What could she have done to warrant blackmail?' She ran the tap and swilled the mugs under the running water. 'And what about the other fly in the ointment? When I had my theory that there could be a claim on the cottage by someone else I'd thought it must be Catherine but now we know who she really is, that bit doesn't add up any more.'

'You haven't forgotten the nephew?'

'Of course not. He's a likely candidate to be involved in some form or other, from what we've found out about him, but I still don't see how the whole thing hangs together. What is Polly being blackmailed about and what's Mary's part in it?'

'So,' said Lucy, shrugging. 'Now what?'

Esme turned round and leant her back against the stone sink, drying her hands on a teatowel.

'What reason might you have for concealing your true identity?' she said, folding her arms.

'You mean why did Catherine remain being Daisy, long after she gave up Elizabeth for adoption?'

'That's exactly what I mean. Maybe it's not Polly who's been up to no good. Maybe it was Daisy. Or maybe,' she said, as the idea occurred to her for the first time, 'maybe Mary has worked out what we just have, that Daisy and Catherine were one and the same.'

Lucy made a hopeless gesture with her hands. 'But Daisy's dead, Esme. What possible difference could Mary's knowing make now?'

'I'm not sure, but it will be interesting to find out.'

'And how do you propose to do that?'

'By seeing what Polly's response is when I tell her what we know. Confronting her with that might just be the key which unlocks the whole secret.'

23

Mrs Roberts was 'as well as to be expected', according to the matron, when Esme telephoned to ask after her. Mrs Roberts had spent much of the past two days in her room, Mrs Rowcliffe explained, but was venturing out into the lounge for an hour or two that afternoon. Esme said that she would drop by for a short time so as not to tire her. She felt a twinge of guilt as she replaced the phone. Pleased though she was that the old lady was feeling better, Esme knew full well that her visit was not simply a courtesy call but had an ulterior motive and it could well undo all the good that her restorative treatment had afforded her. But time was running out. If Polly was well enough to receive visitors, it wouldn't be long before Mary turned up again. Esme must speak to Polly before then.

What would the old lady's reaction be to the fact that Esme had realised that Catherine and Daisy were the same person?

Impatient though she was to unravel the truth, Esme was nervous about the consequences of confronting the old lady with her discoveries. But if they were to make any progress at all it was better that Esme should challenge Polly with an unpalatable truth than that some unscrupulous partnership of Mary and her accomplice, strongly suspected by Lucy to be Leonard Nicholson, should be free to indulge in blackmail and extortion.

Before she'd left yesterday Lucy had elicited a promise from Esme that she would tell the police about Leonard, regardless of whether Polly co-operated or not.

'If you'd read the newspaper reports in full like I have,' Lucy said, 'you'd know that Leonard Nicholson isn't a person to cross. By all means give Polly the chance to come clean but if she chooses to rebuff you, you can't afford to turn your back on what you know.'

Esme smiled at the show of protection. 'You sound like my mother before my first date.'

'Esme, you're not taking this seriously. We're talking threats and blackmail here, for goodness' sake.'

Esme put up her hands, surrender fashion. 'OK, OK, I get the message.'

Lucy continued to look stern. 'I'm not sure you do.'

Esme looked into her friend's worried face. The thought sobered her. She reached out and laid her hand on Lucy's arm.

'Sorry. I didn't mean to be flippant. I understand your concern and I accept what you're saying.'

Lucy looked at her warily, as if she wasn't completely convinced, but then nodded. They hugged as Lucy left, as though it was to be months before they saw one another again.

Being a Sunday the visitors' lounge at Wisteria House was busy with faces unfamiliar to Esme, as relatives took time out of their weekends to make their duty calls. One or two looked as though the experience caused them physical discomfort but others were deeply engaged in convivial conversation.

Polly looked better than Esme had expected, though her face was pale and she looked tired. Had Mary been for her final visit or had Mrs Rowcliffe managed to waylay her again?

Esme tried to assess whether Polly appeared as though a weight had been lifted from her mind, or as though she had a further obstacle yet to overcome. She didn't reach any conclusion, one way or the other.

Esme greeted the old lady and asked her how she was feeling. Polly shrugged and said she couldn't grumble. She glanced around the room, which was getting crowded.

'There's too many people in here,' she said, in an irritated tone. She went to get up. Esme stepped forward to help her.

'We'll go up to my room,' said the old lady. 'I've something to show you.'

They left the buzz of the visitors' lounge and made their way to the first floor where Polly's room, at the rear of the building, overlooked the garden and grounds. The room was spacious, furnished with a heavy sideboard, dressing-table and wardrobe.

The bed Esme recognised as a smaller sibling of the one she'd seen in Keeper's Cottage. The large sliding sash window overlooked the grounds. Long drapes of heavy tapestry-like fabric hung on either side.

Polly went over to the sideboard and took out a small photograph from a drawer. She shuffled over to an armchair beside the window, positioned to take in the view across the lawn. She sat down, telling Esme to fetch the stool from the dressing-table for herself.

When Esme was seated Polly passed over the photograph.

There were three women in the picture, standing in a row with smiling faces. It must have been the photograph from which Elizabeth had taken the miniatures for her locket. Elizabeth was in the middle. The woman on the left was Polly so the remaining figure must have been Elizabeth's mother, Daisy.

Or should that be Catherine? She studied her for a while in the same way as she had looked at Polly when she'd first met her, looking for signs of similarity to Elizabeth.

'Taken the week before she died,' said the old lady.

'It's here, isn't it?' Esme could make out the front entrance of the building on the right hand side of the shot.

'Yes, before I moved in. She wanted me to come and see the place. She knew it was a matter of time, you see. She wanted to know I'd like it here. Then she was going to put everything in place for me to move here when she...wasn't there any more.'

She pulled her handkerchief from her sleeve and looked out of the window. Esme sensed that emotions were close to the surface.

They sat in silence, Esme churning over in her mind as to when was going to be the best time to confess that she knew about

157

Catherine. She was concerned for Polly's state of mind.

What would her reaction be? Distress? Resignation? And would the disclosure lead Esme to what she needed to know? That it was this that Mary was using against her?

Esme looked again at the photograph. The face of Elizabeth seemed to alter as she stared at it. One moment it was familiar, the next it appeared to be of someone completely different, the way faces do change sometimes if you stare at them long enough.

She looked up at Polly who was still gazing out of the window.

'It's nice to put a face to her name.' She handed it back but the old lady was still lost in her own thoughts. 'I'll put it away for you, shall I?' Polly gave a brief nod.

Esme went over to the sideboard. There was one small framed photograph on display which she hadn't seen when she came in. It was of Daisy. Now she could detect something of Elizabeth in her. It was in the eyes and the line of her nose. It was strange to make the first visual acquaintance, at least, of the lady who was so significant in her enquiries, even if it was from such a distance.

She opened the drawer from where Polly had retrieved the picture and put it inside. A small white booklet caught her eye. It was the order of service for Daisy's funeral. She picked it up and read the cover. Daisy Roberts, born 8 February 1939. She knew that date. It was the same date as was on the birth certificate she'd received of Catherine Monkleigh. That confirmed it then.

Daisy was Catherine. As she replaced it on the pile of papers she noticed the date of Daisy's death, 1 December. Why was that date significant? She'd seen it recently or someone had mentioned it.

She closed the drawer and turned back to Polly. Having now confirmed that Daisy and Catherine had the same birth date, Esme knew she couldn't avoid the issue any longer.

She went back over to the stool and sat down in front of the old lady.

'I've found out something about your cottage,' she began.

Polly turned away from her musings through the window and focused on Esme.

'Were you aware of the value of the land?' Esme continued. Polly looked puzzled. 'What are you trying to say, dear?' she said.

'The land next to your cottage. Have you ever had it valued?' Esme briefly summarised what she had learnt from Andy.

Polly shrugged and showed minimal interest. 'No concern of mine. Not now.'

Esme was alarmed. 'You mean you've already signed the contract?'

Polly leant across and patted Esme on the arm. 'Don't fret, my dear. It'll all be sorted out presently.'

'But you're being exploited,' exclaimed Esme, in an exasperated voice.

Polly sat up straight in her chair and regarded Esme with an expression of outrage. 'May I remind you, dear, that as that Mr Evans so rightly pointed out in his letter, the decision is up to me.'

Esme bit her lip. Here she was alienating the old lady, and they hadn't even begun to discuss the contentious issues yet.

'I'm sorry, I didn't mean to be rude, but I'm worried about what's going on.' Esme thought she saw a flicker of something in the Polly's face. Panic? Irritation? It was too fleeting to be sure.

When she spoke it seemed that Polly might have regretted her outburst. 'Esme, I know that you feel that you somehow have to take on Elizabeth's responsibilities while she is ill, but I can't let you do that. It wouldn't be right.'

Wouldn't be right? Was this just another excuse to prevent Esme from getting too close, or did she seriously think Esme was stepping over the mark? Probably both.

Esme made a decision. 'There's something I need to tell you, Mrs Roberts,' she said. Polly looked sternly at her, as though defying her to exceed the line she had just defined. Esme refused to be deterred. She looked into Polly's face and spoke as gently as she could.

'I know that Daisy was Catherine Monkleigh.'

The shock in the old lady's face was unmistakable. 'What do you mean?' she demanded. Now she looked frightened. She pulled at her handkerchief until Esme thought it was going to dissolve into shreds.

'Is it what Mary knows, that Daisy was really Catherine Monkleigh?' asked Esme with urgency. 'Is that what she's using against you? Is that how she's getting you to part with your cottage in some sort of crooked scheme?'

Polly sank back into the chair, being almost absorbed into the depths of the upholstery. She shook her head, slowly, as if the last reserve of her energy was spent and she could no longer resist an inevitable outcome.

'I don't know. I honestly don't know,' she murmured.

Esme tried to grasp the implications of her words. She seemed to be saying that she had allowed herself to be compromised on the grounds that Mary might know something about her past?

'You never challenged her?' she asked.

'I couldn't take the risk.'

Suddenly Esme thought she understood Polly's anguish.

The thought of Mary Watts spelling out what she knew with malevolent pleasure would have been too harrowing for Polly to cope with. As long as it was never spoken of, Polly could convince herself that Mary didn't know. She never need suffer Mary's gloating.

What she still didn't understand, however, was why that particular piece of knowledge could possibly be grounds for blackmail.

Polly slowly turned her head and focused intensely on Esme.

She was shaking. Esme leant over and put her hands over the old lady's.

'What is it? I'm here to help but I can't unless you tell me what's upsetting you?'

160

Polly seemed to come to a decision.

'I thought if she got what she wanted she'd go away and leave me alone.' She sighed. 'But if she does know,' she added in a voice barely above a whisper. 'Then she'll have guessed everything.'

24

'Matron wondered if Mrs Roberts wanted a cup of tea,' said Abigail. She looked beyond Esme's shoulder into Polly's room as if she suspected Esme was holding the old lady against her will.

Esme opened her mouth to answer but Polly had apparently recovered her composure in the time Esme had taken to walk across the room and answer the knock at the door.

'That would be lovely, dear,' Polly called out from her chair. She smiled at the young woman. 'It was a bit busy down there,' she added. 'We came up for a bit of peace and quiet.'

Abigail appeared to relax. 'Of course. You don't need to wear yourself out, do you? I'll pop back with a tray, then.'

She turned away and Esme left the door ajar for her return.

She hovered uncertainly in the middle of the room, frustrated at the interruption. Polly had been on the brink of explaining exactly what she meant by Mary 'knowing everything', Esme was sure of it. Now she might use being disturbed as an opportunity to change the subject.

Esme paced the room, rehearsing in her head how she might word a question and revisit the issue. There was no point in saying anything until Abigail returned with the tea tray or there would be a further halt. She walked back and forth, hoping that in the silence Polly would be reflecting upon what she'd been about to say. Esme said nothing, having no wish to break the spell by diverting her in trival conversation while they waited.

Esme heard Abigail's approach along the landing and met her at the door.

'Thanks very much,' she said taking the tray from her. 'I'll bring it down when I go. I won't be long.' She backed into the room, dismissing the young woman with a smile, and pushing the door closed with her foot. She set the tray on a side table near the window and returned to her stool.

'What makes you think that Mary knows everything?' asked Esme.

'They never loved her you know,' said Polly.

'Loved who?' Whom did she mean?

Polly seemed for the moment to be unaware of Esme's presence but her next words answered Esme's question. 'Her mother was too busy socialising and her father was too wrapped up in his London work. He even thought that Catherine wasn't his.'

'Was he right?' Perhaps Lucy had guessed correctly after all, that Catherine's mother had an affair.

Polly was shaking her head. 'No, the mistress made that quite plain to me but she had this "little game", as she would call it, of teasing him about her admirers. She used to laugh at his furious reaction.' She shook her head slowly and pursed her lips in disapproval.

'Rather cruel,' remarked Esme but Polly had moved on. Her eyes brightened as she remembered.

'She was a bonny little thing, always laughing. A lovely baby. Poor little Daisy. I called her that, even then, on account of her middle name.' Her mouth formed a line of censure. 'They didn't deserve her and that's a fact.'

'It couldn't have been long afterwards that you left?' Albert had said that Catherine had only been a few months old.

Polly turned her head and stared out blankly into the garden.

'I thought she'd keep me on as Daisy's nursemaid.'

Esme was confused. Hadn't Polly been retained as Daisy's nurse? Her words suggested the contrary. Perhaps Albert had got it wrong after all, and it *had* been Polly who was dismissed that day.

'She'd always defended me, see,' continued Polly, 'when Sir Charles ever talked about employing a professional. Stupid man.

Catherine was a baby. She needed love and affection and she already got that from me. Professional, indeed.'

'What happened?'

'Oh, she was all excited about her latest beau. She said he would take her away from all this, you know, the usual Hollywood drivel. Then I began to realise that she was talking about a world that didn't have a place for babies.'

A question stirred something in Esme's subconscious as Polly continued.

'She came and said she was leaving and I dared to ask what was to happen to me.' Polly turned her head to look back into the room, focusing on the wall behind Esme, as though she was viewing the past event as a silent movie.

'I can see her now. She just laughed. "Don't be ridiculous Polly," she said. "I can hardly achieve my freedom with a baby on my hands." She was pulling on a pair of gloves and I remember staring at them, thinking she'd put her thumb through the kid leather, she was being so rough. "He can take her on," she said. "He wanted an heir. Well, he got a girl and he can take responsibility."'

'She planned to leave Catherine behind?' asked Esme, bewildered. She tried to remember what Albert had told her, that Mother and baby had both left. How had Polly persuaded her to change her mind?

Polly continued as though Esme hadn't spoken. 'It dawned on me then, what she'd said about Daisy's father. It wasn't just his work that kept him out of the nursery, he thought a daughter a poor substitute for the boy he'd expected.' The old lady sighed and shook her head. 'I got worried then. With his wife no longer there to defend me I knew it would be only a matter of time before Sir Charles replaced me with the professional employee he was always threatening.' She looked imploringly at Esme.

'Don't you see? I was going to lose Daisy.'

Esme couldn't see, not completely. There was obviously

something she wasn't fully grasping.

'But what happened to change her plan to leave Catherine behind? Why didn't she go through with it?'

Polly tossed her head, wisps of white hair escaping from the neat pleat at the back of her head. 'Oh she went through with it all right,' she said bitterly. 'Poor little mite. I told you. They didn't care about her, either of them.'

Her eyes looked up at Esme, pleading with her. 'What else could I do? No one cared. It was as though she had no parents.'

She pointed agitatedly at herself. 'She only had me. I was like her mother.'

Then suddenly Esme realised what Polly was trying to tell her. There she had been, a young girl facing the loss of a baby she loved and had protected as her own. The mother was about to walk out and the father, emotionally detached from his daughter, was interested only in procedure, and so was a threat to Polly's future with a baby who needed her. To Polly, what she had done must have seemed the only course of action open to her.

'You left and took Catherine with you,' Esme said slowly, watching Polly, daring her to contradict. But Polly said nothing.

She sat looking down at her hands, rolling the wretched handkerchief into a ball.

Hundreds of questions hurtled around Esme's head, the most obvious one was how she had got away with it.

'I didn't think of it straight away,' Polly was saying. 'Why would I? It was after she'd gone and I read the letter she'd left for Catherine's father. She gave it to me to pass on to him, you see.

She thought the staff would steam it open and read it before he got hold of it.' Polly gave a short laugh. 'If she hadn't said that I'd have never have thought of reading it myself. But I did, then. I was curious to know if she'd mentioned me. As I read it, the idea just came to me. It was perfect.'

'Why, what did the letter say?'

'She was teasing him even then. She talked about "we". "We're going abroad", she wrote. She was deliberately omitting to give a name, see, so he wouldn't know who she was going off with, I assume so that he would find it more difficult to follow her. Not that he did, as it turned out. Follow her, that is. But her mockery was a godsend for me. I reasoned that he would assume she'd taken Daisy, as no doubt any father would, and so I had the perfect cover. He'd think "we" was her and her daughter.'

'And she would assume Daisy was with her father, where she'd left her?'

Polly nodded.

Esme grappled with the enormity of the decision Polly had taken. Had she thought it through? Did she have a plan? Did she really believe that it would be as simple as she'd imagined?

'But what did you do? Where did you go?' she asked, fascinated.

Polly sighed and leant her head against the back of the chair. The confession seemed to have drained her.

'I had this mad idea that my sister would welcome me with open arms. She had a brood of six. One more wouldn't make much difference, I thought. Our parents were dead. She was my only family. I used to go there for my days off. I used to help out with the little ones. I loved it. It seemed such a lovely thing to have a family. Perhaps that's why when I saw my chance with Daisy, I took it. I wanted something of what she had.'

'But you were only young. There was plenty of time for you to marry and have your own children.'

'But to my way of thinking, Daisy was my own. I'd looked after her from the day she was born. Don't you see?'

Esme could understand how she could have felt it that way, particularly considering the apparent indifference of both the child's parents.

'So you went to your sister's?'

'She was horrified when I told her. I should have invented a story but I was too honest. I thought she'd understand what neglect I would be subjecting Daisy to if I left her with her father. She said it wasn't my place to judge. She let me stay a week and then we were to go.'

'What did you do?'

Polly looked wistful. 'It was September 1939. War had just been declared and children were being evacuated across the country. People were getting out of London. I joined in the chaos. Then when my sister kicked me out, I took the next train and surrendered to fate. I didn't know where it was going. Somewhere up North. But we never got that far. I got talking to another passenger, an elderly lady. We got quite friendly during the journey. She said she was looking for a live-in housekeeper, here in the Midlands, so I took the job. Like lots of people, she assumed my husband had gone away to war and I had chosen to get out of London for the safety of the baby.'

'She must have wondered, though, when your non-existent husband didn't materialise.'

Polly looked at Esme and smiled sadly. 'I had plenty of time to work on my story.'

Esme tried to picture Polly in her quandary, deciding which way to turn. Then, having acted and settled, wondering whether someone was going to turn up on the doorstep one day, to arrest her for abduction and take Daisy away. The pressure must have been intolerable.

'Did you ever think of going back?'

Polly shook her head. 'Not really. At least, never seriously. I'd lose Daisy, wouldn't I? I wasn't going do that unless they came for me. And the longer time went on, the more I was convinced that my double deception had worked. Each parent thought she was with the other.'

'I can't believe Sir Charles didn't go after his wife and discover Catherine wasn't with her.'

'You don't know his family. They were set against the wedding from the start, so they say. He was mesmerised by Rosalind when they first met and went against their wishes in marrying her. By the time he saw her true colours it was too late. The family probably breathed a collective sigh of relief when she left.'

'But his daughter?'

'What use was a daughter? He wanted a son and heir. He probably thought Catherine would grow up like her mother.'

Esme looked at the tea tray. She had forgotten all about it. She felt the pot.

'Do you want some tea? It's gone a bit cold, I'm afraid.'

Polly nodded. Esme poured her a cup and passed it to her.

'I still don't understand why Mary would guess the circumstances. She left about the same time as you did.'

Polly sipped the tea and then replaced the cup on the saucer on her lap. 'We bumped into one another years later, when Daisy was seventeen.' She pointed to the small cupboard beside the bed.

'Go and fetch something for me, would you? It's right at the bottom. You'll recognise it when you see it.'

Esme placed her cup on the tray and went and looked in the cupboard Polly indicated. On the bottom shelf she found the silver frame with the cracked glass which she had discovered in the cottage. She brought it over to the old lady.

'Is this Daisy?' Esme had asked her that once before and Polly had said not. Had she been lying to protect her? But again Polly shook her head.

'That's Rosalind, Catherine's mother.' Polly gestured to the sideboard. 'Go and put it next to the one of Daisy.'

Esme took the photograph across the room and compared the two images. Although the ages of the two women were different, the likeness was unmistakable.

'Mary would have known Lady Monkleigh,' said Esme, realising Polly's dilemma. 'She would have seen the similarity in Daisy. But it would be a huge leap to conclude that she was Catherine, surely?'

'Possibly. As I said, Daisy was only seventeen, when we met

Mary. The likeness then wasn't strong but I could see it becoming more marked as she grew older. But there was something else.'

Polly clutched the handle of her cup, as though bracing herself. 'On the day I went, she saw me leave. After I'd manhandled the perambulator out of the front door on to the pavement, I turned and saw her watching me from the cellar steps.' Polly looked over to Esme. 'She wouldn't have made anything of it at the time. After all, I was Catherine's nursemaid. I took her out all the time.'

'So why...?' began Esme.

'I took a piece of jewellery, a brooch with a timepiece in the centre. Well, I needed some security, didn't I? I didn't have much money of my own. It was insurance. It would be Catherine's anyway when she grew up. I was just keeping it safe.'

Esme was saddened by the huge burden that Polly had put upon herself as a young girl for the love of a baby who wasn't hers. A moment's decision and a lifetime of dealing with the consequences.

'Mary was accused of stealing it,' Polly said.

'And that's why she got the sack.' Now it made sense at last.

'But how did she know it was you who had taken it?'

'When we came across each other years later, it was because she'd met Daisy. And one day, unbeknown to me, Daisy had worn the brooch.'

'And she recognised it?'

Polly nodded.

Too many coincidences. Esme could see why Polly was convinced that Mary had worked out the truth.

The question now was, knowing the full story herself, could Esme have any influence over Mary and persuade her she no longer had a case for blackmail?

25

Esme sat in her car at Wisteria House clutching the documents Polly had entrusted to her. She understood now why Polly had been unable to confide in her before. The papers showed that the property had been made over to Polly recently from the previous owner – Catherine Marguerite Monkleigh. Sight of the document would have raised questions which were no longer relevant now that Esme knew about Catherine and Daisy. Daisy had apparently acquired the cottage after a reunion with her father, some years before he died. Esme wondered whether his exasperation with Leonard's behaviour had contributed to his change in attitude towards his daughter, assuming what Polly had said about him was correct.

Now Esme intended to tackle Mary. She wondered how much she genuinely knew or whether it had been Polly's response to Mary's threats which had alerted Mary into thinking Polly had something to hide, without knowing the details. Mary had told Esme that Polly had a 'guilty conscience', easy enough to read into Polly's reaction, whilst Polly had been too distressed to call Mary's bluff. What if that was all this really was a bluff? Even if Mary had guessed the truth, she wouldn't know whether Polly taking Catherine wasn't a legitimate instruction from her father to move his daughter to a place of safety from the feared bombing campaign. Mary had left the household immediately after the sighting and wouldn't have known that Catherine had never returned.

After Polly had passed Esme the document she was supposed to sign, she appeared drained of emotion, as though finally unleashing the truth had exhausted her. Or perhaps she had simply reached a state of acceptance, realising that the fight to keep the past hidden seemed suddenly futile and she hadn't the strength to continue any longer.

Esme leaned over and shoved the papers into her bag in the passenger footwell. She hadn't yet worked out her approach with Mary yet, but she hoped that she would think of something before she got there. She fitted the key in the ignition and turned it. The car rumbled into life. Esme reached for her seatbelt and clicked it into place. She hesitated. There was something she had wanted to clarify with Polly but she couldn't place it. She was sure it was significant. She banged the steering wheel with the heel of her hand. Everything about this situation was like this. Something always on the edge of consciousness, which she couldn't quite grasp.

She put the car into reverse to manoeuvre around the Land Rover parked next to her, then engaged first gear and steered towards the exit. The driveway opened out on to a quiet road with little traffic. She paused to ensure the way was clear and then pulled out.

Suddenly a black car shot from nowhere to her right, threatening to ram her in the side. She slammed on the brakes and turned the wheel hard to the left, throwing files and books from the back seat on to the floor behind her. The car roared past.

She cursed the driver but by now the car was almost out of sight. It had been an Audi, she was sure. They seemed to be appearing everywhere she went. Either going very slowly or very quickly.

She took a deep breath and resumed her journey. She was approaching the junction to the main road when she suddenly remembered something. Perhaps it had been the black car which had prompted her to think of funerals. Daisy died on 1 December. She'd known the date was significant when she saw it printed on the front of the Order of Service for Daisy's funeral in Polly's drawer, but she couldn't think why. Now she knew. It was the date the police had said Leonard Nicholson was suspected of stalking Catherine. Which meant, of course, that he'd been following Daisy. Had he caught up with her?

And more significantly, if he had, did his presence have any bearing on her untimely death?

Esme did a U-turn at the junction and sped back to Wisteria House.

*

Esme burst through the front door. Mrs Rowcliffe was standing in the hall putting on her coat, presumably about to leave for home. She looked round in surprise at Esme's explosive arrival.

'Whatever's wrong?'

'Where's Mrs Roberts?' panted Esme.

'Having her tea, I expect. What's happened?'

'I need to talk to her.' Esme sailed past the matron and ran round the corner towards the entrance to the dining room.

Several residents were moving along the corridor on their way to tea. Polly had just reached the door.

'Mrs Roberts?' called Esme. 'Can I have a word?'

All heads turned as Esme caught up with the old lady.

'What on earth's going on?' said Polly. Leaning on her stick, she reached out with her free hand and touched Esme's arm. 'Is it Elizabeth?'

Esme shook her head. 'No, she's fine. There's something I need to ask you.' She looked around at the audience they had attracted. 'Shall we go and talk in the lounge?'

Polly turned and they made their way along the corridor into the visitors' lounge. Polly dropped into the armchair nearest the door and propped her stick up against the arm.

'What is it?' Her eyes were wide open and her lip quivered.

Esme crouched down in front of the old lady. 'The day Daisy died,' she began.

Polly flinched. 'Daisy? Why do you need to ask about Daisy?'

'It's important, please,' urged Esme. 'Was Daisy at home on

her own that day?' This was critical. If Polly had been with Daisy when she died, it would change everything and Esme could relax.

The old lady looked alarmed. 'Well, for a short time...but why? I don't understand.'

Esme hesitated. She couldn't say anything until she was sure. 'Tell me what happened.'

Polly stared at Esme for a moment as if considering whether to speak or refuse and go back to her tea. After a tense moment she chose to speak.

'I'd been here in the afternoon.' Her eyes flickered and she blinked. 'A vacancy had come up and I came to see it. Elizabeth brought me. Daisy had an appointment.'

'With her solicitor?'

Polly nodded. 'We got home about four o'clock. It was getting dark. I remember thinking Daisy couldn't be home yet because there were no lights on. I was relieved in a way. I didn't like leaving her on her own, though Carol would have stayed with her until we got back.'

'Carol?' Esme shifted her position and pulled up a footstool in front of the old lady's chair.

'Her friend. She's a nurse. She went with Daisy to her appointment. She carries oxygen in her medical bag for emergencies, you know the sort of thing. Daisy occasionally needed oxygen, you see. Her condition meant that she had to have it close by.'

'And did Carol stay on after they got back?'

Mrs Roberts shook her head. 'Carol told me later that Daisy had said not to wait as she expected us back soon and Carol needed to collect her children from school.' There she paused for a moment, composing herself before carrying on. 'Daisy was lying on the floor in the living room when we walked in. It was too late.' The old lady reached for the handkerchief in her sleeve and blew her nose.

Esme reached over and squeezed her hand. 'And they thought

her illness was the cause of death?'

'They assumed she didn't reach her oxygen in time.' Polly squeezed her handkerchief into a ball in her fist. 'It was in the hall,' she said slowly. She looked up at Esme. 'Why was it in the hall?' Esme's stomach leap-frogged. 'So it wasn't usually in there?' Polly shook her head furiously. 'No, of course not. It was kept in the living room where she could get to it easily. Beside the armchair. I didn't stop to think about it at the time, but it shouldn't have been in the hall. What was it doing there?' She grabbed Esme's arm. 'Who would have moved it?'

'When the police came and asked about Catherine,' said Esme, 'they mentioned her cousin, Leonard.' Polly looked terrified. Esme wondered if she'd already guessed what Esme was about to suggest.

'They said they suspected him of following her,' Esme continued. 'What if he'd followed her back to the cottage and when Carol left, he'd gone in to talk to her? Could it be Leonard who moved the oxygen? Maybe he pulled it out of her reach as a threat?'

'Why would he?' gasped Polly. Her face was white and drawn but Esme couldn't stop now.

'Because that's what this is all about. Your cottage used to be part of the estate, didn't it? Perhaps he thought it ought to belong to him? Maybe he tried to persuade her to part with it?'

Polly shook her head in bewilderment as if she couldn't cope with the enormity of what she was hearing.

'Don't you see?' urged Esme, unwilling to spell it out but desperate for Polly to understand the true state of affairs. 'He could have been responsible for her death.'

The old lady gave a sob and pressed her handkerchief to her mouth.

'We must tell the police,' said Esme.

'No!' Polly began shaking uncontrollably.

Esme laid her hand on the old lady's arm. 'We have to. The

police don't know that Catherine and Daisy were the same person. They wouldn't realise the significance.'

And neither had Leonard Nicholson.

At first Esme hadn't understood why Leonard believed that Daisy's death would get him the cottage. Daisy had beneficiaries; her daughter Elizabeth and granddaughter Gemma. Surely his investigations would have thrown up that piece of information?

But Leonard wasn't looking for Daisy. He was looking for Catherine. He would have tracked down Catherine and found the cottage registered in her name and would have learned that Catherine had no children. As far as Leonard Nicholson was concerned, he was Catherine's next of kin and in line to inherit the cottage on her death. It must have seemed so simple to him.

Only one thing remained unclear. Why hadn't Daisy told him the truth? Perhaps she had and he had killed her in fury.

And having learned the truth, was that why he'd turned his attention to Elizabeth? Had he intended to eliminate her too?

Esme shuddered. Had that really been his objective? Esme didn't think so. The expectation of inheritance would have evaporated by then and he would have been forced to invent a more complex plan.

Esme looked at Polly. Her eyes were filled with tears which slowly overflowed and ran down her cheeks. Esme felt a tug of sympathy for her. She had seemed so much more at ease with everything a few hours earlier and now her world had been turned on its head, just when she thought the end of the nightmare was in sight.

Polly suddenly blew her nose and dried her eyes with her handkerchief.

'If he did that to Daisy...' She looked up at Esme with reddened eyes, and voiced something which hadn't occurred to Esme before. 'What about, Elizabeth? It was him in the park, wasn't it?' Her next words undermined everything Esme had just reassured herself regarding Leonard's motives.

Polly reached over and touched Esme's arm. 'You don't think he'll try again, do you, in the hospital?'

26

Esme immediately shelved her plan to confront Mary that day. After Polly's fearful question about whether Elizabeth was under threat from Leonard she was anxious to call in at the hospital as soon as possible. In any case, by the time Esme had parried Mrs Rowcliffe's questions about Polly's distress the day had slipped into evening and dusk was falling. Esme had no desire to trawl around Shropton in the dark trying to find Mary's house. Besides, there would be more chance of catching her on her own on a weekday. Polly had told her Mary had a son and grandson who lived with her in Fletcher Street. With luck they'd be at work on a Monday morning.

The matron accepted Esme's explanation that Polly had received some bad news about a friend, though Esme suspected she was not entirely convinced. But she said nothing, probably motivated by her desire to get home after a long day.

There was nothing to report at the hospital. Elizabeth was still sleeping peacefully and to the knowledge of the nurse on duty, no strangers had attempted to barge their way in to see her.

The nurse seemed to take it as an insult that the question should even be raised. Elizabeth's visitors were strictly controlled, she assured Esme. Family and specific friends, and the hospital knew them all. There would be no danger of anyone being allowed in who hadn't already been given permission. She'd looked at Esme briefly as if questioning her sanity but, having decided to put it down to the pressure Esme must be under, smiled reassuringly and returned to her station. Esme hesitated. Should she have made more of the issue, suggested police protection? Part of her thought she was overreacting, part that it was prudent to be cautious. She decided to discuss it with the inspector when she spoke to him.

The answer-phone was blinking when she got in. She'd missed Gemma again. There was a short message which was no more than an echo of the one Esme had left Gemma. They seemed to spend their time trying to catch hold of one another.

Gemma's mobile phone was invariably switched off because she was in theatre and Esme's was because Esme had never been very good at remembering to switch it on in the first place. She had always been careful to turn it off when in libraries and archives, but hopeless at turning it back on when she left.

Making a mental note to become more vigilant, Esme dialled Gemma's home phone. No reply. She got a similar result on Gemma's mobile. She must be at the hospital, probably arriving as Esme was leaving. They seemed to be destined not to make contact.

Esme threw off her coat and fished around in her bag for the inspector's number. She thought it unlikely that he would be at his desk at this time on a Sunday evening and she was right.

The person at the other end asked if she would like to leave a message or speak to someone else. Esme hesitated and asked if Sergeant Morris was available. He wasn't. She left her name and said she would try again in the morning.

She went into the kitchen to make herself something to eat while she worked out how she was going to deal with Mary Watts the following day. She was under no delusions that it was going to be easy.

*

Fletcher Street was the last in a maze of roads which formed an untidy and badly constructed council estate. One end of it fed back towards the town centre where the estate merged with older and more aesthetically pleasing properties. Number twelve was one of the ugly houses. Esme parked a short distance along the street and walked back.

She'd still not managed to speak to the inspector. He'd already gone out when she called first thing that morning.

She'd glanced at the clock, still showing that it was well before eight. He obviously liked an early start. She had still been in her dressing gown, intending to give Mary's family plenty of time to leave the house for work before she arrived. There was no guarantee that Mary would be at home but first thing on a Monday was as good a time as any.

Esme walked past an old Ford Escort, its back half-propped up on two unstable piles of bricks. She was reminded of an episode of a television crime series where the detective had gone to interview a suspect and emerged after the encounter to discover that the wheels had been removed from his car. Esme glanced around and told herself she was letting her imagination run away with her.

When she reached number twelve she stood on the pavement and looked up at the house. The façade was a pinkish shade of pebbledash. Her grandmother's house had had a similar coating. It was a horrible surface, she remembered. Many times she'd brushed up against it and shredded several layers of skin.

She turned down the cracked concrete path, similar in colour to the house walls. There was grass either side of the path, in need of a mow but not excessively overgrown. The sound of the television resounded through the net curtained front windows to the right hand side of the entrance.

She halted at the bottom of the path and looked at the door in front of her. There was no bell or knocker so she rapped loudly on the centre panel between two long frosted panes of glass. She spied a figure through the semi-opaque glass shuffling towards her and a moment later the door was flung open.

Mary stood on the threshold, her straight hair clipped tightly to her head with hairgrips. She was wearing an old-fashioned wrap-around floral apron, the type Esme always associated with Mrs Scrubbit, a character from television's *The Wooden Tops* which she used to watch as a child.

'Yes?' Mary barked.

'Mary Watts?' There was no doubt it was the same woman whom Esme had encountered at Wisteria House. Surely Mary must recognise Esme. How could she not with such a visible signature on her face?

The old woman scowled and peered at her. 'Who are you?' She evidently didn't enjoy receiving visitors unannounced. Perhaps they usually spelt trouble.

Esme returned her hard stare. 'My name's Esme Quentin. I'd like to speak to you. About Polly Roberts.'

Mary narrowed her eyes. 'You're her who was at the home, aren't you?' She puffed herself up and tried to look at Esme down her nose, which was difficult to achieve since she was considerably shorter. 'I haven't got anything to say to you,' she announced and went to close the door. Esme put her hand out and prevented her pushing it to.

'I have a message from her.'

The woman hesitated. 'What sort of message?'

There was a noise from next door's front garden, if it could be called a garden; it had the characteristics of a junk yard, several rusting motorbikes and a tarpaulin half-heartedly draped over another machine in a less dilapidated condition.

Mary glanced in the direction of the sound. At the same time someone else appeared in the hall. Esme could detect a shadow moving somewhere in the background. So Mary wasn't alone. This might be more difficult than she'd hoped. The shadow moved closer and a middle-aged man came into view.

He stopped behind Mary's shoulder and looked quizzically at Esme. There was something incongruous about him as if he didn't fit his surroundings. If he hadn't been in his shirtsleeves Esme would have thought him some sort of visiting official.

'Who's this, Mother?' His voice was surprisingly gentle compared with Mary's harsh growl.

Esme was surprised to see Mary look uncomfortable and fail to reply. Esme took advantage of the old woman's reticence to introduce herself. The man, she learnt, was Mary's son Will. He scanned her face briefly, a flicker of the eyes his only reaction, smiled politely and turned to Mary.

'Mother, are you going to leave the lady on the doorstep?'

Esme suspected that was exactly what Mary wished to do. Better still, banish her from the district. What she clearly didn't want to do was invite her into the house. Esme took comfort in that. It suggested that Mary wasn't keen for Will to hear what Esme had to say.

Mary pursed her lips and after hurling a furious look at Esme turned away abruptly and tramped back down the hall.

Will pulled the door open and gestured Esme inside.

'You must forgive my mother,' he said closing the front door. 'She hasn't yet learnt the gentle art of social interaction.'

'Oh, cut out the airs and graces,' yelled Mary over her shoulder. 'You ain't impressing anyone. Least of all her.' She shuffled into what appeared to be the kitchen and slammed the door.

'Now then, Mrs...?' said Will, hastily. 'Sorry, what did you say your name was?'

'Quentin. Esme Quentin.'

'What can we do for you?' His tone was forced as though he was over compensating for his mother's surliness or maybe he was trying to raise his naturally quiet voice so as to be heard above the noise of the television. The sound of machinegun fire and squealing tyres had increased in intensity and threatened to swamp their conversation.

Will looked at her quizzically, so Esme tried to ignore the noise and address the reason for her visit.

'To be honest, Mr Watts, it's your mother I've come to see. It's about Mrs Polly Roberts.'

Will looked momentarily startled but regained his composure almost immediately. His jolly manner changed to one of

181

indifference. 'Oh?' He seemed suddenly to be interested in a thread on his cuff to avoid her eyes.

Esme looked hard at him. 'I have a message from her. For your mother. There's been a...' she struggled for the right word, ' an arrangement between them but Mrs Roberts has decided to end it. I've come to make that clear to Mrs Watts.'

He said nothing at first. He seemed confused, as though he had been expecting her to say something quite different. Esme stared at him, trying to blot out the roar of swooping aeroplanes coming from the front room. Obviously the chase had taken to the air.

Will pulled himself up straight. 'I don't approve, you know.'

The comment was unexpected. Was he saying he knew what was going on? Mary's discomfort had indicated otherwise.

The front room door suddenly flew open and the sounds exploded into the hall along with a gawky teenager who looked as if a hairbrush was something to which he'd never been introduced. He appeared bewildered at finding two people in the hall and came to an abrupt halt. He peered at Esme and Will in turn through a curtain of lank hair.

'Can't you see we've got a visitor, Billy?' Will sighed. The young man grunted and went back into the room, slamming the door behind him. Esme assumed that Will meant him to turn the sound down, but the volume remained unaltered.

'You said you didn't approve,' prompted Esme. 'What did you mean?'

'This feud between my mother and Mrs Roberts. It started years ago and it is quite ridiculous that it is being drawn out in this way. I have told my mother, begged her even, to let sleeping dogs lie, but I'm afraid she is adamant.'

'Do you know what the feud is all about, Mr Watts?'

His flickered glance implied that he did but his reply was uncooperative. 'I will not be drawn in to going through it all over again.' He frowned at Esme. 'And you should take the same line with Mrs Roberts.'

Esme glared at him. 'I have no desire for this feud to be drawn out any more than you have,' said Esme, cocking her chin. 'I am only concerned about dealing with its consequences.'

He flinched and looked embarrassed at her retort. What had he expected in response to such an officious rebuke?

Esme pulled her bag from her shoulder and took out the document. 'Were you aware that your mother has been trying to blackmail Mrs Roberts?' She was pleased to see that he looked shocked. Maybe she did have an ally, after all. 'Your mother gave Mrs Roberts this to sign.' She thrust the paper at him. 'It's for the transfer of property. Mrs Roberts was being coerced into parting with a parcel of land in addition to her cottage. Valuable land that she was to be paid nothing for. I've come to tell your mother that she can do her worst. Mrs Roberts has no intention of signing.'

The door at the end of the hall opened abruptly. Esme turned to see Mary emerge from the kitchen.

'It was justice!' she shrieked.

Will glanced in the direction of the front room from where the tone of the music suggested that the credits were rolling. He ushered Esme down the hall and into the kitchen. He followed her in and closed the door. Mary stepped back in to the room in surprise.

'What's going on? What you bringing her in here for?'

'It's about time this was sorted,' said Will. 'I've just about had enough.'

Esme watched them as they glared at one another. She pulled out a chair and sat down at the end of the kitchen table.

Her action seemed to break the deadlock. Mary redirected her glare towards Esme and then slowly sank down on to the chair at the other end. Only then did Will take his own seat between the two of them.

Mary had found her voice again. 'It's justice,' she repeated. 'I only did what's right.'

Will was scathing. 'Justice? How can a prejudiced old woman like you know what's justice?' He shook the piece of paper at her and dropped it disgustedly on the table. 'Making her give away what was rightfully hers? Is that justice?'

'But it wasn't hers! They did him out of his rightful inheritance, they did. Left him without a penny. I only did what was fair.' Mary leant forward and stabbed her finger on the document. 'This should have been his.'

'I assume we're talking about Sir Charles's nephew?' said Esme.

There was the sound of a door opening and then footsteps banged up the stairs. Another door banged shut above. The television still blared out its din from the other room. No one made any attempt to go and turn it off. They seemed to be unaware of the way it pervaded the house, how it added to the feeling of claustrophobia. Three aggrieved adults thrown together around a table, arguing over something about which none of them fully understood. Except perhaps Mary.

'Catherine Monkleigh. Turned up out the blue and took it all from him, she did.' Mary spoke the name with unmistakable sarcasm. Was that a deliberate ploy to show that she knew that Catherine was also Daisy? Or was that Esme's interpretation, knowing what she did?

'As I understand it, there wasn't anything to take.'

Mary turned on Esme. 'What d'you mean?'

'The estate. There wasn't any money in it. The cottage was Catherine's. She didn't take anything from him. He just wanted it for himself.'

'Not the cottage. He'll pay her good money for that. He only wanted a bit of land so he could build himself a house.'

Esme scoffed. 'And you believed him?'

Will had been sitting back watching their exchange and saying nothing until now.

'So this wasn't a way to get back at your sworn enemy, Polly

184

Roberts, of course?' said Will with obvious sarcasm. 'You just helped this man out of the kindness of your heart, is that it?'

Mary tossed her head. 'I just acted as go-between. There was nothing in it for me.'

Will scoffed. 'If I believed that I'd believe Jack was still living and breathing.'

'How dare you!' The sound of Mary's hand slapping Will's face startled Esme. Who was Jack and why did his name provoke such a reaction? Mother and son glared at one another. They seemed unaware of Esme, their antagonism smouldering between them in their locked vision.

'Mrs Watts, are you aware what sort of person Leonard Nicholson is?' said Esme. Her brusque question seemed to snap them both out of their trance. They glanced her way.

'What?'

'Leonard Nicholson. Did you know he is wanted by the police?'

'Trust you to get mixed up in the lowlife,' said Will. He rubbed his face.

Mary flashed a look towards him but didn't comment.

'Did you know, Mrs Watts?' repeated Esme. 'They want to talk to him about a suspicious death.' Well, they will do when I speak to them, Esme reassured herself.

'Don't believe it. You're making it up.'

Esme sighed with exasperation. 'I'm not making it up. For goodness' sake, he needs to be caught. You must be able to get hold of him. You could help the police track him down.'

Mary sniffed and looked away across the room. 'Why should I care?'

'Because he's dangerous. Because he caused Daisy Roberts's death.' In Esme's mind there was no question that Leonard Nicholson was responsible. She was sure the inspector would agree with her, as soon as he knew the facts.

'Daisy,' she sneered. 'Oh yes, Daisy.' Again the sarcastic manner. When was she going to own up to knowing the truth?

185

Maybe she simply enjoyed taunting Polly and gloating over her reactions. No wonder Polly had been unable to contemplate challenging her.

'I don't owe her anything,' she continued bitterly. 'She broke Jack's...' Her voice faltered.

Jack again. This was a side of the story that Polly had kept to herself. Esme felt a stab of irritation. She was fighting with one hand tied behind her back. If she had all the facts, she might know how to reach this stubborn and selfish old woman.

Mary composed herself and turned her head sharply in Esme's direction.

'And I don't owe you anything, either,' she sneered.

'Maybe not, but the least you can do is stop him doing to someone else what he's done to Elizabeth.' Esme's voice threatened to betray her emotions. 'She's still in a coma, for God's sake.'

She saw Will recoil in the corner of her eye and turned to look at him. He was staring at her wide eyed.

'Elizabeth?' he was saying. 'Mrs Roberts's Elizabeth?'

Esme frowned and stared at him. 'Do you know her?'

'Are you sure she was attacked by this Nicholson man?' said Will, looking increasingly agitated. Mary was staring down at the table, her face expressionless.

'It looks that way but why...?' But Will had already got hold of Mary's arm and was shaking it frantically.

'Mother, you can't walk away from this. You must stop this man. He's attacked Elizabeth.'

Mary looked as confused as Esme was feeling. She yanked her arm away, attempting to pull it out of Will's grip.

'Let me go. What are you talking about?'

Esme stared at Will, waiting for him to answer Mary's question and explain himself.

'Mother,' said Will, his voice calm now, 'there's something you should know. Elizabeth is Jack's daughter. She's your granddaughter.'

27

Now Esme understood why Polly had been so reticent about revealing everything about Elizabeth's past. She had never come to terms with the incontrovertible fact that Mary's son had fathered Daisy's baby and that therefore Mary had a greater claim on Elizabeth than she had. No wonder she was doing everything she could to extricate herself from Mary's clutches, even if it meant giving up her financial security. Esme wondered whether Polly had ever realised that Mary was unlikely to sever the connection completely if she thought there was still anything in it for her. Esme guessed that she probably knew that, but hadn't wanted to admit it to herself.

Once Will had explained everything Mary walked out of the house.

'Shouldn't you go after her?' asked Esme, anxiously. She had no intention of letting a potential remedy for this crisis disappear from her grasp. Leonard Nicholson needed to be apprehended as soon as possible and Esme was convinced that Mary was the most obvious person to help achieve it. The two of them must have had a means of getting in touch, in order to pass over the signed document and receive payment. She couldn't imagine Mary trusting it to the post with a cheque to follow. She was much too wily for that.

Will looked at her carefully before replying. Maybe he was trying to assess the reasoning behind her apparent concern.

'She'll be back when she's taken it all on board.'

Esme accepted that she would just have to trust his judgement.

'How long have you known about Elizabeth?' Esme asked.

He hadn't yet said whether they knew one another.

'Only a few days.'

Esme was surprised by his answer. So they hadn't met. 'You hadn't tried to find her before?'

'How could I?' He shrugged. 'I didn't even know whether Daisy had had the baby and whether it was a boy or girl. Where would I start? It was only when Mother said she'd found Polly Roberts that I suddenly realised I had the chance to find out.'

Esme couldn't help feeling slightly resentful that he had apparently had a more open response to his enquiries of Polly than she'd had.

'I'm surprised she told you,' she said to him.

Will laid his hands out on the table, thumbs and forefinger-tips touching, and studied them carefully. 'She didn't want to. She tried to tell me she didn't know what I was talking about. But I told her I was Jack's brother and that I had the letter Daisy had written to him telling him she was pregnant. She had to admit it then.'

'Even so, she would have found it difficult to tell you anything given the antagonism between her and your mother.'

'She made me promise not to tell.'

'A promise you've now broken,' said Esme pointedly.

'Yes. I feel bad about that but I didn't have any choice, did I?' He looked reproachfully at Esme. That's what you wanted, his expression said.

'How come your mother never knew, when you did?'

He gave a small laugh as one who knows the full implications of a situation and has been asked to sum them up in a single word.

'The circumstances were unusual, shall we say?'

'How so? Tell me about Jack and Daisy.'

Esme thought for a moment he wasn't going to enlighten her but then he sighed and slumped back in the chair.

'I was a kid at the time. I really don't remember anything about it. Only the bust up at the end. Mother said it was Polly's fault, that she came between them.' He shook his head. 'I don't know why.'

Esme understood why. Polly had to get Daisy out of the way

before Mary made the connection with Catherine. If Mary did know the whole story, she'd obviously never told Will.

'When Daisy left,' continued Will, 'Jack was distraught. He blamed Polly, of course, for turning Daisy against him. Mother was furious but probably not too bothered to be shot of Polly, if the truth be known. But what she couldn't take was what it did to Jack.'

'How do you mean?'

'I don't really know the ins and outs. Like I said, I was too young to fully appreciate what was going on. Anyway, afterwards he got it into his head that he was going to go back down the pit like our father. My father was badly injured years ago. He was never fit enough to work again. He died a few years later. I was just a baby then. I never knew him.'

'And your mother understandably was terrified the same would happen to him?'

Will nodded. 'He was just reacting to the hurt, I suppose, being careless. People go around driving fast cars or getting drunk and do reckless things these days, don't they? But whatever his reason, Mother couldn't persuade him otherwise.'

Esme guessed the outcome. 'There was an accident?'

'A cave-in. Jack didn't get past the fall in time, it blocked his way out. He was trapped for three days. When they dug them out it was too late. He was dead.' He bowed his head. 'I often wondered whether he did it on purpose.'

'As you said, he chose a dangerous job deliberately.'

He shook his head. 'No, more than that. His mate reckoned he could have got out but when the opportunity came he didn't move. It made me think of a war story my granddad told me once, about when he was in the trenches. They were all reading their letters from home. Suddenly one of the men cried out and rushed for the ladder to go over the top. They went to drag him back, but he'd gone too far and they couldn't reach him. Then they heard artillery fire. It was too late, then. They found his letter in the mud.

His girl had written to say she'd met someone else.'

'And you saw Jack in the same position?'

'Makes you think, doesn't it? An honourable way out.'

Esme nodded. Suicide would still have been illegal back then in the 1950s, despite the growing understanding which would change the law in the following decade. Jack had seen a moment to end his despair without bringing shame on the family. She felt an overwhelming sadness that his desperate action had deprived Elizabeth of knowing her father.

'Does your mother have any idea of your theory?'

'God, no. She was in a bad enough state as it was. Believing that would have sent her over the edge.'

'It must have been pretty awful for you too?'

He stared at the table top. 'She was terrible when he died. I missed the worst of it because my aunt looked out for me. She could see that I was being neglected. Mother hardly noticed me. Slowly things got a bit better, but Jack's name was never to be spoken. Then, now and again, she started to mention him, but usually as a complaint aimed at me, you know: "Jack would never have done it like that." That sort of thing. I let her get away with it, if the truth be known, because he was my brother, and I thought a lot of him. If she said Jack would do it better, I believed her. He'd always been my hero, he knew best because he was older. And I missed him, of course. Not that she'd ever stopped to think of that. She never looked at it from my point of view. All she could think about was how it affected her.'

'And she saw all this as Polly's fault for taking Daisy away?'

'Always. It's eaten her up ever since.'

'So what about Daisy? She must have found out that Jack had died.'

'I suppose. She'd written to Jack about the baby just before. I never knew at the time. I only found out much later. A mate of Jack's came round to the house after the funeral. Mother was well out of it. He spoke to me and told me that Jack had always said he was going to encourage me to better myself, not go down the mines, or even take some dead-end job. I remembered that. It's what made me work hard and get my qualifications.' He tossed his head towards the back door. 'Despite all the put-downs.'

'Did Jack know about Daisy, d'you think?'

'Apparently. His mate gave me the letter that Jack had on him when he died. He said to keep it safe. Private it was, he said. Of course I couldn't read it. It was in joined writing and it was as much as I could do to decipher print in those days. I hid it away along with a few of Jack's things. Mementoes, you know. By the time I was capable of making sense of the letter I was too scared to tell my mother. She still wasn't over it. I didn't know what it would do to her. I assumed one day, when she trusted me...'

His words tailed off and Esme could see that it had never come to that. From the outburst she'd seen earlier, she guessed that Jack had never moved from Mary's number one spot. He'd become her god and as a result he'd displaced her surviving son.

'The fact that she'd written and told him she was pregnant,' Esme suggested, 'wouldn't it have given him hope that there might be a future for them?'

Will shook his head. 'No. The letter made it quite clear. The baby was to be adopted.'

Esme tried to imagine Daisy's state of mind. Had there been any wistful hope behind the purpose of her letter that Jack might respond in some way? Was it a test to see if he'd come and find her, perhaps? Or was it simply that she thought that he had the right to know he had fathered a child?

'I thought Mother'd drawn a line under things of late,' Will was saying. 'But then this private investigator chap came round asking questions about the old family and it stirred everything up all over again.' He shook his head and sighed, his face drained. 'Nothing I say seems to make any difference. She's obsessed with the idea of getting even with Polly Roberts, even after all these years.'

They both turned sharply as the back door opened. Mary stood and glowered at them. She stepped inside and shut the door behind her.

'He lied about it,' she said sullenly. 'I never knew he was violent. He seemed a bit of a gentleman.'

'Gentlemen don't go in for blackmail,' said Esme with cynicism. Will flashed a look as if to say, don't antagonise her.

Mary pursed her lips and looked at Esme. 'What do you want me to do?'

28

'I can see why you suspect Leonard Nicholson, Mrs Quentin, but it's going to be difficult to prove.'

Inspector Barry pulled up the collar of his coat around his ears against the blustery wind that whipped at them as they emerged from the shelter of Wisteria House and walked across the gravel. Much to her relief he had taken her concerns seriously and suggested that he should talk to Polly. The only down side was that it made Polly the centre of gossip once more.

Mrs Rowcliffe had been given the rudiments of the situation, that foul play was suspected in Daisy's death and the police were keen to investigate.

'The oxygen cylinder will be long gone back to the health authorities by now, I suppose, for things like fingerprints to be of any use.' Esme adjusted her bag on her shoulder and put her hand on it to stop it flapping about. It was in danger of being dislodged by the strength of the wind. 'But you might be able to prove that he was at the cottage, perhaps?'

'Being her cousin, his defence would argue that he had legitimate reason for being there even if there was evidence to place him at the scene.'

Esme sighed. 'It doesn't look very hopeful.'

'We need to speak to him anyway, on this other matter of a missing person. That's what we were hoping Miss Roberts, or should I say Miss Monkleigh, could help us with.'

'I hope you don't think Mrs Roberts was being deliberately obstructive when you came to see her. I think she was genuinely shaken by your visit. Catherine had become Daisy some years ago. A personal matter. Family estrangement. It's not illegal to operate under a different name, as I understand?'

'Only with the intention to defraud,' clarified the inspector.

'Yes, of course,' said Esme, focusing on the rooks circling above the huge beech trees beyond. 'But I'm sure that wasn't her intention.' She hoped the inspector wasn't seriously questioning the reasoning behind the name change. Polly wouldn't cope with the indignity or the stress.

'So you haven't caught up with Leonard Nicholson, then?' Esme said as they arrived at their cars.

The inspector climbed into the large grey Vectra parked next to Esme's Peugeot. 'We will,' he said. 'And don't worry about him turning up at the hospital. Too many potential witnesses. He wouldn't take the risk.'

'So how are you going to track him down?'

'Something'll turn up, you can be sure of it.' He nodded his goodbye and slammed the car door. Giving Esme a wave, he sped off.

She watched him until the sound of the engine faded into the distance. 'Sounds to me,' she murmured to herself, 'that you need a tip-off.'

*

As soon as she got home, Esme picked up the phone and rang Lucy. She took some persuading.

'I don't understand why you can't suggest it to him yourself,' whined Lucy.

'Because I'd have to go into the whole background and everything. It's so much simpler this way. Mary has agreed a meeting with Leonard Nicholson and I need someone to tell the police. Easy as that.'

'Surely you can make the call? You don't need me.'

'They're bound to record all their telephone calls. I don't want them to recognise it's me.'

'Why not?'

'For the same reason I can't suggest it to the inspector outright.

If they work out it's me they'll want to know the full story.'

'How could some receptionist possibly put two and two together and come up with you? They wouldn't know your voice from Adam. You're being paranoid.'

'Perhaps, but I can't take the risk. I've promised Polly they don't need to know.'

There was a pause. 'Amateur dramatics aren't really my thing, Esme. I'm not sure I'm up to it.'

'Please, Lu. Use a phone box. One in the middle of town.'

Eventually Lucy caved in and Inspector Barry received an anonymous tip off that Leonard Nicholson was meeting someone in the café at Kingsway Shopping Centre at 3.30 p.m. the following afternoon.

As the inspector was hardly going to give Esme a call and involve her in police operations, Esme planned to be shopping in the centre herself. She arrived with about fifteen minutes to spare and wandered into W.H. Smith, opposite the café in question.

With the large floor-to-ceiling windows that the store boasted, it was a perfect place to observe events. As the minutes ticked by her apprehension grew. She reached up nonchalantly to take a magazine from the shelf and noticed that her hand was shaking.

'Good afternoon, Mrs Quentin,' said a voice next to her.

She jumped as if she'd been shot and spun round to see who had spoken. Sergeant Morris was peering at her from over a Top Marques magazine. Esme got a sudden urge to giggle, the situation was so surreal. She thought the sergeant would consider her behaviour very odd, given that she supposedly knew nothing of why he was here, so she purposefully thought of Elizabeth and pulled herself firmly in check.

'Oh, hello Sergeant,' she said as casually as she could.

'Choosing your next car?'

'All out of my price bracket, more's the pity,' he replied. He replaced the magazine on the rack. "Bye for now.' He strolled out of the store.

Esme watched him until he was out of sight and then began to look at the books on the shelf closer to the door. That way she could read the blurbs on the backs of the paperbacks while observing the entrance to the café. Sergeant Morris had disappeared from view and she didn't see which direction he'd taken.

Her heart gave a jolt. There was a man hovering at the café's entrance, apparently undecided as to whether to go in.

He looked at his watch. She strained to see if he looked like the photo-fit image she had looked at, but he had his back to her. She replaced the book on the shelf and slowly made her way towards the shop door, keeping her eye on the man. As she stepped out into the shopping centre the man suddenly spun on his heel and marched straight at her. She stopped dead in surprise, right in the entrance. He breezed up to her...and past her and into the shop.

She closed her eyes and let out a long breath. It wasn't Leonard Nicholas. Not unless he had used a fast-acting hair-growth hormone since the sighting in the park. This man had a thick black beard.

She composed herself and looked at the time. Twenty to. He was ten minutes late. She casually walked along the concourse to a shoe shop and peered through the window. Glancing across to her right she realised that she could see the reflection of Sergeant Morris on the opposite side of the concourse. She let out another long sigh and decided she wasn't the right type for covert surveillance. She kept forgetting to breathe.

By quarter past, when she had studied every shop window several times over, without actually registering a single item, she felt a presence next to her.

'We meet again,' said Sergeant Morris.

'You still here?' asked Esme. 'You must have a long lunch hour.'

The sergeant grinned. 'There can be a lot of standing around in this job, you know.'

'Really? Looking out for pickpockets, are you?'

'Something like that, though I think we're wasting our time today.'

Esme instinctively glanced towards the cafe only to see Mary marching off at a brisk pace. Her body language said it all. Don't think I'm doing that again in a hurry.

A young woman came over and spoke to the sergeant. 'Shall we call it a day, Sarge?'

The policeman shrugged his large shoulders. 'Yeah, I think so, don't you?' He turned back to Esme. 'I'll be off, then, Mrs Quentin. Happy shopping.' She nodded and she watched the pair leave the building.

So, Nicholson hadn't shown. Why not? Had he been tipped off? But by whom? Mary? She surely had no loyalty to him after she had heard what he was accused of. Anyway, Mary hadn't been able to complete her part of the deal, so she had nothing to lose by exposing him.

But then she'd nothing to gain either. And she might have persuaded him that he owed her something for not giving him up to the authorities.

If Mary was behind his non-appearance, he would know by now that the police were aware of his activities. Esme wondered what his reaction might be to that piece of information. From what she'd heard about him she didn't think it would be good.

29

Esme walked through the hospital reception area and into the lift on her regular visit to Elizabeth. Early afternoons had become the pattern, recently. Gemma generally called in later so the two of them had still not seen one another since their confrontation. Esme thought it was time that they tackled their differences. What was to be gained by prolonging their estrangement at a time when support was most needed? Surely Gemma must feel that she had made her point by now. Esme decided she must leave a message on Gemma's answering machine suggesting she dropped into the hospital one evening when Gemma was there, and see what response she got.

The lift doors opened. Esme stepped out and walked along the corridor towards Elizabeth's ward. Helen was on duty at the desk. They exchanged a few words about Elizabeth's progress.

'Is Gemma not well?' asked Helen.

'No idea,' confessed Esme. 'Haven't spoken to her for a while. Why?'

'I haven't seen her today, that's all. She always says if she can't make it.'

'She'll still be in theatre, won't she?'

Helen shook her head. 'Day off.'

'Perhaps she's planning to come in later. I was going to give her a call when I get back anyway. I'll see if she's OK.'

'I've already tried phoning her home number but there was no reply. Though if she's ill, she might have been asleep, I suppose.'

Esme wasn't particularly concerned. Gemma was quite capable of looking after herself, as Gemma had tersely declared to Esme when she'd accused her of fussing.

'Did you try her mobile?' asked Esme.

'Switched off.'

'Odd. It's usually only off when she's working in theatre. How long ago did you try?'

Helen looked up at the clock and pulled a face. 'About an hour ago, I suppose.' She leant over the counter of the nurses' station and reached for the telephone. She turned it around and placed it on the shelf next to Esme. 'Do you want to try her?'

Helen left the station and disappeared towards the other end of the ward. Esme dropped her coat and bag on the chair and picked up the receiver. She punched in the numbers and listened. The line was connected and the ringing tone echoed in her ear. No immediate response. She hung on, becoming mesmerised by the monotony of the sound. How long should she let it ring? Twenty rings? Thirty? On the one hand she didn't want to drag Gemma out of bed if she wasn't well, but on the other there were the beginnings of anxiety stirring in her head and she would rather be assured that Gemma wasn't suffering from something.

Esme had lost count of the number of rings when the telephone clicked at the other end and a woman's voice answered.

'Gemma?' It didn't sound like Gemma but then if she wasn't feeling well...

'No, she's not here. Who is that?'

Esme explained.

'I'm Annie,' said the woman. 'I live next door. I called in to feed Gemma's cat. I sometimes do if Gemma has to work late. I wouldn't normally answer the phone but it kept ringing and I thought it must be important if they were so persistent.'

'Gemma's not there then?' said Esme.

'No, of course not.' She obviously thought Esme was stupid to ask such an obvious question. 'Otherwise...'

'Otherwise you wouldn't be there. Yes, I see that. You don't know where Gemma is?'

'I assumed she'd stayed over at the hospital,' said Annie. 'She sometimes does.'

'No one's seen her today and we were concerned she wasn't well.' Esme tried not to sound alarmist. 'Perhaps she's gone to the supermarket or something. Sorry to trouble you...'

'She did that yesterday,' interrupted Annie. 'Saw her unloading her car. But I told you, I thought she must have stayed at the hospital. She never came home last night, see.'

'But she didn't phone you to tell you she wasn't coming home?'

'No but then if she's in theatre late, she can't always. I keep an eye out usually.'

Esme glanced up and saw Helen striding down the corridor at speed. She looked agitated. Patient problems, probably.

'I must go, Annie. Thanks for your help. I expect she'll turn up in a minute. If you do see, her perhaps you'd let her know I've called. Bye now.' She dropped the receiver on to the cradle with a sigh and looked up at Helen who was looking decidedly anxious.

'What's up?'

'Peter, one of the nurses, saw Gemma's car when he came on duty yesterday.'

'Where?'

'Here, in the hospital car park. He's just gone down to see if it's still there.'

'Her next-door neighbour says she didn't go home last night,' said Esme. They stared at one another, working out what they should make of it, thinking of possible scenarios.

Helen grabbed the phone. 'I'll get on to security and see if anyone noticed her leave last night. She arrived just as I was going off duty yesterday. I was on a late so it would have been about 9.45 I suppose. Hello?'

Esme switched off from Helen's conversation as she tried to fathom out what this meant. Was she being unnecessarily edgy about this? Wasn't Gemma capable of organising her own life, visiting friends, staying over in whatever way she wanted?

She had a good arrangement with Annie which meant that she

didn't have to worry too much about telling her if she wanted to stay out, so didn't that suggest that it was her usual way of operating? But Annie had said she didn't bother to phone if she was in theatre and couldn't make the call. But she hadn't been in theatre, she had been here with Elizabeth. If she had intended to go elsewhere, surely Gemma would have let Annie know her movements.

Helen put down the phone and looked across at Esme.

'She definitely left the building. Tom Christie saw her in the lobby and said goodnight.'

'So she didn't stay here, then. Perhaps she went to a friend's.'

'At midnight?'

'Is that when she left?'

Helen nodded. 'Apparently.'

They heard the door to the stairs swing open and a male nurse, whom Esme assumed to be Peter, came hurrying up the corridor out of breath.

'It's still there, in the same place.'

'She could have parked in the same place again when she came back,' suggested Esme.

'Are you kidding?' said Helen. 'It's a nightmare finding a parking space at the best of times. What are the odds of getting the same one two days on the trot?'

'No, she never,' wheezed Peter. 'The car's not been moved.'

'How do you know?' demanded Esme.

'Because the bugger in charge of the parking has given her a ticket.'

*

Esme could just imagine Gemma's reaction if she reported her to the police as a missing person and then Gemma rolled up having spent the night with a friend. On the other hand she couldn't ignore it. She thought of her conversation with the inspector. He had thought it completely unlikely that Elizabeth would receive

201

any unwelcome visitors, so what was it that was making her anxious?

She made a nervous telephone call to Inspector Barry. He was sympathetic but he cautioned her against overreacting.

'She could have been collected by a friend after she left the hospital, gone out for the evening and be sleeping it off at their place,' he said reasonably.

'Yes, I've thought of that.'

'And you say that she has this arrangement with her neighbour. So it's not unusual for her to come home late or even not at all.'

'Yes, but only when she's at work and isn't able to get to a phone and warn her. If she was with a friend she'd have the opportunity to let the neighbour know. She's not a thoughtless person.'

'Maybe she didn't decide until it was too late to phone. You said she left at midnight.'

Esme sighed. 'That's true. So what should I do?'

'Well, it's not twenty-four hours yet, is it? Give her chance to surface, assuming she's had a heavy night. I'll put an unofficial word around. Let me know if you hear anything.'

*

Esme updated Helen on what the inspector had said. Helen accepted the logic. After all she didn't know the whole story so she was more inclined to be convinced than Esme. Later, on her way out, Esme asked Helen to phone her if Gemma turned up at the hospital. Esme had left a message on Gemma's mobile to ask her to confirm that everything was all right, and of course Annie would be looking out for her too. She'd tried to keep the messages upbeat. She didn't want Gemma giving her an earful about her private life being invaded. As things were between them at present, it would be her first reaction.

Esme felt at a loss when she arrived home. The uncertainty of Gemma's situation highlighted the uncertainty of Elizabeth's.

Watching Elizabeth lying there at the hospital was a strange experience at the best of times. It was like sitting in an auditorium waiting for something to happen on stage when you didn't know what time the programme started. Was anything going to happen this time? Were there any clues that suggested something was about to change?

It had been more intense in the early days. Now it was waning a little. Esme suspected the task was slowly becoming a routine of sitting and watching, without expecting anything.

Was she losing faith that Elizabeth was going to wake up? The thought made her feel uncomfortable. She chastised herself. The hospital staff were highly optimistic. So should she be.

When Esme got in through the front door she dumped her bag and coat on the floor and went through to the kitchen to put the kettle on. She needed a cup of tea before addressing anything else. As the kettle boiled she went over the reassuring words of the inspector in her head. Ninety-nine per cent of the time there's a perfectly rational explanation, he'd reminded her.

But she couldn't help being concerned about that one per cent.

She took her tea into the sitting room. The answer-phone was blinking so she pressed the 'play' button. Maybe there was a message from Gemma. That would be a weight off her mind.

She slumped down on the armchair and sipped her tea. There was an enquiry for a research assignment which sounded quite interesting. She got up to find a pen and paper to take down the details. She put her pad on the desk and stood poised to press the replay button once the messages had played through. The next message, though, fixed her to the spot.

It was a man's voice, well-spoken, but there was something about its manner which set her teeth on edge before she even registered what he was saying.

'Your interference has been a grave mistake, Mrs Quentin.

I can assure you that Gemma is not very happy about it.' Then there was a click. That was the end of the message.

She replayed it. Twice.

It was the last message. As far as she could tell, no one else had called since. There was a chance. She dialled 1471. The automatic voice began, 'You were called...' She knew what that meant but she listened through to the end any way. 'The caller withheld their number.' Of course they had. It wouldn't be that simple.

Shaking, she managed to dial Inspector Barry's number.

30

The techno-wizards had been let loose on Esme's phone, the police told her, as Leonard Nicholson would need to call her again to make his demands. They hoped to establish his location. Inspector Barry also arranged for a uniformed constable to be on hand at Esme's cottage. Esme called Lucy for moral support. She came over immediately.

Esme found herself explaining to Inspector Barry what she knew about the cottage and its connections with the Monkleigh family. Not surprisingly the inspector was annoyed that she hadn't passed on the entire information before. Given the circumstances, Esme almost agreed with him. Maybe Gemma wouldn't have been a target if she had done so. Esme gave a reasoned defence that the police would have only seen it as a petty family disagreement over an inheritance, but she had to admit that once she had discovered the unsavoury truth about Leonard Nicholson she ought to have realised that there might be more to the situation than a family squabble. She openly acknowledged her misjudgement, and she and Lucy proceeded to tell the inspector almost everything they had uncovered.

However Esme chose not to mention the added complication of Polly and the unauthorised 'adoption'. She couldn't see how it could be seen as relevant. She sensed that Inspector Barry suspected her of not being completely candid but he didn't press the point. She envisaged a conversation sometime in the future, she justifying her decision and being told 'I'll be the judge of what's relevant, Mrs Quentin.' Esme would have to disagree.

Leonard Nicholson wanted that land; he had failed with his first plan and now he had an insane idea that he was going to get it through Gemma. There was nothing more to know that was going to alter that state of affairs.

*

Three hours passed and there was nothing. They had one false alarm when the telephone had shrilled and panicked them all. Esme had snatched up the receiver without allowing herself to think about who might be on the other end. In the event it was the bookshop in town to tell Esme that the book she'd ordered had arrived. Esme thanked the shop assistant and replaced the phone. They all breathed again.

The clock ticked soothingly in the silence. Esme concentrated on it, trying to use its rhythm to calm her nerves. It was only part successful. She got up and began pacing. If the others were irritated by it, they kept their thoughts to themselves. Waiting for anything disagreeable was worse than the actual event but the strain of this was agonising. Esme remembered a similar feeling when watching Elizabeth and dealing with the uncertainty of when or whether she would wake up.

The constable, a young man by the name of Harris, offered to make yet another cup of tea. Esme declined but Lucy accepted. He went off to the kitchen for the umpteenth time.

Lucy watched him go and then took Esme on one side.

'Surely he isn't holding Gemma so that Polly will sign that document,' she said in a low voice. 'It wouldn't be legally valid, under those circumstances. He must have something else up his sleeve.'

They heard the constable's radio crackle in the kitchen and his voice answering. Esme and Lucy exchanged glances and anxiously turned towards the kitchen. Constable Harris emerged but without the smiling face that the women had hoped for. At least he didn't look distraught.

'Any news?' asked Esme.

'CCTV footage at the hospital shows Miss Holland getting into a car after she left the building.'

An idea flashed into Esme's head. 'What sort of car was it?'

P.C. Harris consulted his notebook. 'Black Audi A6.'

'With tinted windows?'

The constable nodded. 'That's right.'

'What is it?' asked Lucy urgently.

'I've seen it around here a few times recently. That's if it's the same one.'

'You didn't report it?' said the constable.

'What was there to report? I thought it was the new people down the lane.' Esme thought about the black car which had tried to ram her as she was coming out of Wisteria House but there didn't seem much point in mentioning it now. She had nothing to add, no registration number, no driver description.

She shuddered at the thought that she might have been so close to Leonard Nicholson.

'Did Gemma get into this car of her own accord?' she asked the policeman.

'Nothing to suggest otherwise.'

Esme frowned. 'Why would she get into his car?'

'Perhaps he spun her a line?' suggested Lucy.

'But it was midnight. Who in their right mind would fall for a con under those circumstances?'

'Maybe she knew him,' said the constable. He shuffled and turned pink. 'I don't mean he was a friend. I mean he could have chatted her up in a bar, or something. Opened a door for her and got talking, so she recognised him when he drove by.'

'It was all part of a plan, you mean?' said Esme.

'It could be. The other thing is they found her car'd been tampered with.'

Lucy continued the scenario. 'So he comes along, knight in shining armour, to give a lift to a damsel in distress with a broken-down chariot.'

'And because she's met him before she doesn't smell a rat,' finished Esme. 'Malicious bastard.' She stormed over to the window and stared out into the gloomy lane. Earlier, a heavy mist had all but eliminated the view of the Georgian house over the road. Now with darkness falling, the mist had become an impenetrable black thickness.

Esme thought back to Lucy's comments a moment ago. What were his demands going to be? And what would he threaten to get them? He must know that his identity wasn't in question. How did he think he'd get away with it? Perhaps he didn't expect to. Maybe it was a matter of revenge.

At 1.15 a.m. they thought it wise to get some sleep. They had sat zombie-like through several mind-numbing television programmes until Esme had been on the point of screaming.

She had even debated doing some gardening in the dark, but then decided she'd feel vulnerable and unnerved in such a surreal situation, so she dismissed the idea.

She showed Lucy to the spare bedroom and then lay on her own bed without undressing. If there was a call in the middle of the night, she'd feel more able to deal with it fully clothed. She fell into a fretful sleep and woke before light, wishing she'd gone to bed in the usual manner. Her clothes were twisted around her, she was shivering and when she threw her legs over the bed to stand up, they felt twice the weight they usually did.

She didn't even want to look at her face in a mirror. Her scar itched and she knew she would be more affected than usual by the sight of it, should she catch her own reflection in the glass.

Instead she crawled off to the bathroom for the solace of a hot shower.

It was close to six o'clock by the time she'd showered and changed. She came down stairs to find Constable Harris pacing about waiting for his relief to arrive. Esme supposed that he had been up all night but it seemed likely he would have snatched what sleep he could in the armchair.

Lucy emerged from downstairs and they commented on how awful they both looked. It prompted some much-needed relief in the form of laughter as they exchanged insults. Constable Harris's replacement arrived and he went outside to brief her.

The temporary humorous outburst fizzled out as Esme and Lucy faced the fact that there had been no progress in the situation. They were exactly in the same position as yesterday.

'How long is he going to play about with us?' Esme snapped.

She frowned with annoyance at the collection of used mugs which adorned her desk. Didn't the police force train their minders to wash up after they'd helped themselves to tea? And drinking chocolate she noted. And goodness knows what had been in the last one. She peered in to the grunge at the bottom and sniffed it. It smelled of tomatoes. Some sort of instant soup.

He must have brought that with him, she didn't keep in such disgusting substances. Perhaps he'd needed the E numbers to keep him awake. She snatched up the mugs more in frustration with the situation than any genuine annoyance with the officer, but her action was careless and her elbow caught the heap of papers stacked on her desk. Before she could stop it the pile slipped over the edge and cascaded to the floor.

'Oh, that's all I need,' she cried. She banged the mugs back down on the desk and knelt down by the chaos. Lucy appeared from the kitchen and helped her collect them up.

'The Shropton Canal?' commented Lucy as she glanced at one of the pages.

'A research job. Some guy wanted to know about it. They're hoping to restore it.'

'Yes, I know. I've a friend who's on the committee. They've just got funds for a feasibility study on it.'

'My brief was to find out about the canal and where they'd got to on the project, amongst other things. I assumed my client was planning to make a donation.' She continued gathering up the papers and passed a batch up to Lucy.

'Did you know that the Shropton Canal went across the Monkleigh's land?' said Lucy absent-mindedly.

'Did it? I don't remember seeing it,' said Esme, thinking back to the maps she'd studied.

'No, I mean way back. During the canal era, in the late eighteenth century. The estate lands were more extensive in those days.'

'Oh, I see.' She picked up the last of the sheets of notes and stood up. 'It was a bit odd, this job. He instructed me to do the work, to e-mail him regularly with progress reports, then a couple of weeks after I'd started he suddenly told me to stop.'

'Did you ask him why?'

'Well I e-mailed him, but he didn't reply. I wondered if he'd decided he couldn't afford my fees, but then he knew the score before I started. He paid a retainer quite happily.'

'Did he pay you for what you'd done?'

'Oh yes. There was no problem there. In fact,' Esme began ferreting through the letter rack on the desk, 'his last cheque's here somewhere. I haven't paid it into the bank yet.' She produced it and studied the handwriting as though it would reveal something.

'A bit of a coincidence, though, don't you think?' said Lucy.

'What is? That the canal is on what was once Monkleigh land? You said yourself that it was a couple of centuries ago. It's a bit tentative.'

'What was he like, this client?'

Esme shrugged. 'No idea. Never met him. Never spoke on the phone even as I would normally with a new client. E-mail only. He was most insistent on it.'

The two women looked at one another.

Esme pulled a face. 'I see what you mean. Given the circumstances, it does sound suspicious.'

'Should we mention it to the inspector?' said Lucy.

'Mention what? That one of my clients seemed a bit odd? He'll think I'm just being neurotic.' She looked over at the untidy heap of notes now back on the desk. 'Perhaps I'll trawl through that lot, though, and see if it triggers something.'

Suddenly the telephone rang out. They both looked at one another. The front door opened and Constable Harris returned with a woman constable in tow.

'I heard the phone,' he said. 'It's a bit early for a social call.'

Galvanised by his words Esme pounced on the phone and picked it up.

'Yes?' She could feel her heart hammering in her chest. Any harder and it would give out.

His voice was sneering. 'Your meddling, Mrs Quentin, has denied me my right to land which should have come my way.'

Anger exploded out of her. 'What have you done with Gemma, you creep?'

'Come now, Mrs Quentin, we won't get anywhere trading insults. As I said, you have been the cause of my loss. I am now unable to acquire the land so you are going to buy it from me.'

'What?' He had clearly dropped into some sort of fantasy world. 'Don't be ridiculous. I can't buy it from you. It's not yours to sell, as you have just pointed out. I want to talk to Gemma. I want to know she's all right. Put her on the phone.' There were echoing sounds as the phone was moved around. Esme cast an anxious glance at Lucy who was leaning against the receiver so she could overhear.

'Esme?' Gemma's voice was shaky.

'Gemma, are you all right?'

'He tricked me,' sniffed Gemma. She was almost in tears.

'What's going on, Esme? I've told him, I don't know what he's on about but he won't believe me.'

'Where are you?' Esme desperately tried to think what she should be doing to try and help locate where he was holding her.

There were more noises and Esme heard Gemma's distant voice complaining that she hadn't finished talking.

'Two million sterling should do it,' said Nicholson.

'What? Are you mad? Where am I going to get that sort of money? You haven't kidnapped a millionaire's daughter, you

211

know?' But the line had gone dead.

31

The new constable was PC Williams. She had a gentle Welsh accent and came from an unpronounceable village in South Glamorgan. She quickly settled into a routine of tea making and communicating with the rest of her team. The inspector and his sergeant had been and gone, presumably off to follow up leads and source information. Nicholson's call had been traced to a call box so no doubt witnesses were being sought. The waiting game continued.

What would Leonard Nicholson's tactics be? Was he seriously under the impression that Esme was in a position to put her hands on £2 million? The inspector had said not, that there was still much negotiating to do and this was only a starting point. The thought of the present uncertainty being long-drawn-out was agonising. Esme questioned her ability to handle it and wondered about the parents of child kidnap victims. Their sense of helplessness must be infinitely worse, with their particular vulnerability.

The telephone sat like a malevolent force in the corner of the room. Esme felt her eye drawn to its threatening presence every time she walked nearby. She needed something to distract her. She remembered their conversation about the client and the Shropton canal. She hadn't been back to check his credentials.

She walked over to her desk and booted the computer. Perhaps rereading his e-mails would throw up some ideas. From the outset she'd felt a sense of unease about the client but when her work was paid for so promptly she had dismissed her initial misgivings.

Lucy had been gazing out of the front window. She turned round as the computer sang out its signature tune and looked questioningly at Esme.

'Just checking on something,' said Esme, with a loaded glance. Lucy picked up the message and came to look over Esme's shoulder. Esme murmured 'Shropton Canal client' under her breath, as the screen went through its procedures and sat ready for instructions. Esme clicked on to the appropriate file and opened it to find the e-mailed brief she'd received. They both read through everything.

Silently Esme pointed to the screen. The client had asked for the route of the canal, but the words Esme was indicating were, 'and details of derelict buildings and their proximity to occupied properties.'

'Maybe he was planning to do them up,' whispered Esme, thinking of the development issue associated with Polly's land.

'He could be a property developer.'

'But British Waterways still owns most of the canal buildings,' answered Lucy. 'He'd have to buy them first.'

'He may have already done so. They do sell them off now and again and they've been involved in various partnership developments recently.'

'Maybe.' Lucy sounded unconvinced. 'Or perhaps he was looking for a nice out-of-the-way place for keeping a kidnap victim.'

Esme looked at Lucy aghast. 'That's a bit far-fetched, isn't it? Anyway, this is his Plan B? The time scale doesn't fit.'

'But maybe development was the original idea but the information came in handy.'

Esme took a quick glance at Constable Williams. She was looking out of the window, engrossed in something happening in the lane.

Lucy rubbed her eyes. 'Sorry,' she said. 'Take no notice. I'm tired and I'm letting my imagination run away with me.'

'But what if you're on to something?' asked Esme. 'How could we establish whether there's a connection?'

'What's his name? It's obviously not Leonard Nicholson, but what about the same initials or something.'

Esme shook her head. 'Arthur Cranfield. A. C.'

'Not even close.'

'What other tricks do people use? What about family links?'

They looked at one another. Esme stood up. It was time to consult.

'I need to speak to your boss,' she said to the WPC.

By the time they'd tracked the inspector down Esme was convinced there was something in Lucy's hunch. She hoped she wasn't going to hear the wrong information. Leonard Nicholson could have taken any sort of random name, off a billboard, out of a magazine. There would be no way of knowing. At least Arthur Cranfield could be checked out. At least then they'd know if he was legitimate.

'Why would he employ you, though, given your link?' said Lucy as Esme waited for the inspector to come to the phone.

'He wouldn't have been aware of one, probably, until later. That's when he dropped me.'

'Amazing that he picked you though, don't you think?'

'Not really. I'm the only professional researcher listed in the phone book in this area.'

Lucy gave a wry smile. 'Hobson's choice, then.'

Esme heard the line crackle and the inspector's voice came on. 'Mrs Quentin? What's this? You need to know something?'

He sounded bemused.

'What were Leonard Nicholson's parents' names?'

'Pardon?'

'Humour me, please, Inspector. It could be important. On the other hand it could be nothing.'

'If it's important you ought to explain.'

Esme curbed her impatience and quickly summarised.

'I had a strange client recently. There may be a link with the Monkleigh family. His name might be a clue, or tell us if he's genuine.' She willed him not to ask her to explain in what way she thought her client strange.

'What's his name? We'll run a check on him.'

Esme told him.

'OK, wait a moment.' Esme imagined him scratching around on his desk. She heard his voice in the background talking to someone. Lucy came and stood next to her. She pressed her ear to the phone.

'We'll run a check anyway but since you ask his father was Arthur Nicholson.' So far so good. Esme held her breath. 'And his mother was Lillian Monkleigh.' She cursed. Of course it would be Monkleigh. She was Sir Charles's sister.

Lucy mouthed something at Esme.

'Did his mother have a middle name?' said Esme quickly.

She thought for a moment that he was going to protest she was wasting his time, but he just sighed. There were voices again in the background.

'I'll have to call you back.' He disconnected. Esme put down the phone and bit her bottom lip.

'Well, the Arthur bit fits,' said Lucy. 'Even if the other doesn't match up, at least they'll be able to check him out.'

Esme started pacing again. Constable Williams looked on from her post by the window. Lucy dropped into the armchair.

The clock ticked. The voices of children passed by the window.

School was out. A delivery lorry pulled up over the road and the sounds of the metal bolts being drawn back grated on the tense silence in the room.

The telephone rang. All eyes looked at it and then at one another. Was this the inspector phoning back? Or Leonard Nicholson?

Esme strode over and grabbed the receiver.

'Leonard Nicholson's mother,' said Inspector Barry, 'had two middle names, one unusual one. I'm told it was probably her mother's maiden name.'

'What was it?' said Esme, clutching the phone.

'Cranfield.'

32

'You'll wear a hole in the carpet,' said Lucy from the armchair.

Esme was pacing again.

She halted by the window. 'It keeps me busy.'

'And stressed. You must be pumping so much adrenaline.'

Esme sighed. 'I keep looking at that phone, desperate for it to ring and yet terrified it will do.' She looked out into the lane in an attempt to find something to divert her thoughts, but it was empty. Inside was quiet, apart from the sound of Constable Williams's radio occasionally crackling into life in the kitchen.

'Do you think they've set out yet?' said Esme.

'Give them a chance. You only told them five minutes ago. They will have barely had time to decide on their plan.'

'I ought to have arranged to meet them out there, to show them where I'd researched. They might go blundering about all over the place and frighten him off.'

'Esme, they're quite capable of reading the map you faxed them. You've got to trust them. The trouble with you is you always want to be in the thick of it.'

Esme shot Lucy a glance. It was a measure of the pressure Lucy must be feeling that she was so biting in her remarks.

Lucy avoided Esme's gaze. 'Sorry, that was a bit insensitive.'

Esme flapped her hand. 'You're trying to make me see sense, I know.' She knew Lucy was only trying to protect her from stumbling into a perilous situation. Perhaps it would be better to sit by the phone and let the police do their job.

'Anyway there's no guarantee that that's where he'll be holding her,' Lucy was saying. 'It was only a wild guess.'

'The fact that the inspector reacted must mean they think there's a good chance.'

'He's probably glad to have a lead to follow.'

Esme thought for a moment. She glanced towards the sound of radio exchanges and sat down on the sofa trying to calm her frantic thoughts.

Her resolve lasted five minutes. She couldn't simply sit around waiting for something to happen. She got up and perched on the arm of Lucy's chair. She lowered her voice. 'I want to go there. To the canal.'

Lucy almost leapt out of her seat. 'Are you mad?' She nodded towards the kitchen. 'She wouldn't agree to it, for a start.'

'She might not notice for a while. We could get a head start. It would be too late by then.'

Lucy frowned. 'But you're supposed to be here, waiting for him to phone again.'

'I can get around that.' Esme picked up the phone and pressed a series of keys. She listened for a moment, then replaced the receiver.

'What was all that about?' said Lucy looking alarmed.

'Call diversion. I use it all the time when I'm working. Incoming calls go straight to my mobile.' Esme snatched her mobile phone from off the desk and her coat from the newel post at the bottom of the stairs. She slipped the phone into one of the pockets.

'But won't they know? They've got the line tapped, don't forget.' Lucy was looking pale.

'It doesn't matter if they do. It'll be too late by the time they've put two and two together. Anyway, we're not running out on them, just getting out of here. We can make contact once we're in place.' She looked down at Lucy's terrified face.

'Now's our chance,' she hissed, 'while she's talking to HQ.'

Lucy was still sitting upright in her chair as though cast in stone.

Esme looked at her. 'You can stay here, if you'd rather. Say I disappeared while you were in the loo. I don't want to drag you into this if you don't want to.'

Lucy stared for a moment. Then she shook her head and stood up. 'I think I'd better come and stop you doing something stupid.'

Esme grabbed Lucy's coat and threw it over to her. With one last glance in the direction of the kitchen, she seized the Ordnance Survey map from off the desk and they stole out of the front door.

*

Threatening clouds were beginning to crowd the sky as Esme and Lucy arrived at a patch of wasteland which was the closest place you could get a car to this section of the canal.

'So where are they?' said Lucy looking around.

Esme opened the map and studied it. 'The canal originally came along here,' she said following the route with her finger.

'That's where I guessed that he might be, because there were all sorts of old buildings along that stretch. And there's the entrance to the tunnel, as well.'

'But that's miles away. What are we doing here?'

'This is the south end of the tunnel. It's been bricked up for years so I didn't attach any importance to it. I thought the other end would be more likely.'

'So what's changed?'

'It's changed,' said Esme, folding up the map, 'because it's perfectly possible for someone to unbrick it. If it looks as though that's happened, the inspector can redirect some of his men to look out here.'

Esme opened the car door. 'I'll go down and see and report back. You hang on here.' She climbed out of the car.

'Esme?'

Esme popped her head back inside. 'Yes?'

'Is this wise? Just call them anyway and say you've thought of it. Don't go poking round on your own. He could be out there.'

'He'll be keeping his head down, won't he? He's not likely to give himself away. I could be just taking a walk. He doesn't know who I am from Adam.'

'How do you know?'

A momentary flicker of uncertainty flashed into Esme's mind. True, how did she know? He'd known who to call, hadn't he? He'd employed her. How did she know he'd not been watching her? An image of the black Audi came into her mind.

Had he ever been close enough to see her properly? Not on the couple of occasions she'd noticed him, but what if there had been other times?

She decided she hadn't time to ponder on such trivialities. She still wasn't convinced he'd blow his cover. 'Look,' she said, 'if you'd feel better about it call the inspector and tell him where we are.' She handed Lucy his crumpled card from out of her pocket.

Lucy fished her mobile phone out of her bag. 'Don't worry, I will.'

Esme closed the car door and set off towards the line of the canal. The grass was long and wet, and in no time her boots and jeans were soaked through. She forced her way through the areas of arching brambles which snagged her hair and jacket sleeves, until she reached the edge of the cutting. There was no water in it now but, overgrown though it was, there was still a discernible path down the middle. She set off in the direction of the tunnel entrance. She couldn't see very far ahead of her because of the wide bend in the canal. Then, as it began to open out, she could make out the stonework of the original arch on the left hand side. Soon the end of the tunnel came into view.

She halted abruptly. Even though she had considered the possibility, the sight of a hole in the wall large enough for a person to crawl through made her flesh creep. The bricks lying at the base of the opening were bright and clean, in complete contrast to those which remained in the wall. They had been removed recently. Of course it might mean nothing. It simply extended the possibilities. She backed off and scrambled up on to the bank.

She called Lucy to get her to alert the inspector.

'I've already spoken to him. Someone's on their way,' said Lucy. 'But I'll update him. Are you on your way back?'

'No, not yet. I'll have a look around first.'

'You're not thinking of going into the tunnel?'

Esme laughed. 'Don't worry. I'm not that stupid.'

She disconnected and looked around. She could vaguely make out a solid shape across the other side of the canal. It was buried under a mass of branches and half-dead brambles.

It looked like the remains of a building. When the branches were in full leaf it would be indistinguishable from the undulating landscape but the new shoots hadn't yet filled out enough to screen it.

She dipped down into the cut and climbed back up the other side towards the structure. It was most likely an old storage building, perhaps for housing coal to fuel the old steamboats. There were no windows in it that she could see.

By pushing her way between the undergrowth and the wall she managed to manoeuvre her way along one side. If she could find the front entrance she might establish, discreetly, whether the building had been used recently. Buddleia had seeded deep into the base of the wall in places and it took considerable effort to shove her way through the tangle of branches which grabbed her jacket tails and pressed against her face. She stopped to take a breath and peered out. She had almost reached the end of the building. As she was about to force her way through the last knot of brambles she heard a car approaching. She pulled back, staying hidden behind the brickwork as it swung into view.

Her stomach leapfrogged when she recognised the vehicle.

It was the black Audi.

33

Esme stared, unable to move. A figure climbed out of the car.

So this was Leonard Nicholson. Had to be. Although she could see the similarities to the police's picture, he was different from the image she had formed in her mind. She'd envisaged a rough, coarse individual, which clearly this man was not. He was slight, almost fragile. She recalled Mary referring to him as a gentleman, a concept at which Esme had scoffed. Now she understood why Mary had described him that way, even if his conduct didn't warrant the label.

What should she do? Confrontation, while satisfying an urge within her, was not the wisest move. Irrespective of whether she would be risking physical injury – she had to remind herself of Elizabeth's circumstances – it made more sense to keep Gemma's predicament in mind and hope that he might lead them to her.

But she couldn't chance making a call on her mobile to summon assistance until he was out of earshot, and if she stayed back too long she might lose him. Already he was he was moving quickly away across the rough grass. In a few seconds he would be out of sight.

She started after him. If she could just hang on to his route long enough to determine in which direction he was going, she could make her call and the inspector's team could take over.

She stumbled over the tufts of grass, cowering low so as not to attract his attention while trying desperately to keep him in view. But she was losing ground.

Just as she was debating whether it would be more effective to stop and make the call, a particularly large and slippery clump of grass defeated her. She lost her balance and rolled off it, turning her ankle. With a groan of frustration she went down. She put her hand out to stop her fall but instead of the rough grass her fingers felt the roughness of a rusting metal grid. It gave way under the pressure of her hand and she found herself tumbling into some sort of void. She plunged into an empty blackness. She landed with a thud, losing all sense of orientation.

For a moment all she could hear was the echoing of her attempts at gasping for air. She slowed her breathing and when she was able she held her breath, listening. She was in some sort of chamber. She heard the drip, drip of water coming from what she realised was the roof of the tunnel. She must have fallen down one of the ventilation shafts. A musty, rotting smell accosted her nose. She felt sick.

She tried to sit up. Her back and right hip felt bruised but there were no acute stabs of pain. Hopefully that meant nothing was broken. It was utterly dark around her. She couldn't see anything but liquid black. She reached out and touched something. She flinched and withdrew her hand. It felt wet and slimy.

She blinked. Slowly the light from above began to penetrate the blackness. Her eyes adjusted little by little and she looked up. She could make out the roof of the tunnel above her, around the narrow shaft down which she had fallen. Slowly she scanned down the wall. Her eyes fell on the object beside her. The shape compelled her attention. Even in half-light she knew that she was looking at a body.

Suddenly someone started screaming, deafening and out of control. Esme put her hands over her ears to cut out the terrifying sound. Then she realised who was screaming. She was.

*

Lucy sat in the car, absently tapping her mobile phone against her chin. Occasionally she looked over her shoulder to see if Esme was coming into view. Surely she should have come back by now. What was she doing? Should she ring her? Lucy glanced at her watch. She'd spoken to her not three minutes ago. Esme would only complain that Lucy was overreacting.

She sighed. She still thought it was mad to go wandering around where they thought Leonard Nicholson might be holding Gemma, but once Esme had got something into her head, Lucy knew from experience that it was all but impossible to steer her on a different course.

She had already defended Esme's actions to the inspector on the phone, as far as she could. Though from what she had heard in the background, the inspector was more furious with someone else than he was with Esme. Something to do with not making the proper checks at the exchange, which meant that they were unaware of the call diversion facility that Esme had on her line.

Lucy took another glance over her shoulder. It was eerily quiet. The clouds were still hanging heavy overhead threatening to discharge a hefty shower at any moment. It created a menacing light which heightened Lucy's disquiet. She opened the door of the car and stepped outside. She slowly made her way towards the direction Esme had taken. She stopped when she reached the top of the rise and scanned the distant landscape. Nothing.

She tried to stay rational. From her first leaving the car, it had been a good fifteen minutes before Esme had phoned to say she had reached the end of the tunnel and that the wall had been breached. She had said she was going to look around before she came back. Lucy reminded herself that if she had done that, she wouldn't be on her way back for at least another five minutes, assuming she'd only had a brief look around, and Lucy wouldn't be able to see her coming for at least another ten.

She was being over-anxious. She didn't convince herself, though.

She knew why Esme had felt the need to go in search of Gemma. It was partly because she felt it was her fault that Gemma was in this terrifying position and partly because of her past demons. When Esme's husband Tim had been killed, it had been

225

Esme who had found the body. Lucy prayed that the current crisis wouldn't result in a similar tragedy. Esme might not recover from such a horrifying experience a second time around.

And although Lucy told herself that one quick phone call to Esme's mobile would resolve her anxieties she found she couldn't make the call. She knew she was being weak. She wasn't really deterred by the fact that Esme might moan at her for fretting unnecessarily. She was terrified that by telephoning she would discover that her worst fears were confirmed.

34

Lucy realised that she was gently rocking back and forth when the sound of fast-approaching cars startled her. She turned her head, terrified at what she would see. A convoy of patrol vehicles came hurtling on to the wasteland along with a posse of other unmarked, presumably police, cars. It was a relief not to be alone any longer.

She saw Inspector Barry emerge from an unmarked car and she made her way over to him. 'Any sign of Mrs Quentin, yet?' asked the inspector as she came into earshot.

Lucy shook her head. She lifted an arm and pointed down the canal route. 'She went off in that direction. That's where the tunnel entrance is.'

The inspector turned and began directing members of his team. Lucy watched as two officers headed off with reassuring urgency along the empty canal. The inspector turned back towards Lucy but before he could say anything, his mobile phone began ringing. He reached in his inside pocket and snapped it open.

'Barry,' he barked.

Lucy studied his face, trying to discern something from his expression. He gave a couple of instinctive curt nods as he listened, then abruptly severed the call.

'You say Mrs Quentin's got her phone on her?'

'Yes.'

'Call her. She needs to get back here.

*

When she managed to stop screaming, Esme sat shivering, partly from the cold and damp and partly from shock. After steadying her breathing she forced herself a sideways glance at the body. It

227

took all her strength and determination to focus long enough for her eyes to become accustomed to the gloom.

There was no way of telling whether it was Gemma. It was too dark to make it out properly and it was wrapped in plastic sheeting of some kind. It had been tied tightly, though there wasn't enough light to see detail. She supposed that that would be to stop the whole thing from coming loose while it was being transported. She certainly had no intention of unravelling it to look further.

When they lifted the sheet for her to formally identify Tim it had been a devastating experience. It had taken many years before she was able to cope with the memory. But now the demons were threatening to take over. What hope was there now for her sanity if she looked beneath the shroud?

She turned away. How had it come to this? Gemma had never wanted her to go digging about in Elizabeth's past but Esme had ignored her because of her own overwhelming need for answers. Why should the need to know become so dangerous? Such danger existed if one was investigating serious crime or corrupt government officialdom in unstable countries, as she and Tim had proved. But this time all she had been doing was looking into Elizabeth's family history.

She took a deep breath and tried to stand up, deliberately looking away from the terrifying shape beside her. She looked up towards the shaft. It wasn't so far up, which explained why she hadn't broken any bones, but it would be another thing altogether to climb out. Her only way out was to let someone know she was here. She was about to start shouting when she remembered her phone. Would she get a signal though? She got an immediate answer to her question. As she took it out of her pocket it rang.

She felt a moment's panic as a thought occurred to her. She'd re-routed her landline to this number. Was it Leonard Nicholson phoning to discuss their next move? What had she done? Just when she should be at home with the police nearby co-ordinating Gemma's rescue she had gone off on a wild-goose chase. Had her impulsive actions caused Gemma's death and scuppered hope of her own safe rescue? Or was he playing with them, having disposed of Gemma already?

Before she had time to consider how to deal with what he had to say, she stabbed the receive button. She had to believe that Gemma was still alive.

'Hello?' she croaked.

Silence. She brought the phone round to look at the illuminated screen. The bars which indicated reception levels were fluctuating between one and completely dead. She stuck the instrument back on her ear again.

'Hello?' she called desperately. 'Can you hear me?'

'Perfectly,' said Leonard Nicholson's voice.

Esme froze. The voice hadn't come from the phone. It was behind her.

*

Lucy clicked off her mobile phone and looked up at the Inspector.

'I can't reach her. It just keeps switching to voice mail.'

'There's probably no signal. She must be in a dead area.'

Lucy winced at the description. 'Well she wouldn't have switched it off. Where could she be? I spoke to her all right earlier on.'

'Sir!'

The inspector looked round and headed over to join his colleagues, who were huddled over a map laid out on the bonnet of one of the vehicles. Lucy climbed out of her car and walked across to join them. As she approached, two officers hurried away, shouting instructions to other policemen in the car park.

'What's happening?' Lucy asked the inspector.

'The tunnel looked as though it had been breached, you said?'

'Yes, but she promised she wouldn't go down there.' She looked up, her eyes wide. 'You think she's followed him into the tunnel?'

The inspector sighed. 'It's possible, if she thought he'd lead her to Miss Holland. His car's been sighted, so it's likely he's in the area. But we would have seen him if he'd gone in the tunnel at the north end. Unless there's another way in. A maintenance entrance, perhaps.'

'British Waterways might know, if anyone does.'

The policeman nodded. 'We've already spoken to them. They're trying to find someone who can help us.' He fished out a packet of chewing-gum from his pocket, unwrapped a stick and put it in his mouth.

'Mrs Quentin is understandably distressed by Gemma's disappearance,' he said, chewing thoughtfully, 'but it's not the usual course of action to go off in hot pursuit. Not in my experience, anyway.'

'No,' agreed Lucy. 'I thought she was over all that.'

'Oh?'

Lucy hesitated. It seemed to be betraying a confidence but then in reality it wasn't. It was a fact. 'She used to be in journalism. The investigative sort – unearthing the unpalatable, that sort of thing. Her husband was Timothy Quentin.'

The inspector frowned then slowly nodded. 'I thought her surname rang a bell. Haven't seen his name around for years.'

Lucy stared out across the bleak landscape. 'You wouldn't have. He died.'

'Ah.'

'Killed. In the line of duty, you might say. Esme was caught up in it all, too.' She glanced sideways. He was looking at her, perhaps aware that she had more to add. She shivered. 'Esme always maintained that they would have killed her too if there hadn't been some sort of disturbance nearby. They obviously decided it was time to get out. They made a run for it but not before slashing Esme's face.'

'And her husband?'

'They implied they'd already caught up with Tim. She went

230

looking for him but it was too late.'

They stood in mutual contemplation. Lucy focused on the straw-like quality of the couch grass on the edge of the bank in front of her and tried to blank out the horrors of Esme's past, whilst willing for them not to recur somewhere below her.

The inspector's phone rang. He snapped it open.

'Barry?'

He grunted something back and put the phone back in his pocket. He turned to Lucy.

'They're ready. They're going into the tunnel.'

35

Esme slowly turned her head and looked over her shoulder. There was a dim light about two or three yards further down the tunnel and she could just make out a figure in the gloom.

There was no mistaking the voice.

'Well, well, what have we here?'

Esme twisted round. 'What have you done with Gemma?' she demanded, with more self-assurance than she was feeling.

She drew some comfort at the sound of her voice echoing around the cavernous space. She felt as though she was taking control, however false the illusion.

Nicholson started to move towards her, the light source, a battered old lantern, strangely incongruous against the suit he was wearing, swinging ahead of him and creating disturbing shapes on the pitted walls of the tunnel. 'It's most kind of you to come and bring the cash with you so promptly.'

Esme was alarmed by his statement and the cool assumption implied within it. He was clearly deranged if he seriously believed it to be as simple as that. How could she even begin to convince him otherwise?

The flickering light continued to move relentlessly towards her. 'I don't hear you, Mrs Quentin. That was our arrangement, was it not?'

'Not our arrangement, only your demands. There's a difference.' Esme backed away slightly and considered her options. She wouldn't get six feet in the dark if she tried to make a run for it. The tunnel hadn't been in operation for years. The canal bottom would be covered with the debris of neglect, not to mention a thick layer of mud. Hardly ideal for an effective escape. She glanced around for a potential weapon to defend herself but could see nothing in the blackness.

'You have caused me a great deal of trouble, Mrs Quentin,' said the ever-closer voice. 'Because of your flagrant interference you have deprived me of my birthright. You now have to pay for that error of judgement. It's a question of justice.'

'What birthright?' Esme watched him warily, aware that her heart was pounding in her chest. He was coming into focus now.

'It was my inheritance and she tried to trick me.'

'Who?' Was this another of his delusions?

'She told me she was dying. She said it would all come to me, but she lied. Like they all do.' He stopped in front of her and held up the lamp. It emphasised his gaunt features, giving his face a grotesque quality. His smile was a grinning skull in the shadows. 'But I had the last laugh, didn't I?'

Esme's insides jolted. He was talking about Daisy, had to be.

In her concern for Gemma the suspicion of Leonard Nicholson's involvement in Daisy's death had slipped from the forefront of her mind. She stared into his face, afraid to move. So her assumptions had been right. What else could he mean by having the last laugh? She was staring at Daisy's killer. She felt giddy.

'What do you mean?' whispered Esme. She imagined Daisy trying to catch her breath and the man in front of her pulling her life-saving oxygen out of reach. She shuddered.

He flicked his head up. 'Catherine, of course. She thought she'd been so clever.' His eyes glared. 'No matter. You're here to put things right.'

'Perhaps she didn't understand,' suggested Esme. Perhaps she could keep him talking. But for how long? No one knew where she was. She had gone blundering into danger again, as usual. Would she never learn?

Leonard glowered at her. 'She knew all right. They're all the same. They tell you something but they lie.'

'Who? I don't understand what you're talking about.'

He sneered at her. 'And you, Mrs Quentin, are you to be trusted or are you the same as the rest of them?'

'The rest of them?'

He looked straight into her eyes. 'Women, Mrs Quentin. Are you another lying, cheating bitch like the rest your sex?'

Esme held his stare, her distaste for him increasing by the second along with her anxiety. She thought of the many nannies and nursemaids who, Albert had said, had left because of Leonard's insufferable behaviour. She was being subjected to the damaged legacy that such events had left behind. Rationality was not going to defuse this situation. Comprehension of the reality of her situation gripped her insides and turned them to water.

'Of course you are,' Leonard continued when she didn't answer. 'You have already shown your true colours, haven't you? You interfered.' His voice was rising now. He took a step towards her.

Esme shrank back. 'I don't know what you mean?'

'The old lady was about to sign, but you made her change her mind.' He was pointing an accusing finger at her. 'I have been cruelly deprived of what was due to me and you prevented her from restoring that justice.'

Esme's disgust and fury finally empowered her. 'Justice? By blackmailing a vulnerable elderly lady? What sort of justice is that? You're just a self-centred little shit and, from what I hear, you always have been.'

His face erupted into a mass of scarlet. For a moment Esme thought he might physically explode. She took a tentative step backwards. If he dropped the lamp she might evade him in the darkness. If he held on to it he would be hampered. Even if he attacked her maybe she could fight him off. He couldn't be very strong, slightly built as he was, and she was no lady weakened by illness, as Daisy has been. Yet she didn't underestimate the significance of his emotional state. If her own anger gave her strength then the rage she could read in his face could arouse a force she'd rather not test.

Turning suddenly she darted away from him and ran blindly out of the lantern's pool of light, to one side of where he stood.

She calculated that if she then circled back behind him she might disorientate him enough to give herself time to reach the tunnel's entrance. If the police had removed more of the bricks there might be enough light coming through to guide her way.

But her optimism was short-lived. Instead it was exactly as she'd feared. She had run no more than ten yards when her legs became caught in a tangle of wire. She went crashing to the ground.

She felt him run up behind her. His hands seize the back of her jacket and with surprising strength he dragged her up on to her knees. He pushed his face into hers.

He forced the words out slowly, one at a time, as though they caused him pain.

'If I say justice, that's what it is.'

Esme swung her arm round as hard as she could and aimed for anything she thought was within hitting distance. She made contact with his lamp-carrying arm and the light sailed through the air.

She was gasping for breath now, the anxiety and the exertion taking its toll. She sensed that he was still near and she struggled to her feet. She could hear his vicious words and she scrambled in the opposite direction from the sound.

Then suddenly there was light. And noise. Shouting and hurried footsteps. Esme winced against the sudden radiance which all but blinded her and she put up her arm to shade her eyes. People surged past her.

Someone grabbed her arm and she flinched.

'Are you all right, Mrs Quentin? It's Sergeant Morris. You're safe now.'

Esme felt suddenly weak. She grasped his sleeve.

'Down there,' she said, pointing in the general direction behind her. 'There's a...' She swallowed. 'It looks like a body.'

'It's not Gemma,' said the policeman. 'Gemma is fine. We found her in Nicholson's car boot.'

'Thank God.' Esme slumped against the policeman.

'Now, let's get you out of here.'

As she was led out of the tunnel she shivered at the thought of the unidentified body lying a few yards away behind her.

Whose body was this? The inspector had mentioned to her that they were keen to question Leonard about a missing person. She recalled Albert saying that Leonard had been into drugs and...what was his last comment? And worse.

Esme shuddered. She hadn't stopped to think at the time what he'd meant by it. She hadn't expected their paths to cross.

If the victim was connected to Leonard Nicholson and he had dumped the body here, work to restore the canal would have led to its discovery. No wonder he wanted to know how the project was progressing. It all made sense now.

36

Esme watched and smiled, amused by Gemma's clucking around her mother's bed, smoothing sheets and pumping pillows. When she reached for the hairbrush Elizabeth flapped her away.

'For God's sake stop fussing,' she said, surprisingly forcefully considering her weak state.

'Oh, go on, Elizabeth,' said Esme. 'Let the girl fuss. It's a good way to get all those anxious weeks out of her system.'

Elizabeth sighed. 'Well, for one day only. Then please behave normally or I'll go completely mad.'

Gemma grinned and set about dealing with her mother's wayward hair, pulling it back into a ponytail and tying it at the back of her neck. She stood back looking pleased with herself.

'A great job,' said Esme, standing up from her slouch against the ward wall. 'Are you ready now? Shall I go and find her?'

Mother and daughter nodded. Esme left the ward and took the lift down to reception. She glanced at her watch as she stepped out of the lift. It was close to two o'clock. Polly should be here by now.

As yet Elizabeth had only been told of the attack itself, of which she remembered nothing, and that during her unconsciousness Esme and Gemma had learned of Polly's existence. She remained in ignorance of anything else concerning her true ancestry and Polly had agreed that she would tell her the full story. As Esme had speculated, their parents had taken the then commonly held view that Elizabeth had no need to know she was adopted, believing she would feel an outsider in the family, even more so when, to their surprise, Esme was conceived. It was many years later, after their father's death, that their mother began to worry that they had made the wrong decision, not least because Elizabeth had begun to ask awkward questions. When their mother eventually admitted the truth, Elizabeth kept from her that she had requested a copy of her birth certificate and the subject was never discussed further.

'Mother just needed to know that I understood and that I didn't blame her,' Elizabeth had explained. 'That was enough. It was our secret.' Searching out her birth mother had come only later after their mother had died. By then Elizabeth confessed she didn't know how to broach the subject with Esme, though Polly had been correct in what she had said – that Elizabeth had come to a recent decision that the time had come to tell her sister and daughter about her true past. It was ironic that for the moment Esme and Gemma knew more about it than Elizabeth did herself.

There was an argument taking place at the hospital's front entrance but Esme ignored it and scanned the area for the old lady. She was due to arrive by taxi. Esme wandered over to the foyer to look out for her.

The altercation at the entrance was reaching a climax.

Esme could now see what the problem was. A taxi was parked at the front of the building, blocking the entrance. The driver was arguing with a hospital employee. As she got closer, she could see a passenger in the rear of the car. She bent down and peered inside. The two men arguing stopped in mid-sentence at the same moment that Esme realised that the passenger was Polly.

She turned to the men. 'Is something wrong?'

The man in hospital uniform spoke. 'Yes there is. He can't park there.'

'Have you come from Wisteria House?' asked Esme, addressing the driver.

He looked relieved. 'That's right.' He nodded towards his cab. 'She won't get out. I've got another pick-up in ten minutes, but she refuses to budge. Do you know her?'

'Yes I do. I'll come and have a word with her, shall I?'

He almost bounded towards the door. 'Please.'

The official called after them. 'You'll have to move the car.'

Esme climbed into the back of the taxi, receiving a surprised then glowering look from Polly. She turned away and stared out of the window. Esme suggested that the driver find an empty slot in the car park.

As the car pulled to a halt the driver turned round and tapped his watch.

'Five minutes,' Esme said, firmly. He got out of the car and wandered off aimlessly across the car park.

Esme turned to Polly. 'What's the matter? The driver said you wouldn't get out of the car. Are you feeling ill?'

'I can't go in,' said Polly, still staring out of the window. 'I don't have the right.'

'What are you talking about? Of course you have the right?'

The old lady turned quickly, her eyes on Esme. 'How can you say that? It's my fault that Daisy died. All these years I pretended to myself that I saved her from a loveless, miserable upbringing but what did I do instead? Deprived her of a loving family life, tearing her away from the man she loved and persuaded her to give up her own child.' There were tears in her eyes. She turned away again. 'Why would Elizabeth want to see me, when she knows all that?'

Esme reached out and laid a hand on the old lady's arm.

Polly fumbled in her coat pocket for a handkerchief and dabbed her eyes.

'You must have already talked to Elizabeth about why Daisy gave her up for adoption. She must have accepted that, or she wouldn't have carried on visiting.'

'But I have another secret to reveal, don't I?'

'That you aren't really her grandmother? It will be a shock, but why should it alter anything?' Esme was jolted by the words. The situation was comparable to discovering that Elizabeth wasn't her sister. She'd experienced a gamut of emotions from shock to anger to loss, but she was still here. She doubted Elizabeth would behave any differently.

'I had a visitor yesterday,' Polly was saying. 'Will Watts came to apologise for breaking his promise and telling Mary about Elizabeth.'

'He didn't have any option. It was the only way he could get her to help.'

Polly shook her head. 'I know that. I don't blame him. Anyway, it's the truth, isn't it? He and his mother are really Elizabeth's family. Not me.' She looked at Esme. 'So you see, even if Elizabeth does understand, she doesn't owe me anything.'

'This isn't about owing anyone. In virtually every sense of the word you are Elizabeth's grandmother, you brought up Daisy. If you don't keep in touch with Elizabeth, she'll lose the only link she has left to her mother's memory.'

Polly resumed her pensive stare out of the taxi window. Did her silence mean she accepted Esme's argument?

'You can't abandon Elizabeth now,' said Esme, which earned a sharp look from Polly.

Esme spread her hands. 'I'm only making the case that she needs you.' No answer. Polly looked away.

The driver returned. He began pacing up and down outside the car.

'Come on,' said Esme, brightly. 'This poor guy's going to be late for his next job, and you've got someone waiting.'

Esme looked at the old lady for a sign. Polly turned her head and gave a weak smile.

'Good,' sighed Esme. 'Let's go.'

She knocked on the window and alerted the agitated chauffer, who leapt back into his seat and drove them back to the front entrance.

Esme found Polly a wheelchair and wheeled her over towards the lift.

'I never claimed to be Daisy's mother, you know,' said Polly. 'She always knew she was adopted. I was – what is it they say? –

240

economical with the truth. Until that day, of course, when I had to make her see the danger and what would happen if the truth came out.' She shook her head. 'It was too much to ask.'

They arrived at the lift doors. Esme leant over and pushed the call button. 'But she made her choice and did what you asked. She didn't want to lose you.'

The lift hummed and the doors slid open. Esme wheeled Polly inside and selected the correct floor.

'She was furious,' continued Polly, as the doors closed. 'That's how the glass on her mother's photograph got cracked. She threw it across the room. I showed it her to make her see why Mary might guess who she really was.' Polly fell silent for a moment. The drone of the winding mechanism filled the empty space. The lift slowed, then halted and the doors opened.

As they approached the ward, Esme stopped the chair and came around in front of the old lady. She crouched down.

'Ready?' she whispered.

Polly attempted a brave smile, her rheumy eyes only giving the slightest hint of the foreboding she felt about the task ahead of her. Esme squeezed her hand. 'If she kicks you out,' she said with a wink. 'I'll still come and visit you.'

Esme's flippant remark seemed to bolster the old lady and her smile widened.

'We're a bit in the same boat, you and I, aren't we, Esme?' she said, as Esme wheeled her along the last leg of the corridor.

After delivering Polly, Esme made her excuses and wandered off to the day room. As she passed the lift the doors opened and a familiar figure stepped out.

'Inspector Barry,' called Esme. 'What are you doing here? She can't remember anything, you know?'

'So I understand. It's not uncommon with head injuries. No, it wasn't about her attack, exactly. Her daughter said she'd mentioned a man trying to speak to her earlier that day, but she didn't understand what he was talking about. She might remember that.'

Esme hadn't realised that Gemma had passed that on. Gemma had changed her attitude towards the police since Elizabeth had regained consciousness. No doubt partly because of her gratitude for her rescue from Leonard Nicholson's clutches.

She had also been magnanimous about Esme's investigations, which had led to her unfortunate experience. Esme was grateful for that but saddened, and not a little frustrated, that the situation might not have arisen at all if Gemma hadn't at first been so hostile towards Esme's enquiries into Elizabeth's past.

It was pointless to fret about it now. Both of them had survived their ordeals. What it had taught either of them it was, perhaps, too soon to tell.

'This man,' said Esme, guessing the inspector's line of thinking. 'Are you suggesting that Leonard Nicholson approached her before?'

'It's possible.'

Esme bit her lip, as something occurred to her. 'Inspector, I'm not sure if Gemma's explained everything to you, but Elizabeth didn't know the whole story about her true parentage. As none of us did until this all blew up.'

'Go on,' said the inspector, eying her carefully.

'If it was Leonard Nicholson who approached her and was asking about Catherine Monkleigh, the name would mean nothing to her and she would have told him so.'

'Which he might have taken for deliberate non-cooperation.'

'Perhaps he attacked her out of frustration, thinking she was stonewalling him?'

'It's possible. Patience isn't one of his strong points. It would certainly give him a motive.'

'One other thing,' continued Esme. 'I said that Elizabeth didn't know everything. She still doesn't. She's still getting to grips with the attack. We've only told her so much for now.'

The inspector picked up on her message. 'And you don't want me marching in with my size tens asking about things which will confuse her?'

Esme tipped her head to one side, appealing to him. 'If you could give it a day or two. While she takes it all in.'

Inspector Barry looked at her as if mulling over her request. 'I'll look in tomorrow,' he decided.

It was the best she could hope for in the circumstances. He was obviously keen to tie up the loose ends.

'I saw the papers,' said Esme. 'You've charged him with murder.' She shuddered at the thought of the body at the bottom of the ventilation shaft. 'Who was she?'

'Ex-girlfriend. Parents are devastated. He'd seemed such a gentleman, they said.' Esme thought of Mary's comments along the same lines.

She shook her head. 'Poor girl. What happened?' The inspector didn't reply. 'Sorry, you're probably not meant to be talking to me about it. *Sub judice* and all that.'

He smiled. 'To be honest, we're not sure what happened. Her best friend seemed to think the girl was planning to finish with him. Whether it's true and whether it's relevant we don't know at this stage.'

Esme thought back to Leonard's rage in the tunnel. 'He didn't have a good word to say about the women in his life, from the way he was ranting on at me.' She looked up at the policeman with concern. 'His whole theme was "the bitches". My guess is he meant his mother, his nannies, Catherine, me... he saw us as the cause of his ruined life.'

The inspector folded his arms. 'So if his girlfriend had told him she was leaving, he wouldn't take it calmly.'

Esme gave a small laugh at the understatement. 'Not from what I saw.' Esme felt a cold chill as she recalled his frenzied behaviour. She turned away. 'I think I need a cup of tea.'

Inspector Barry strode ahead of her to the drinks machine in the day room.

'You may have a point about Nicholson,' he said as he pressed

243

the relevant buttons. 'He seemed to get his kicks from terrorising women when he was involved in those bogus burglaries.'

'Lucy told me. She read the newspaper reports.'

'They always chose their targets when the woman would be alone.' He handed Esme a polystyrene cup full of strong tea. She took it from him and sat down on the edge of a chair.

'They were the mothers of his friends, weren't they?' The policeman nodded. He sat down opposite her. 'Perhaps he was taking it out on his own mother, because she had left him,' Esme added.

'I thought she died?' said the inspector.

'She did. I was talking figuratively. From a bereaved child's perspective. Then after that he was such a nightmare child that no nanny would stay more than a few months so the pattern of mother figures abandoning him kept repeating itself. His girlfriend telling him she was leaving followed the same pattern. He couldn't cope.'

'You could feel sorry for him if he wasn't such a ruthless bastard, couldn't you?' said the inspector sardonically. He stood up. 'No doubt, it'll all come out in the psychiatric report. Are you OK, Mrs Quentin?'

Esme looked up and smiled. 'Yes. Thank you, Inspector. I'll be fine. Thanks for the tea.'

The inspector nodded, saying he would call back the following day to speak to Elizabeth, and made for the lift.

Esme wandered over to the window and looked down into the grounds of the hospital. The inspector must encounter the consequences of damage done to people, or dysfunctional relationships every day, manifested in the crimes that he had to handle. She wondered why it didn't get to him. Perhaps it did.

Another occupational hazard for a police officer, along with assuming everyone had something to hide.

She sipped her tea and thought about Mary. Polly had chosen not to involve the police even though Esme was concerned that

Mary might try to use her knowledge again.

She was equally fearful that Polly's blackmailer would escape justice. But what about Polly's offence, the abduction of a child? Esme reflected that, ironically, both women had been guilty of crimes which, in their different ways, had resulted in self-inflicted punishment. Polly had spent her life in a continual state of fear of exposure following an impulsive decision as a naïve young woman. By contrast, Mary had wasted a huge portion of her life eaten up, almost to the point of destruction, by the anger with and hatred of the person she saw as the cause of her son's death. Her suffering was the realisation of that fact.

Esme had seen it in her face when she returned to the kitchen after Will had confessed his own secret.

Esme realised with some alarm that Mary's circumstances mirrored her own. Hadn't she been in a similar destructive spiral? It had taken years of isolation and withdrawal after she lost Tim, before Lucy had been able to persuade her to let go of her anger and rebuild her life. She would be forever grateful that Lucy had never given up on her.

Below her an ambulance arrived at the entrance to the Accident and Emergency department. Esme had a birds-eye view of the A & E staff, milling around as though on wheels, manoeuvring the patient out of the vehicle and into the building.

What effect would that patient's accident or illness have on his life and the people around him? What decisions would be made and what would be the consequences?

Esme's thoughts turned again to Polly. It was exactly as Polly had said that she and Esme were in the same boat. They both had emotional claims on Elizabeth but were not her true family. Soon Elizabeth would find out about Mary and Will.

And the young lad, Billy. What would she make of him? Esme was amused by the thought. They might be connected by birth but they were such different people. In the bigger picture, what did that really mean?

She glanced at her watch. Time enough for stories to have been told and truths revealed. She turned away from the window. She wouldn't make the mistake of the past and withdraw. Not this time. She might have experienced a shift in perspective, but Elizabeth was still the same person and so was she. If they had been related, would it have changed anything? How could it? They would be different people.

The question wouldn't arise.

She dropped the empty cup into the wastepaper bin and headed out of the day room. It was time to join the family, blood-tied or otherwise.

A message from the author

Thank you for reading *Blood-Tied*. If you enjoyed the book and have a moment to spare, writing a short review on Amazon or Goodreads (or your favourite site) would be greatly appreciated. Authors rely on the kindness of readers to share their experiences and spread the word.

Join us!

To keep updated on giveaways, special promotions and new releases, and to receive my quarterly newsletter, join the Readers Group mailing list.

You can sign up on my website **www.wendypercival.co.uk.**

Subscribers also receive a FREE copy of the Esme Quentin prequel novella:

LEGACY OF GUILT

The shocking death of a young mother in 1835 holds the key to Esme Quentin's search for truth and justice for her cousin.

With the tragedy of her past behind her, Esme Quentin has quit her former career, along with its potential dangers, and is looking to the future.

But when she stumbles upon her cousin in traumatic circumstances, Esme realises that her compulsion to uncover the truth, irrespective of the consequences, remains as strong as ever.

You'll also find me on:
Facebook: www.facebook.com/wendypercivalauthor
Twitter: @wendy_percival

I look forward to hearing from you.